VIPER'S RUN

JAMIE BEGLEY

Viper's Run

ISBN-13: 978-0615910901
ISBN-10: 0615910904

PROLOGUE

"Touchdown, and the Bulldogs pull ahead six to zero!" A cheer went up from the crowd as the first half ended. Winter and Emily braced themselves for the flood of customers that would take advantage of halftime to buy a snack.

"Here we go," Emily said as the fans began to arrive.

"We might get lucky and set a record crowd tonight," Winter said, hoping her words proved correct. The money they earned in the concession stand would go towards buying a new scoreboard. As principal of the high school, she was expected to be at home games, though typically as a spectator. Tonight, she had volunteered to work the concession stand so one of the parent volunteers would be given an opportunity to watch their son play in the game. Emily, her secretary, had also volunteered, but her reasons hadn't been so altruistic. Emily was determined to pursue the football coach.

They worked steadily until the game finally resumed then the customers returned to being sporadic.

"What are you doing after the game?"

"Going home and putting my feet up," Winter replied. "You?"

"I plan on asking Mr. TNT for a ride home then asking him to come inside to show me his play book."

Winter rolled her eyes at Emily's reply. The football coach had quickly been given the nickname TNT. Winter had laughed the first time she'd heard the nickname, but after she had been introduced to the new coach, she'd had to agree with their assessment. He was good-looking enough to knock any woman off her feet.

"May all your fantasies come true," Winter joked.

"You're not seeing Loker tonight? Is he still out of town?" Emily asked as she scooped popcorn into a bag for one of the students.

"Actually, he's here somewhere watching the game." Winter bit her lip, wishing she was brave enough to be as assertive with men as her secretary. She had been seeing Loker James on and off for the last two years. Unfortunately for her, he didn't seem to want to fulfill any of her fantasies.

They had met during a school committee meeting and developed a casual friendship. When he was in town and needed a date, he would always call her. Winter had never turned him down, always hoping each time that their friendship would develop into something more. It never did, though; he had barely tried to kiss her.

"I bet it's hard on him having to constantly fly back and forth between Kentucky and Washington."

Winter nodded her head, "I told him he needed a vacation, that he was looking tired, but he said now isn't a good time. His business is keeping him busy in Washington. Then, when he flies back to Kentucky, his father Ton is always in some kind of trouble."

"I heard about his father hitting Beth Cornett's car when he was drunk," Emily said, taking a handful of popcorn for herself.

"Loker said he wasn't drunk and that her sister, Lily, was actually driving the car," Winter corrected her. She was used to gossip being more fiction than facts and she usually didn't respond to it, but Ton was Loker's father. She didn't want anyone to think that he had been driving under the influence when it wasn't the truth.

"So if he's in town, why not hook up with him tonight?"

Because I've been trying to put some space between us, Winter thought to herself. He had called earlier, offering Winter a ride to the game, which she had politely refused, yet now she was regretting her decision.

"I'm tired of beating my head against a closed door. He only sees me as a friend." Winter had even considered the possibility of him being gay. Treepoint was a small town with old-fashioned morals. He was on several school committees and was even thinking of running for a soon to be vacant seat on the school board. If anyone found out he was gay, he would find himself ostracized.

"Maybe you just haven't used the right bait."

"There's not a lot here to bait a hook with," Winter said wryly. She was under no illusions about her looks. She was average height, neither pretty nor coyote ugly, with brown hair and eyes that accompanied a body that was so thin that her friends would bluntly ask if she was anorexic. Even when she loaded herself with carbs, she barely weighed a hundred pounds.

"Don't put yourself down like that, you're really striking," Emily responded.

"For a middle-aged high school principal," Winter finished for her. Emily began to disagree with her, so Winter decided to change the subject. "Since we haven't had a customer in a few minutes, do you mind if I take a break?"

"Not at all. I'll start doing the cleanup so we'll be ready to close as soon as the game ends."

"Okay, I won't take long."

Emily nodded, already starting to clean the grill.

Fixing herself an order of nachos and taking a bottle of water, she left the concession stand. Seeing a small table with a view of the game, she sat, picking at her nachos. Watching the crowd more than the game, she spotted Loker talking to Ben Stiles, a member of the school board. She wondered what they were talking about that had them looking so serious. Winter saw Ben say something before going to the restroom a few feet away, leaving Loker standing alone.

She rose from the table, carrying her empty containers to the trashcan, stopping in her tracks when The Last Riders walked by Loker. The motorcycle club had moved into town three years ago. Since then, it had become a familiar sight to see them riding throughout the town on their motorcycles. Every so often, a group of them would attend a sporting event in town. They had so far, to Winter's knowledge, never caused any trouble, other than nailing every female that threw themselves their way.

It was the look that Loker was giving one of the women in the group that had Winter coming to a full stop. His usually cold expression had changed into one of predatory intent and the slight smile on his lips left no doubt as to what he was thinking. The woman was everything Winter was not.

She had short, spiked blonde hair and was wearing tight jeans with high-heeled biker boots. Top that off with her white shirt, which was low cut, showing an abundance of cleavage that Loker seemed unable to keep his eyes off, and any doubts she had about his sexual preferences were laid to rest. The woman gave Loker a provocative smile, but kept following behind her friends. Loker continued to watch her until Ben returned and then his expression once again became an impassive mask.

Winter went back to the concession stand, sick with jealousy. Loker had never looked at her the way he had looked at the seductive blonde. She helped Emily finish cleaning up, and laughed when she left with a determined look on her face. Then Winter turned off the lights, locked the door and began to walk towards her car when she saw Loker standing in her path.

"Busy night?"

"Yes," Winter responded nervously as she started walking briskly towards the parking lot. Loker, calm like always, leisurely followed by her side.

"Would you like to get something to eat before you go home?"

"No, thanks, I'm not hungry," Winter answered.

"I have to go out of town tomorrow, but I'll be back in a couple of weeks. Your cousin Vincent is having his birthday party the fifteenth, isn't he?"

"Yes."

Loker gave her a sharp look at her curt reply.

"Do you need a date?" Her cousin was president of the local bank and a member of the local school board. Loker was constantly asking to go to the various functions that Vincent invited her to, but she couldn't stand Vincent. She often only attended because of Loker's insistence.

"I don't plan on going."

"Why not?"

"Because I don't want to, Loker. Now, if you don't mind, I'm tired and want to go home." Loker took her arm, preventing her from getting into her car.

"Are you mad at me for something?" he asked sharply.

"Why would I be angry?" Winter snapped.

"I don't know. That's why I'm asking."

Winter sighed to herself. He was clueless. For the last two years she thought they would eventually move toward a more intimate relationship, but after seeing his reaction to the blonde, she was finally admitting to herself that nothing was going to change.

Over her shoulder she saw Emily getting inside the football coach's car as he held the door open; she was blatantly flirting with him. Perhaps that had been where she had gone wrong.

"I could fix us dinner at my house," she said with a soft smile, ignoring his question.

Loker's eyes narrowed and his hand dropped from her arm.

"I don't want you to go to any trouble. I thought we would just grab a quick dinner. My plane leaves at six in the morning, so I need an early night."

"You could stay at my house tonight and leave from there," Winter suggested, shamelessly asking him to spend the night with her. Holding his eyes with hers, she felt her cheeks redden in embarrassment.

Loker studied her flushed face for a minute before replying. "That's a tempting invitation, but I haven't packed yet. I'll call you when I get back in town. We could go to Vincent's party and make a night of it."

"I'd like that." Instantly changing her mind about going to the party.

He glanced at his watch. "I should go, it's getting late." He leaned forward and brushed his lips against her cheek. After telling her he would call, he left her staring at his abrupt departure.

There was no doubt in Winter's mind that, if it had been the blonde issuing the invitation, he wouldn't have refused. He had shown no hesitation in refusing hers, however; seemingly more concerned with Vincent's party. She had been a high school principal long enough to tell when she was being manipulated. The sad part was, she let him get away with it.

Winter frowned. She wasn't wealthy, and even though Vincent was her relative, she had no influence over his business decisions. She sighed silently, getting into her car. Loker would be back in two weeks and it was past time they had a conversation about their relationship.

* * *

The Pink Slipper was busy tonight, Winter thought while looking around the busy bar.

"Would you like something to drink, Winter?" Shelly asked politely.

"I'll take an iced tea, thank you." She gazed around the

room as Shelly Scott and Lexi Clark talked. The president and vice-president of the PTA had asked her to accompany them to pick up a large donation for the new scoreboard, which was being made by the owner of the Pink Slipper. Usually the athletic director would go, but his wife had gone into labor that morning and Winter had been asked to extend her gratitude on behalf of the students. She loved her job, but she was getting tired of the politics involved.

Loud, feminine laughter drew her gaze to a table a few feet away where Winter was surprised when she recognized a familiar face within the boisterous group. Beth Cornett had helped care for her mother toward the latter stages of her cancer. They also attended the same church every Sunday. She almost choked on her tea when she heard Beth call them by their names; Sex Piston, Crazy Bitch, and Killyama. Her eyes widened when she realized the group of women Beth was with must belong to a motorcycle club, a conclusion that was easily confirmed when their male counterparts entered the bar and didn't seem happy about their women being in there.

Winter tried to be polite, but was unable to restrain her curiosity from watching the argument take place, since she practically had a front row seat. She was beginning to become concerned for Beth when the door to the bar opened again. This motorcycle club Winter recognized from the jackets they were wearing. The Last Riders took command the second they entered the bar, heading straight to Beth's table.

"Beth."

"Razer?"

"Let's go."

"Bitch isn't going nowhere with you or your men." The woman with her hair teased and crazy eyes answered for Beth then turned to the man who had taken a seat beside her at the table. "Y'all need to get back on your machines and leave us to our fun."

"Beth, let's go, I'm not telling you again."

Beth's eyes narrowed in anger. "You don't have the right to tell me shit. Crazy Bitch is right; you guys need to leave us alone. We were minding our own business until everyone interfered."

"Minding what was in the pants of those pussies you bitches were dancing with when we showed up is more like it," snapped one of the bikers.

"Yeah, I don't care what you think, Ace. We came to celebrate my shop opening Monday. The same one you, or any of you assholes, didn't want to help paint or do shit to help with. I don't want you guys here tonight; you don't deserve to be part of our party."

"I didn't see that douche bag whose throat you had your tongue down doing any hammering there, either."

"Yeah, well, he was going to do plenty later tonight," Sex Piston taunted the biker.

"Was he, or were they?" He jerked his head towards the other club. "Did you plan on hitting their clubhouse next?" the one named Ace asked in a menace-laden voice.

"You kidding me? We were going to fuck around, not betray the club. If we were going to do that, we would have picked one worth the punishment of breaking a rule."

"Did she just put us down?" one of The Last Riders asked. Winter couldn't believe how huge the bald-headed biker was. He was easily the biggest one in the bar.

"Yes, she did, dumbass," Sex Piston mocked.

Winter saw four women push to the front of the men, standing by The Last Riders. She recognized the attractive one from church. Pastor Dean had even introduced the woman to the congregation as Evie.

"What the fuck are you doing here?" an angry voice asked. Winter's eyes looked toward the biker who spoke sharply to the women, unable to believe what her eyes were telling her.

"Loker James?" Beth's questioning voice reverberated through Winter's shocked mind. She couldn't suppress the gasp from escaping her lips, drawing his attention.

Their gazes met across the room as she took in his tight leather pants, boots and black t-shirt with a leather vest. The Last Rider's patches were on the back, proclaiming his membership. The tribal sleeve down one arm was another shock; she hadn't even known he had a tattoo, much less one so large. She had never seen him in anything other than expensive suits with his hair immaculately brushed. Now, the dark mass was longer than she would ever believe he would wear it, making him appear just as dangerous as the others standing next to him. Loker had always displayed a brooding presence with his sophisticated appearance. In his biker gear, there was no appearance of sophistication; nothing was civilized about this man. This Loker James was someone to watch warily then get the hell out of his way, which is what everyone in the restaurant was doing.

"He's Viper," Evie said.

"Well, that's none of my business, is it?" Winter saw Beth's hand tremble when she picked up her drink.

"To answer your question, if Beth was in trouble, we were going to be here to help," Evie answered Loker's angry question.

"Who the fuck are you?" Killyama asked.

"Evie," she answered in a tough voice.

"You're the bitch who left Beth high and dry! Damn, girl, you got balls to stand there after you fucked her man then watched her man fuck these other bitches."

Winter noticed the other club was beginning to look at The Last Riders members with dawning respect.

"How d'you manage that, man? My bitch would cut my balls off in my sleep if I touched another bitch," Ace asked Razer.

"We did it to protect her. We had a brother who was a crazy fuck and the only way we could protect her was to put space between us," Razer answered.

"Yeah, was the hand that was playing with that girl's

titty imaginary? Any one of these fucks do that to one of my bitches, I'm gonna cut his hand off," Killyama warned before leaning back in her seat. Winter noticed the other motorcycle club lost their admiring expressions.

"No, it wasn't imaginary…"

"Let's go, Winter." Shelly and Lexi were grabbing their purses. Winter picked her purse up, but hearing her cousin's name drew her attention back to the bikers.

"…Bedford was arrested or he would never have made a clear move against us. We had to have proof he betrayed the club. We couldn't take someone outside the club's word as proof without evidence," Evie explained.

Winter had heard that her cousin Vincent had been arrested for conspiracy to commit the murder of an investor that had disappeared four years ago. The killer who Vincent had hired must have been a member of The Last Riders.

"So instead, you betrayed Beth. She's not club, so she didn't matter," Killyama threw the explanation back in Evie's face.

"She matters." This time it was Razer who spoke.

"Not enough," Crazy Bitch answered. "But I have a question I need answered." Turning to Beth she asked, "The one with all the tats, he do anything to hurt you? Because my fingers are dying to see how far down those tats go."

Winter didn't have to guess which Last Rider she was referring to because the women's eyes all turned toward the heavily tattooed biker standing next to Razer. Both men had dark brown hair, but the one with the tattoos was cut short and was leaner than the other bikers. It didn't make him look less dangerous than the rest of the men, though. The woman must be crazy to be attracted to him. Even from where she was sitting, Winter could see that he would be a merciless opponent.

"No, he is the best of the bunch. Never saw him laying a hand on the women. Never drunk, didn't see him at the parties. I have no problem with Shade."

Winter noticed that The Last Riders, both male and female, all had mouths dropped open. One of the women began laughing with the other women from the club also joining in.

"Are you serious? He's the wor—" The woman's voice was cut off immediately.

"Shut-up," Shade's voice gave Winter a chill down her back.

"Damn, you had to go and blow it, telling her to shut-up. Don't let him talk to you that way, bitch. Still, if you fuck as good as you look, I could always tape your mouth shut." Winter didn't doubt Crazy Bitch could.

"You aren't going to be touching nothing of his, bitch. Get on the back of my bike; we are leaving," a biker behind Ace yelled.

"I am not going anywhere with you, Joker. We're going to Beth's house after we get done here. Sex Piston is going to cut her hair."

"No, she's not." Razer and Beth spoke at the same time. "I was going to make an appointment next week, remember?" Winter could understand Razer's concern. The woman determined to cut Beth's hair had hair that was teased and tortured until it stood several inches high.

"I'm going to save you the trip," Sex Piston said, slamming her drink down on the table, sloshing what little was left over the side of the glass.

"She's going home with me. You're not touching her hair," Razer warned the woman.

"I am not going home with you," Beth argued back. This amazed Winter because she had never known the woman to ever give a sharp reply to anyone.

"Yes, you are," Razer said between gritted teeth.

"No, I am not."

"Beth is not going anywhere with you." Crazy Bitch put her arm across the back of Beth's chair while the rest of the biker women scooted their chairs closer to Beth.

"Back off," Evie cautioned.

"Listen to the bitch," Crazy Bitch taunted the men.

"I was talking to you," Evie said, taking a step closer to the woman who was practically sitting on Beth's lap.

"Evie." The woman who had laughed at Beth's description of Shade tried to pull Evie back.

"Who are you?" Sex Piston asked.

"Natasha."

"What kind of name is that?"

"I haven't really been given a nickname yet."

"You the new member Viper fucked a couple of weeks ago and you let Beth think it was Razer?" Winter didn't think it was possible to hurt so badly, humiliated that she had ever believed it possible that Loker could want her. Staring at the gorgeous club member, she realized why he had no trouble keeping his distance from her.

"Viper didn't want anyone to know he was in town." Winter's hands clenched on the table. She was one of the people that weren't supposed to know he was in town.

"Instead, it was easier to stick a knife in Beth's back. I can think of several names for you, but first there is something I wanna know, been wondering ever since they walked in the door. He fuck as good as he looks?" She pointed to Loker.

Natasha laughed. "Better."

All the time she had thought he was in Washington, he had been here in town having sex with the woman standing right in front of her. Winter stood, deathly afraid she was going to break down in front of everyone. She didn't look towards Loker, aware he hadn't taken his eyes off her.

"Damn."

"It don't matter how he fucks; none of you bitches are going to find out. Hell, he's keeping his own clubhouse of pussy warm, he's not getting mine. Now get on the fucking bikes!" Ace's face turned a mottled red.

Winter winced, realizing that Loker had obviously been

with more than one of the women who belonged to their club.

The women just sat at the table, ignoring the men as The Last Riders looked at the other motorcycle club in sympathy, which Winter was sure had to sting their pride.

"That's it." Ace moved forward to grab Sex Piston, who threw her drink glass at him. When he dodged it, he accidently shoved the bald-headed Last Rider, who shoved him back.

"Let's get out of here," Shelly said, jerking Winter toward the door. Both groups of bikers began a free-for-all with the women joining in with just as much violence.

"Which of these bitches is Bliss? I'm going to take care of her tonight, too," Winter heard one of the women yell.

Shelly and Lexi were both grabbing her arms, trying to get out of the way of the escalating fight when a hard shove almost sent the women to the ground. A scream left Shelly as they found themselves held upright by Loker and the tattooed man.

"Get the fuck out of here," Loker ordered.

Winter tore her arm free from his grasp. "We're trying to." Shelly and Lexi were pushed through the doorway first while Loker blocked the fists flying his way. A grunt escaped his lips when a vicious punch landed on his ribcage. Another biker slammed his friend in the face with a tray that the waitresses used to carry drinks.

Loker managed to push her outside before the rival bikers bombarded him. Winter's face was ashen as she tried to remember where she had parked her car. Shakily reaching into her purse, she located her keys while Shelly and Lexi, scared stupid, were standing by her car, trying to get in while the doors were still locked, causing the shrill car alarm to fill the parking lot.

Quickly, Winter hit the alarm button on her remote then unlocked the doors. The women scrambled into the car, locking the doors behind them. Exasperated by this point, Winter was afraid she was going to lose what little control she had left. Taking a deep breath, she unlocked the doors again, opening the driver's door before they could lock her out once more.

Winter's shaking fingers put the key into the ignition as the three women watched Razer walk out of the Pink Slipper with Beth struggling on his shoulder.

"Let's get the hell out of here," Shelly screamed.

She turned the key in the ignition before realizing they were trapped in the parking spot by dozens of motorcycles.

They could do nothing except wait and watch until the police were finally able to break up the fight, arresting all of the men and The Last Riders' women. Beth's friends came outside to taunt everyone as they were loaded into the waiting squad cars while Loker was brought outside with his hands handcuffed behind his back and put in the back of the Sheriff's car. Winter hoped they locked him in jail and threw away the key, but didn't have high expectations that her prayers would be answered.

* * *

Winter heard the knock as she stepped out of the shower. Hastily pulling on a pair of pink sweats and pink t-shirt, she rushed to answer it only to find Loker in the doorway. He was not what she wanted after the revelation that she had been nothing more than a pawn used to get closer to Vincent. She hadn't been home ten minutes before the small town rumor mill had been at work. After hanging up from the third call, she had known everything there was to know about the president of The Last Riders.

She tried not to appreciate his muscular frame dressed in jeans and a black shirt. The suits he had worn disguised how physically cut he was. Winter was embarrassed that she had ever believed a man like him would want her. In the two years she had known him, he had never come to her house dressed so casually. She figured now that the whole town knew his true identity, there must no longer be a need to pretend.

"Loker, why are you here?" Her tone was less than welcoming.

"I would like to come in and explain."

Winter held the door firmly. "I don't think that will be necessary."

Loker reached out and pushed the door open, easily forcing her back from the door.

"We need to talk." She was smart enough to realize there was no way to avoid the humiliating end to the farce of a relationship they'd had. Sighing, she closed the door. This time it was her turn to paste on an expressionless mask.

"I was just about to pour myself a cup of coffee, would you like one?"

"No, thanks." He followed her down the hallway to her bright kitchen. The sunny room was warm and inviting with touches of her personality. She loved to cook, spending her free time in the room. She had even padded the chairs at the table because she preferred to do her paperwork there instead of in her office.

"Take a seat," she offered, not turning around to see if he had taken her suggestion. Removing a cup from the cabinet, she poured herself a cup of coffee. Out of habit, she did not add sugar, even though she liked her coffee sweet. With the sweetener, it tended to put her in hyper drive. She already felt on edge, she didn't need the added stimulation.

Unable to put it off any longer, she turned to face Loker to see that he was sitting at her table, grimacing as he adjusted himself carefully in the chair.

"I see you're a little worse for wear today. I did notice they seemed especially intent on you and the one with all the tattoos," Winter said unsympathetically.

"They were."

"I don't think they appreciated their women wanting to fuck you two."

Loker froze at her use of the explicit word. Winter had

never even said damn in front of him since they had met.

"Winter—" She broke in before he could continue.

"Of course, from what I heard, the women would have to wait in line. A long line."

"Sit down and I will explain." At one time she would have done just that—did whatever he told her, how he told her—those days were over.

"I don't need your explanations. I am not stupid or even as blind as I obviously was. I can understand English and can figure out exactly what happened. I was a way to get close to Vincent, wasn't I?"

"Yes. Ben Stiles, also. I didn't know which of the two was responsible for my brother's death."

"Congratulations, mystery solved." Winter could not prevent herself from tacking on, "I am sorry about your brother."

"Thank you."

"Now will you leave, Loker, or do you prefer Viper?"

"Whichever you prefer," he said, trying to remain patient.

"Very well then, Viper, get out."

"I am not leaving until I explain. I want to maintain our friendship, and whether you believe me or not, I care about you."

"As friends?"

"Yes." A knife to her gut would hurt less. It was time to level this playing field.

"I am afraid that's not going to work for me. I don't want or need a con artist for a friend."

"You think because I'm in a motorcycle club that I am a criminal?"

"You stole something from me that I will never get back. Well, to be honest, two things; my time and trust."

"I was very careful to maintain a platonic relationship with you. I never led you to believe that it was an exclusive relationship."

"But you were aware my feelings were not the same."

His silence said it all.

Winter sat the coffee cup down on the counter before she threw it at him. Viper's dark eyes followed the movement. She had put on her shirt without taking the time to properly dry off and put on a bra, therefore the thin material clung damply to her breasts. Her hair was drying in a mass of curls that she always blow dried out and styled into a professional look, well aware she needed to maintain a certain image with her job. She had always been aware that she had to project an appearance of authority and professionalism or the students and parents wouldn't respect her position. She only relaxed her guard in the privacy of her own home.

"Wow. You are a complete and utter ass. I thought we had a relationship; you knew I thought that. I waited patiently for you like a fool when you were out of town; while you were fucking your own personal stash of women in not one motorcycle club, but two."

"They are not my own personal stash. The women in The Last Riders don't belong to anyone," Viper sighed. He had not wanted the conversation to turn ugly, but he could see that had been a false hope. "The members are not exclusive to anyone; neither male nor female."

Winter could only stand there with her mouth open, her mind unable to comprehend the sheer magnitude of his deceit.

"Like a sex club? You share the women?"

"It is a motorcycle club first and foremost. We share different interests, one of those is sexual. To answer your question, as best as I can, we have sex with whomever we want within the club. We are very careful with safety and have stringent rules that are followed."

She felt her retort bubbling up her throat, unable to prevent it bursting free. "Two freaking years."

"Winter, I had to find out the truth about my brother."

"You could have been honest with me. You know I would have helped you and never opened my mouth. You knew that!"

"I couldn't take the chance."

"Because it was easier to let me be hurt. You met my mother; you let me introduce you to her knowing that I was hoping we would eventually become more than friends. You could have made it perfectly clear you had no interest in me that way. Instead, you played me, using my desire to be with you to manipulate yourself into situations where you would come into contact with the men you believed killed your brother. Any man would realize when I introduced you to my mother that it meant something. She died with that lie.

"I… hate… you. You are a liar and a deceitful man. You could have made sure anytime within the last two years that I knew our friendship wasn't going to grow into something else, but you didn't! Instead, I felt like it was something I was doing wrong." Winter furiously blinked back her tears. "Did you even realize how embarrassed I was to ask you to spend the night? I offered myself on a silver platter and you couldn't run away fast enough. You practically fucked everyone you came in contact within two states except me." Taking deep breaths, Winter tried to regain control of her boiling temper.

Viper stood, coming towards her, and she put out her hand to stop him. "If you come near me, I will slam my fist in those ribs, and by the look of you, they are extremely painful." He came to a dead stop. "I think it is past time for you to leave." He stood there silently, taking in how deeply he had hurt her, unable to make excuses for himself. He had done exactly what she had accused him of doing.

"I'll go. I wanted to explain, but now I can see I should have given it time. I hope you will be able to forgive me someday. I am sorry." Winter followed him to the door, trying to maintain what little control she had until it closed behind him. As he was going out the door, she asked him the question that had been on her mind since last night.

"Which woman at your club has blond spiked hair, about average height?"

"Bliss?"

"She the one that group of biker women wanted?"

"Yes." Viper's jaw tensed.

"That's what I thought." Winter took a step back and slammed the door in his face.

CHAPTER ONE

The fenced in backyard of the church was filled to capacity with the congregation and the members of The Last Riders. Winter carefully balanced the potato salad she had prepared, thankful the buffet table was empty of guests as she slid it among the colorful array of choices.

Glancing around the yard, she saw her friend and secretary drawing flags on children's faces.

"Hello Emily." A highlighted strand of hair had fallen across her forehead into her eyes. With her paint-stained hand, she was unable to move the irritant, so Winter casually brushed it away, receiving a thankful sigh in response.

"Keeping busy?" Winter grinned.

"I could use some help," Emily admitted.

Winter jumped into the fray, organizing activities for the children in different areas of the yard so that Emily was allowed a breather. She was setting up the horseshoe game when a large cheer from the picnic table area drew her attention.

The Last Riders were gathered around Beth and Razer. It was obvious what the cheers were for as she was holding out her hand to the women in the group to examine the ring on her finger. Winter went back to handing out the horseshoes to little hands anxiously waiting for them, her face carefully blank. She had been conscious of Viper's eyes on her, but she ignored him, turning her back so that she could no longer see the group.

Winter hadn't seen him during the last four months, yet the small town rumor mill had been active. She had stayed away from the gossip, though her friends—self called— had made sure that she was aware of Viper's actions. No longer hiding his connection to The Last Riders, her friends spitefully let her know each and every time he was seen out in public with one of the women from the club. She eventually quit taking their calls and avoided them in public. She had quickly learned not only to hide her reactions from the viciousness of the gossip, but also to suppress them until she no longer felt much of anything.

The only reason she stayed in Treepoint was because she loved her job and the few true friends she had left. She hoped eventually the gossip would die down, however having grown up in Treepoint, she realistically knew that it would be a long time coming.

Winter was playing freeze tag with the rambunctious preschoolers when Lily joined the group with a grin. She smiled at the beautiful girl as she chased the children around the yard. Lily was one of the few friends she had remaining. Winter had been a student teacher when she had tutored Lily, then eventually taught her in high school for a couple of years before she had been promoted to principal.

When her mother became ill with cancer, both of the sisters had been there for her. Beth had been an excellent caregiver and made it possible to let her pass away at home. Winter didn't know if she would have been strong enough to do it without their help. Lily had also helped by giving her time to rest; she would stay by her mother's bed when exhaustion would claim Winter. She felt she owed both women a debt of gratitude.

A touch on her arm had her freezing in place not far from where one of her female students was standing. Carmen was leaning against a tree with her boyfriend standing next to her and they appeared to be arguing. Winter was about to interrupt them when Carmen caught her eye and shook her head. Just after that, a small family arrived, distracting her attention from the arguing couple.

"Hi, Jenny," Winter greeted the parents of nine-month-old twin boys. Dressed in matching blue jean overalls, they were adorable. Her hands were reaching out for one of them before she had finished her greeting.

"Hello, Winter." Laughing, Jenny released her child into Winter's grasp.

Lily was already snagging the other twin from the proud father.

"I remember when everyone was glad to see us, now it's all about the boys," Jenny mocked reproachfully to the two baby thieves.

"That's what happens when you have two adorable babies," Winter complimented. "Why don't you let Lily and I watch them while you two go eat?"

"Are you sure; they can be a handful?" Dan replied.

"Don't question our luck." Jenny laughed.

"Go ahead," Lily agreed.

"All right, if you're sure?" Dan questioned once more before taking his wife's hand, leading her towards the buffet table.

Winter and Lily grinned at each other with their prizes in hand. The other children quickly regained their attention, both of them running with a baby balanced on their hip. Their laughter sounded sweetly through the yard, drawing attention to the women.

About that time, Lily's boyfriend approached and Winter watched him hand her a drink. Lily looked at him with a grateful smile. Winter's heart lurched at the emotion evident in Charles's eyes. He had always loved the girl, and everyone in town knew it. Winter had experience being around hormone crazy young adults and knew when the chemistry was there. With them, it wasn't. Something was missing, and whatever it was, it was missing on Lily's part. The passion was plainly visible in Charles's face and body language while Lily simply treated him like a friend. They had dated since high school and now that Lily was in college, she didn't see them together as often. It hurt Winter to see someone make her own mistake of caring for someone who would never return their feelings. She had a feeling Charles would one day learn his own painful lesson.

Lily handed Charles the cup, and as he took it, he reached out to place his arm around her shoulders and pulled her closer to his side. The two with the baby between them gave a false image of a small, happy family. Winter could almost imagine them one day looking just as they did now with their own family.

A sudden movement from across the yard where The Last Riders were standing drew Winter's attention. The guy with all the tattoos was flipping out. He was heading towards Lily with an expression of lethal intent, and it was focused on Charles, who had never been in a physical altercation in his life.

Razer tried to hold him back, and Winter gasped as he was punched in the face. Viper moved forward and tattoo guy's boot flew out to nail him in the balls. Winter fell in love. She was unable to keep the smirk from her lips as Viper laid on the ground in a crumpled mess. Two of the other bikers ran forward to stop him and were promptly smashed together. They were just infuriating him even more. Winter looked for Beth, and not seeing her, knew she was going to have to take charge.

"Charles, I left a couple bags of clothes in my car for the rummage sale. Could you get them and take them to Pastor Dean's office for me?"

"No problem. I'll be right back," Charles told Lily before moving towards the parking lot.

Lily went back to playing with the kids while Winter wasn't able to stop herself from looking back at The Last Riders. The four men who were holding tattoo guy released him and quickly backed away. Winter felt the questioning gazes of the group on her, wondering why she had interfered, and truthfully, Winter didn't know. Giving them her back, she began rounding the children up to play horseshoes.

The game was fun and the excited pleasure from the children made Winter forget that Viper was nearby.

"The little hellions are going to wear us out," Winter said, out of breath.

Lily laughed. "I know."

As Lily's laughter trailed off, the sound of an argument began drawing the attention of those close by to Carmen and her boyfriend. He had her pinned against the tree with his hand at her throat. Winter moved forward before she remembered the baby on her hip. Motioning for Emily, who had seen her signal and was hurrying towards her, Winter was unable to believe what was happening before her eyes. A metal horseshoe was flying across the yard, striking Jake in the back. Surprised into releasing Carmen, he turned to see Lily glaring in his face.

"Don't touch her," the girl hissed. Winter couldn't believe it was Lily standing up to the young man. There she stood, with the baby on her hip, demanding that he didn't lay a hand on a cringing Carmen. Quickly, Winter passed the baby to Emily and hurried to Lily's side.

"What business is it of yours?" Jake tried to intimidate the young girl.

"I am making it my business. You were hurting her," Lily replied.

"Perhaps, Jake, you could take a breather until you calm down," Winter interrupted, using her authoritative principal voice.

"You two cunts need to back off."

Winter stiffened. Jake had dropped out of school last

year. She had done everything she could to persuade him not to leave, however he had a hostile attitude then and now it was even worse. She was smart enough to know that there were situations better left for someone else to handle and this was definitely one of them. The problem was extracting Carmen and Lily from the volatile situation safely.

"We can do that. Lily and I were just going to get the kids a drink and we could use some help. Carmen, would you mind?"

"She isn't going anywhere. We're leaving." Jerking Carmen to his side, he shoved Winter out of his way. Almost losing her balance, she felt an arm go around her waist, holding her steady until she was able to regain her balance. Jake and the women found themselves surrounded by The Last Riders.

Stiffening, Winter didn't need to turn around to see who was behind her.

"That was a mistake," Viper said at her back. Winter quickly moved away from him, finding a place to stand to the side of the group.

"You need to let the girl go and take a walk with me." The cold voice of tattoo guy drew everyone's eyes as he stood directly in front of Lily, blocking her from view.

"What's going on?" Pastor Dean hurried toward the group with Beth at his side. She immediately went to her sister while, thankfully, Dan and Jenny came to retrieve their baby from Lily. They had drawn a crowd around the couple, preventing Jake from leaving with a frightened Carmen.

Winter moved forward, taking Carmen's hand in hers, tugging her away from Jake. For a second he looked like he was going to explode, but even as furious as he was, Jake knew he was outnumbered. Gratefully, Carmen let herself be led away from her boyfriend and Winter left The Last Riders to handle Jake.

"Can I get you a drink?" she asked Carmen.

"Yes, please." Winter went to the cooler and took a soda, placing it before Carmen as she sat down next to her.

"Are you all right?"

"Yes, it's not the first time Jake has lost his temper with me. He will cool down and apologize," Carmen excused her boyfriend's behavior.

"Of course he will, honey, but, Carmen, he shouldn't be laying his hands on you when he's angry."

"He doesn't mean anything," Carmen argued.

"Carmen, he could hurt you. Does he lose his temper often?" The girl instantly became guarded. Winter took that as a definite yes.

"He was just mad because he caught me staring at those bikers. He was jealous."

"It doesn't matter what the reason was, he doesn't have the right to hurt you."

"Look, Ms. Simmons, Jake was just angry at me for doing something I shouldn't be doing. I made a mistake. Where is he?"

Winter saw her trying to find him in the crowd, but she wanted to get Carmen out of there before he returned. She didn't have as much faith as Carmen that his temper had calmed down.

"Why don't I take you home and he can call you later?" The girl did not want to leave, however Winter ushered Carmen to her car despite her protests of leaving Jake behind. She only lived a block away from her, so she was able to reach the small house without asking for directions.

Following her to the door of her house, she could tell Carmen just wanted her to leave. "Are your parents home?" Winter asked.

The girl thought about lying, yet all the years of experience of dealing with teenagers enabled Winter to push the doorbell with confidence that her parents were home.

"I was going to go in," Carmen lied.

Before Winter could answer, Carmen's mother

26

answered the door.

"Carmen? Ms. Simmons?" The woman was obviously surprised to find her daughter's principal on her front porch.

"Mrs. Jones, can I come in and speak to you and your husband for a few minutes?" Winter requested politely.

The door opened wider, allowing her entrance with a sullen Carmen following reluctantly behind.

Winter tactfully explained what had happened at the church picnic once both parents were present. Carmen's parents were understandably upset when Winter explained what had occurred between the young couple. Winter exited soon afterwards, feeling it best if she left the family to deal with Carmen privately, praying they would be more successful in convincing the girl that Jake had a serious problem.

Winter could only hope that the girl would wise up before someone was hurt.

* * *

Winter shut off the vacuum, pulling the plug from the wall. She was about to put it back in the closet when she heard the doorbell ring. She opened the door without thinking and was immediately sorry.

"Go away." She tried to slam the door in Viper's face, but his hand caught the door, forcing it to open wider before he brushed passed her as he walked inside. Winter was getting tired of Viper thinking he could simply barge his way into her home.

"Don't you check before you open the door?"

"I will from now on. Get out."

"I want to talk to you."

"As I told you the last time, we have nothing to talk about."

Viper's face-hardened, he was angry already and she was making him angrier by refusing to listen to what he had to say.

"What were you thinking to confront that punk?"

27

"I was thinking I might save Lily from getting hurt."

"He was never going to get a hand on Lily."

"Really? I have news for you; tattoo guy wasn't going to reach her in time. Jake was about to punch her for throwing that horseshoe and he didn't care she was holding a baby."

"Shade?"

"Is he the one covered in tattoos?"

"Yes."

Winter shrugged. "Anyway, it worked out. I took Carmen home, had a talk with her parents who were unaware their sixteen-year-old daughter was dating a scumbag who lays his hands on her when he gets angry. It's now their problem to solve. Now will you leave?"

"You're wrong if you think it's over. That punk has a real problem. Make sure you stay out of it and let the family deal with him." Winter's jaw tightened. Viper stood in her living room, ordering her around and not listening, just like old times. She turned her back and went to the phone, dialing the sheriff's office.

"Maggie, this is Winter Simmons. I have an intruder at my home."

Viper's eyebrows rose as he listened. His arms folded across his chest.

"Thank you." Winter hung up the phone. "Now will you leave?"

"What, and have the red lights chasing after me? No thanks." Viper went to sit on the couch and came to a stop. Turning around in a circle, he noticed all the changes. Winter stood there silently.

She had completely redecorated her home. The stiff, formal living room furniture had been donated to charity and a large, overstuffed tan sofa had replaced it. All the flowery prints were gone; they were instead replaced by neutral colors with hints of coral and turquoise. The hard wood floors had been covered in thick, lush carpet and panels of white sheers fluttered in the early evening breeze.

Redecorating the house had given her something to occupy her mind and time over the last few months, but more importantly, it had allowed her to erase all the memories of Viper being in her home. The memories of them sitting on the couch or having dinner at the table had been wiped clean with the precision of a surgeon using a scalpel. Now he was back inside her house, wearing sexy leather pants and a Harley t-shirt, stamping his presence in her memory with her new things.

He had to leave because she could not afford to redecorate again.

"What in the hell did you do to your house?"

"I redecorated."

Viper had not cared for the flowery furniture that Winter's mother had obviously picked, however this was the complete opposite. Anything homey had been removed; all the personal touches, all the knick-knacks that she loved to collect—several of which he had bought her himself. It looked like it had come out of a decorating magazine. Anyone could live here; no personal photographs of her growing up with her parents, or even the picture of her at an award banquet with him.

That was when it hit him. She had cut anything that hurt her out of her life. She had made a sanctuary for herself. Viper felt his gut clench.

"I can fucking see that." That wasn't all he was seeing. He became aware that she was standing there in blue jean shorts that barely covered her curvy ass he hadn't been aware she had, and a pink top that showed her midriff that was toned and flat.

"I can understand you trashing my picture, but Sue's, also? Why?"

"Don't you dare mention my mother. You are not allowed to have her name in your lying mouth." Winter lost it. "Get out now." She went to him and began shoving him toward the door. Viper didn't move; instead, he took her arms and pulled her towards him. Her shrieks of anger were going to draw every nosy neighbor in the neighborhood.

Viper lowered his head and caught her mouth with his in an attempt to shut her up. . Her mouth was open and sweet tasting like the strawberries and cream gum she loved to chew; it was as if lightning struck his balls. He had made sure never to kiss her open-mouthed while they had been seeing each other, but he gave himself leeway now that she knew exactly who he was. He kissed her, no holds barred, as her struggles ceased, letting him kiss her as she lay limply against his chest.

Winter felt overwhelmed as Viper kissed her as she had fantasized him doing;   passionately and without restraint. His tongue explored her mouth as he released her hands so his hand could grip her jaw, tilting her head to the side in order to deepen the kiss.

Winter tried to take a step back and break contact, but his other hand grabbed her ass, pulling her into his body. His fingers splayed out until they lay against the bottom flesh of her ass to hold her in place.

Fire raced through her as her bare belly came into contact with his cock behind his leather pants. He tightened his grip on her ass, fitting her snugly against him. Winter moaned into his mouth as she felt him swell…

"Humph…." The clearing throat had her tearing out of Viper's arms.

Before she could make explanations, the Sheriff spoke, "I had a report of an intruder entering your home."

"He was getting ready to enter something else," the deputy at his side said crudely.

"That was uncalled for," Winter snapped, angry enough at herself without some jackass of a deputy making her feel worse.

The Sheriff frowned at his deputy. "Yes it was, Deputy Moore. Apologize and wait in the car." The Sheriff's commanding tone left the deputy no choice other than to do what he was told.

The deputy apologized, leaving without another word when Viper glared at the smug bastard.

"Sorry, Winter, Viper. Mayor's nephew. I'm stuck with him until I can get enough write ups to fire his ass; this incident will go into my file. Now, back to why I was called. What's going on?"

"I told Viper not to come in and he forced his way in."

The Sheriff's brow rose. "That true, Viper?"

He shrugged. "Yes."

"You want to press charges?" He turned back to Winter.

"Yes," Winter answered.

"All right." He pulled his notebook out of his pocket, beginning to write. "Of course, it will make the newspaper. You'll have to go to court and testify. I will have to testify that I walked in and found you two being intimate."

Winter's mouth dropped open. "Is this the good ole boy system at work?"

The Sheriff's eyes grew cold. "Actually, I was trying to save you some embarrassment."

"How exactly is that, Sheriff? Your deputy comes in here, insults me to my face, gives a half-ass apology that he didn't mean and didn't care that I knew. To add insult to injury, you tell me that, even though Viper admitted to coming in without my permission, I will be the one made a fool of, which was probably why he grabbed and kissed me. Why don't you both just leave? Can you at least accomplish that for me?" Winter demanded.

"Yes, I can. Let's go, Viper."

Viper stared intently at Winter, but went out the door with the waiting sheriff without an argument. Winter locked the door behind them before going into the kitchen to make a drink for herself. Pulling a soda out of the refrigerator, she went to the table and sat down, burying her face in her hands. Her mind kept replaying the kiss with Viper.

After several minutes, she straightened her shoulders

and dragged her mind back to the present, opening her computer to bury herself in work. Keeping busy was the only way she had learned to drive Viper out of her mind.

* * *

Viper slammed the door to the clubhouse; the members were sitting around the living room relaxing. Some were talking and a few were sitting back, drinking a cold beer after being out in the hot sun of the picnic. He went to the bar, selected a glass and poured himself a glass of whiskey before taking the bottle and sitting on one of the stools.

"What's got you so mad?" a seductive voice asked at his side. Viper lifted his glass, taking a long swallow. Bliss was on him constantly since she needed his vote to become a full member and so far, she had been patient.

She wanted to fuck him and he didn't think it was about the vote. The woman was the picture of nubile sex on two gorgeous legs. The nickname of Bliss had been earned when several members had remarked her pussy was that good. The problem was, he couldn't get a hard on for her. He kept remembering the way Winter described her before slamming that damn door in his face.

The weird thing was, before then, he had been anxious to sink his cock into that nubile body, yet that one little look had taken the life right out of it. He had fucked around on Winter for two years—guilt free—until she had found out the truth then the guilt had kicked in with a vengeance. He took another drink, smothering the conscious that was trying to rise once again.

"Nothing, Bliss. I just need a drink." The pretty blond moved away to sit next to Knox on one of the large couches in the room.

He managed to throw back the rest of his drink before pouring himself another while studying the women in the room. Each had their own particular way of satisfying men. Natasha, if you wanted a quick fun time. Dawn, if you needed a good workout. Ember, if you wanted to go

32

slow and play the seductive games she liked to play. Stori, if you didn't mind the chatter. Jewell and Evie were the ones up for anything.

Not seeing Evie, he caught Jewell's eye. She wandered over to him, sliding her arm around his neck, her breasts in the white tank visibly showing her rose tipped breasts. Jewell liked sex and lots of it. She made no apologies for it and The Last Riders gave her what she wanted on a regular basis.

"What do you need tonight, Viper?"

His hand went between her thighs and slid under her short skirt. His fingers found her already wet and ready. Jewell's hand went to his zipper, pulling out his long, thick cock before she licked her lips and went down on him. Viper's hand left her pussy to slide under her gaping top, playing with her breasts as she sucked hungrily at his cock. The thing with Jewell was, she loved to give blowjobs; they made her hotter than hell. That made the men even hotter because, when she would stare at their cocks, they knew exactly what she was thinking.

Finally, Viper felt his balls tighten in the beginning of his release. The fire that had started when his tongue had entered Winter's mouth was about to be put out. As he came, Jewell moaned as his hand grabbed her hair, forcing more of his length inside her mouth. When she let his cock go, a shudder shook his body.

"You done for the night?" Jewell asked, her body in desperate need of relief.

"What do you think?" Viper moved his glass and bottle to the side, lifting Jewell onto the bar until her pussy was right where he wanted it. He jerked her skirt up around her waist, aware the whole room was watching. His cock was already hardening again and his conscious was easing.

This was what he had spared Winter from. The uptight woman would never have been able to give him what he needed sexually, and if he had fucked her while he was trying to find his brother's killer, then he would have felt like an even bigger fraud. He had kept his distance from plenty of women, waiting to keep him satisfied the way he needed.

Pulling her nether lips apart, he found her namesake and went down. His mouth repaid her in kind as she lay back on the bar, giving everyone a clear view. Viper drove her into one peak after another. Finally, after another hard orgasm, he let her down from the bar. Her legs were too weak to hold her up, so Viper's hand slid around her waist and lifted her into his arms.

"Aren't you done?"

"We're just getting started," Viper replied.

Jewell moaned as he carried her upstairs to his bed, leaving the door open.

CHAPTER TWO

The school bus rolled to a stop in front of Treepoint High School. Winter and her assistant principal, Jeff Morgan, rolled their eyes as the boisterous teens stormed off the bus.

"Another year begins," Jeff groaned.

"Oh, come on; it's not that bad." Winter's cheerful voice could barely be heard among the loud voices.

"Yes, it is," he said, watching two football players pick on one of the band students.

Winter laughed at his glum attitude, her smile dying when she saw Carmen's mother walking towards her from the parking lot.

"Why is Mrs. Jones here?"

"She has an appointment to see you first thing this morning," Jeff spoke, looking at the schedule in his hand.

"I'll talk to her then call the students to the gym for the 'Welcome to the New Year' speech." Winter mentally reorganized the start to her day.

"Better you than me." He hated dealing with parents, and Winter was more adept at dealing with the problems the students and parents would unload on the school.

"Ms. Simmons."

"Mrs. Jones, I understand we have an appointment this morning. My office is this way." The two women walked through the busy hallways to reach Winter's office. Informing Emily to hold her calls, she escorted the woman inside.

"How are you today?" Winter asked, concerned because the woman looked so tired.

"Fine," she said abruptly. "I will cut to the chase and tell you that Carmen will be leaving Treepoint High. Her father and I have decided that it is better that she live with my sister for her senior year. When we find a buyer for the house, we'll be moving also."

Winter had not seen Carmen since the picnic a month ago and was hoping things had improved.

"Has she ended her relationship with Jake?"

"Unfortunately not. They feel that we are trying to keep them apart, which truthfully, we are. Carmen snuck out of the house last week and did not return until the next day. She had a black eye, yet refuses to admit he is responsible. He frightens her father and me. After we told Carmen she was no longer allowed to see him, our tires were slashed and someone set our shed on fire. We called the sheriff, but there is little he can do until he can find proof or Carmen admits he hit her. My sister lives in New Jersey and doesn't work, so she can keep an eye on her until we can join her."

"Usually I would hate to lose a student of Carmen's caliber, but in this case, I wholeheartedly agree with your decision." She wasn't about to talk the parents out of taking their daughter to another school when her safety was in question. Winter pushed the button for the intercom, requesting copies of Carmen's records.

"I think it's best if I just give you notarized copies of her records, that way there will be no trail for Jake to follow unless Carmen tells him."

"We haven't told her yet. We're going to pack her things when I get home. We aren't going to let her have a phone, so she won't have the opportunity to call him."

Emily entered, carrying the requested records. Taking the papers, Winter looked through them, making sure all the correct forms for entering a new school system were there and then imprinted them with her notary stamp. Placing the paperwork in a large envelope, she handed it to Mrs. Jones.

"I wish you all the best. Please keep me informed on how Carmen does in her new school," Winter requested, truly concerned for Carmen's safety.

"I will, and thank you, Ms. Simmons. If you hadn't brought Carmen home after the picnic, it might have been too late for my daughter."

Winter smiled, escorting the woman outside to her car. She was walking back towards the school when she saw Jake sitting in his black mustang in the lot, watching her. The hatred on his face was plain to see even from a distance. She pulled the phone from her pocket and called school security.

"Tom, this is Ms. Simmons. There is a black mustang on the south lot. The young man inside is no longer a student. Will you see that he leaves the school property?"

"Yes, Ms. Simmons. I will be right there."

"Make sure you bring someone with you. I don't want you confronting him on your own. Notify the sheriff's office also that you will be asking a trespasser to leave the property."

"Yes, ma'am."

She entered the school and stood there until Tom and another male security guard approached the car. When they were within a few feet, he spun out of the lot. Relieved he had left without a confrontation, Winter went to her office to call for the assembly to greet the new students and give encouragement for the year ahead.

* * *

The parking lot was dark as she locked the doors to the front of the school. She was angry with herself for staying so late. She knew better, however the paperwork had been piled up with it being the end of the first week. She had wanted to sort what needed to be done and take the rest home to work on leisurely over the weekend. Thankfully, her car was parked nearby. Placing her briefcase on the hood of the car, she bent to unlock the door.

Suddenly, a rough hand grabbed her hair, pulling her backwards and almost off her feet before slinging her forward, smashing her face into the driver's side window. Winter didn't know how she didn't lose consciousness; the pain was that horrendous. She crumbled to the asphalt by her car, crying softly.

She knew there was no one around to hear if she screamed since the school property was isolated on the edge of town. Pain and fear filled her body as a boot kicked her in the ribs while she lay helpless on the ground. Winter had never known real terror in her lifetime, but she felt it when she realized he was not done with her.

Forcing herself to move, she tried to get to her feet. The agonizing pain in her ribs stopped her upward movement then a fist to her jaw flung her backwards. Blood from the cuts on her forehead ran into her eyes, blurring her vision. The parking lot light above her head obscured any vision she had left. Winter rolled onto her belly, trying to crawl away from the person attacking her. Her nails, that she had polished and buffed just that morning, broke as she used them to claw herself from the source of her agony. She knew whoever was hurting her was intent on killing her, but she had to try. The final agony came when the booted foot slammed down on her spine releasing her from consciousness.

* * *

The cell phone ringing on the table next to the bed woke Cash from a deep sleep. Rolling over, he snagged the phone and raised it to his ear.

Viper came out of the bathroom, leaving Evie to finish her shower alone, and saw that Cash was sitting on his bed talking on his cell phone with Bliss lying naked by his side. The club's usual Friday night gathering had ended up with the four of them in his room. Now he just wanted them all to leave so that he could get dressed and go downstairs for breakfast. Ignoring the others in the room, he went to his chest and pulled out his jeans and shirt. By the look on Cash's face whatever news he was receiving was bad.

Evie waved on her way out the door, giving Bliss a look that couldn't be mistaken. Taking the hint, Bliss climbed out of his bed. Coming to stand in front of him, she reached up to place a kiss on his lips. He wanted to turn away, but didn't, letting her have her moment.

"Thanks, Viper."

"Thank you, Bliss." Giving a cheeky grin, the woman left. He was sure she was in a hurry to gather the women together to make a run to town to get the tattoo proclaiming her a full-fledged membership.

"Viper."

Viper sat down on the bed, putting his boots on. He turned to see Cash getting dressed. "What's up?"

"Don't know how to tell you this, so I am just going to tell you like it is. That was the sheriff's office. They need me to track a suspect into the mountains that almost beat a woman to death last night. They didn't find her until this morning when security got there to open the school for basketball practice."

Viper sat there in the chair, knowing whom Cash was talking about. He had warned Winter a hundred times about staying at school so late.

"How bad?" Cash tugged on his boots while grabbing his bike keys off the nightstand. He hurried to the bedroom door, pausing just long enough to tell him what information he had been given.

"Bad. He almost beat her to death and then she lay in the parking lot, exposed to the elements all fucking night. The sheriff doesn't think she is going to make it. Sorry, man, but I have to go. They are waiting for me."

"Go." Cash didn't have to be told twice.

As Viper was walking out, he could hear the sound of Cash's bike as he throttled it down the mountain road. His hand reached out to grab the handlebar of his bike, but he couldn't climb on. He was too busy vomiting.

* * *

Pain. That was all she knew for the longest time. At first, when she would try to wake up, the pain would drive her back into unconsciousness. When she was able, after the longest time, to open her swollen eyes, her screams of pain could be heard down the hallways and the nurses would rush to inject her with more pain medication.

Winter learned eventually to wake slowly with as little movement as possible until the pain medication could take effect. Lying still was a torture in itself to someone as active as she had been. Completely at the mercy of various nurses, they cared for all her basic needs, taking away what little pride she had left. Her mind would drift away when they would impersonally clean her, changing the pads and sheets underneath her broken body.

The worst was when the doctor considered her lucid enough to give her details of her condition. The medical terms were hard to understand with the pain medication clouding her mind. The nurse, understanding her confusion, waited until the doctor left to explain that she had a vertebral fracture, which they had to operate on in order to stabilize. The brace she was in would be on for several weeks and she was going to require therapy to return to normal.

The concussion must have come from having her head slammed into the car window that had left a large gash across her forehead, requiring sutures that would undoubtedly leave a scar. Her jaw had been fractured, and two of her ribs were cracked. When she was finished answering Winter's questions she reassured her that she would heal, given time.

The gossipmongers that came by to see her were never

given admittance to her room. The first words Winter spoke were to keep visitors out. She had no family left and the few friends she wanted to see were put on a list. A security guard was placed outside her door when Viper tried repeatedly to gain admittance. She didn't want his sympathy and she certainly didn't want him to see her looking like a prizefighter after twelve rounds.

Viper would sit in the waiting area, which luckily for him, was a few feet away from her door. He became a master at reading the nurses' and doctor's expressions as they left her room on whether she was having a good day, or one in which even medication didn't help. He knew what the doctors were going to tell her before she did. He had bribed the nurses on duty to see her doctor's notes and to make sure she was taken care of the way he wanted.

He was watching her door when he saw the sheriff coming down the hallway. Their eyes met before he entered Winter's room. He also knew that she was about to find out who was responsible for putting her in the hospital; the man that Viper had every intention of killing.

CHAPTER THREE

The door opening didn't even draw Winter's attention because she had become so used to the nurses coming and going. It wasn't until the Sheriff moved to stand in front of her that she lifted her eyes. Even a man who had been through two tours in the military and cleaned up many fatalities flinched when he saw her face.

"Winter."

"Sheriff."

"I waited until the doctor said it would be okay to let you know what happened." Will Hunter had been sheriff for several years and, while she liked and respected him, she couldn't help holding a grudge that he hadn't taken her more seriously when she'd called to report Viper's trespassing.

"I already know what happened. What I want to know is who?"

"Jake. He blamed you for telling Carmen's parents that he was mistreating her."

Her eyes deadened even further, if possible.

"He ran off into the mountains and we tracked him down. He's in custody. What I need to know is, did you see his face?"

"No, he attacked me from behind. I was too disoriented to see who did it. How do you know it was Jake?"

He really did not want to tell her this part, but knew if he didn't that someone else would.

"He paid Carmen's parents a visit before you. Luckily, they weren't home. Trashed everything in the house then set it on fire. One of the neighbors saw him running out of the house."

"The doctor told me I almost didn't make it."

The sheriff nodded. "You're going to recover, Winter."

He wanted to reach out and touch her hand, but there wasn't a place that wasn't covered in bruises.

"That's what they say." Winter turned her head away, not wanting the sheriff to see how upset she was that one of her former students had hated her enough to almost kill her.

"You will heal. It will be a long journey, but you will make it, Winter. You have a lot of people who care about you and want to see you."

Winter turned her head back to face him. "Is he still outside?"

"They say he's been here since the day they brought you in."

"Make him leave. I don't want him here."

"I'll take care of it. Anything else?"

"No." Winter closed her eyes, letting the medication put her to sleep with a click of a button. The sheriff stood by her bed until he was sure she was asleep before he left.

Viper watched closely as he came out the door and sat down silently next to him, his hat in his hand.

"She wants you to leave. I told her I would get you to."

"I'm not leaving."

"I know, but I am telling you now it's a wasted effort."

"I don't know what you mean."

"Yes, you do. You're not going to earn her forgiveness sitting outside her closed door. Go home, get some rest, and take care of business. Winter has a long road ahead of her. When she gets out of here, she'll need you then. You won't be any help if you're burned out before she's even released. Right now, she has good care; you've seen to that. Reserve your strength for when you'll need it the most."

"I can't leave until I see her."

"You'll go home if I let you in for a minute?"

"Yes." He couldn't leave until he assured himself it was her living and breathing behind that door.

"Okay, I shouldn't be doing this, so make sure you don't wake her. She's still pissed about the last time."

The sheriff went to the door, telling the security guard he would keep an eye on the door while he went and got a cup of coffee. He motioned to Viper as soon as the guard turned the corner and then opened the door for Viper to enter after checking to make sure she was still sleeping.

"One minute," he warned.

Viper gave him a nod and entered the room. A few minutes later, he quietly closed the door behind him. With a grim nod, he kept his word.

CHAPTER FOUR

"Do you understand these instructions?" The nurse waited patiently for Winter to sign the release papers.

"Yes."

"I will send someone in to help you to your ride."

"Wait, they aren't here yet." Winter tried to keep the worry out of her voice.

"Yes, I am." Beth smiled brightly as she pushed open the door.

Winter released a relieved breath. She had broken down a week ago and called Beth to work for her until she was back on her feet again. It was either hire Beth or a convalescence home. Beth had helped when her mother was ill, and Winter, not knowing where else to turn, called her. Beth had immediately accepted.

"I was outside, talking to your doctor. I also found a physical therapist that is going to start tomorrow." It always amazed Winter how Beth could be a little oblivious about what was happening around her, but when it came to her job, the woman was completely OCD.

"Thanks, Beth. I don't know what I would do without you. The thought of having to stay even longer in this rehab center is getting to me." The hospital in Treepoint had released her to a rehab center in Lexington where she was gradually learning to walk again after six weeks, but Winter wanted to go home.

While it would be a long time before she could return to work, she would be able to go home with certain conditions. Someone would have to stay with her until she was a little more mobile. The doctors had assured her she would fully recover, but in the meantime, she had to use a wheelchair as she regained her strength. She would also need physical therapy if she was going to continue to progress in her recovery.

"I plan to have you back on your feet in no time, Winter. I just hope you don't hate me for my methods."

"You get me back on my feet, I will be grateful," she assured her.

"I am going to hold you to that," Beth replied. "Let's hit the road. We have a long drive home." Beth grasped Winter's suitcases and followed as the nurse pushed her outside to the waiting car. Once they were situated inside, they were on their way.

The drive home took several hours. Winter fell asleep in the backseat where Beth had made her comfortable with several pillows and a blanket. She woke up when they pulled up in front of a drive-thru twenty minutes from home.

"I was hungry. I hope you don't mind."

"No, I'm starving myself." They ate burgers and fries and it was the best meal Winter had ever tasted.

"I need to use the restroom. Will you be all right for a few minutes?" Beth turned around in her seat to ask Winter.

"Of course, I'll wait here." Beth smiled at Winter's show of humor as she left the car to go to the restroom. It didn't take long before she was sliding back into the car.

The rest of the ride didn't take long. Winter stared out the window as they drove through the town. Nothing had changed since her attack. The same businesses and signs were there, the same potholes, even the same regulars going into the diner for a meal. Everything was the same except her.

Winter noticed that Beth had quit talking, her fingers tight on the wheel. Thinking she had something on her mind and wasn't paying attention, Winter casually reminded her when she drove past the street her house was on.

"Remember when I said you were going to hate me? We aren't going to your home. I'm taking you where you will have plenty of help." Beth's voice was soft, but firm.

Winter had a terrible, sinking feeling. "Your house?"

"No, the problem is my schedule is so full you would be left alone for long periods of time. You need a hot tub to relax those muscles. You are going to need help maneuvering around until you regain your strength, and I have the perfect place." Beth took a deep breath and released it. "Razer's house."

"But he lives with The Last Riders."

"Yes."

"No. Take me back to the rehab center or drive me to a nursing home, but I am not going there," Winter said adamantly.

"Yes, you are," Beth replied firmly. Winter sat in stunned silence, not knowing what to do.

"Beth, listen to me. Take me home." Her voice wobbled on the demand. She could tell by Beth's determined face that she wasn't going to listen.

She turned into a large parking lot. A house sat above on a small hill, overlooking both the lot and a huge building. Everyone in town had learned that this was where the Last Rider's clubhouse was located.

There were three men waiting in the lot. Beth drove the car to where they were standing.

"I am never going to forgive you for this," Winter told her.

"I know," Beth said with tears in her voice. Winter

47

watched as Beth's fiancé opened her door and pulled her out into his arms, moving her away from the car. Her own door opened and Winter could only stare helplessly into the one face she had never wanted to see again.

"Hello, Winter," Viper said.

"Take me home. This isn't going to happen, Viper. I am not going to stay here."

"I'm sorry, Winter, but I am not giving you a choice." He carefully lifted her into his arms. When she would have struggled, he held her in a firm hold and talked to her in a voice that had her shivering in reaction. "I know right now you're mad as hell and I understand, but I am not going to let you hurt yourself. Stay still or else I will make you sorry."

"You're going to hurt me to keep me from hurting myself?" Winter watched as the huge biker from the bar pulled her suitcases from the car and Razer lifted out the hated wheelchair.

"I wouldn't lay a hand on you, but you would get my message." Viper packed her up the long flight of steps without losing his breath. Winter stared at the steps, knowing they were going to trap her inside the house. She would never be able to manage them on her own.

Evie opened the door as they approached.

"Hi, do you remember me from church? Believe it or not, I'm a nurse. I also worked with Beth for a while, so you'll be in good hands while you're here." Winter could only stare in amazement at the cheerful woman greeting her. If she weren't being so freaking nice, Winter would have snapped a reply back at her.

Viper continued through the entry, going to the stairs not far from the door and carrying her up another flight of steps, which just added insult to injury as far as Winter was concerned. She looked around and could only see a large living room with several couches and chairs placed in different groupings. Several people were sitting, talking; all of them with their eyes on her.

She was amazed at the size of the house as Viper carried her down a long hallway, passing several doors until he came to the one standing open at the end. The house was more the size of a hotel.

Inside the last room, he gently laid her down on a huge, king sized bed. The room was overly large with a couch and two chairs in a small sitting area. A desk and chair took up space along another wall with a dresser and chest on another.

"I am not staying here, Viper…"

He ignored her, walking out of the room, leaving her alone with Evie, who began opening Winter's suitcases that Razer and the other man had set on the floor.

"Thanks, Knox and Razer." Both men left without a word, closing the door behind them.

Evie began unpacking Winter's clothes with a running dialogue. "I'm a certified nurse and have served in the military. I have also dealt with several spinal injuries, Winter. I want you to know this so that you will feel that you are in capable hands. Right now, you're angry with Beth and we can understand that, so we feel, until you calm down, that I will be the one working with you. Razer has become very protective of Beth." At this, she stopped putting Winter's clothes into one of the drawers of the chest to look at her. "I wouldn't fuck with him by hurting Beth's feelings. I can, on the other hand, take anything you care to dish out."

She pushed the wheelchair beside the bed within Winter's reach. "Let me help you to the bathroom and get you more comfortable." Winter could only sit, trying to force back the tears. She didn't have a cell phone and no one to turn to. No one who would even care if she was missing, she was at their mercy.

Left with no choice, she let Evie help her to the bathroom. Evie matter-of-factly waited while she emptied her full bladder then helped her into the shower in which someone had placed a bath chair and installed a safety bar.

Evie let her wash herself then took over to wash and rinse Winter's short hair before helping her out of the shower. It was another humiliating experience that Winter added to her growing list.

Once back in bed, a soft, blue gown was pulled over her head and settled around her.

"Beth was supposed to feed you before you came here."

Winter nodded, feeling exhausted.

"We were afraid you would throw plates at us if you didn't eat before getting here. Yet the pain medication needs to be taken on a full stomach." Evie opened the prescription bag the rehabilitation center had sent with them, giving just enough of Winter's medication until the prescriptions could be filled tomorrow. Evie gave her the night meds with a glass of water.

Winter didn't even consider refusing because, right now, she welcomed oblivion. Evie pulled the covers over her.

"I am going to sit right over there and read a magazine until you fall asleep. I'll see you in the morning, bright and early."

"It's not necessary for you to stay. I'll be all right for the night."

"I'm just staying until you fall asleep. With the pain medicine and a sleeping pill, you won't last long."

"Okay." She didn't have the strength to argue; lying back against the soft pillows, within minutes she was asleep. Evie read half the magazine before getting to her feet to check on Winter. After making sure she was comfortable and her pulse was steady, Evie went to the door, opening it quietly. Viper walked in.

"She should be out for the night. You need anything, I'll be in Knox's room tonight."

"Thanks, Evie," Viper said, not taking his eyes off the woman lying on his bed.

"No problem."

Viper moved to Winter's bedside on silent feet, looking down at her sleeping face. She had lost a lot of weight she couldn't afford to lose. He had been shocked to see how pale and frail she had become over the last two months. Her hair had been cut short and it no longer shined with health. Reaching out with his thumb, he traced a tear that had slid down her check, leaving a damp path.

Going into the bathroom, he took a shower, drying himself off before going back into his room where he turned off the bedside lamp then carefully climbed into bed, pulling Winter towards him. Unconsciously, she tried to roll away from him, tossing and turning several minutes before she was able to get comfortable against his shoulder with her arm over his waist, pinning him down. When her knee rode up close to his cock; Viper gently moved it down to rest against his thigh. He didn't want that knee anywhere near his cock when she woke in the morning.

CHAPTER FIVE

Winter woke up stiff and unable to move for several minutes. In that time, she realized she was lying on someone. Panic soared through her body and she tried to jerk away, but was held immobile, unable to hurt herself.

She was gently turned until she lay on her back with Viper above her. His chest held her down as his hands surrounded her face, keeping her from jerking her head. His hair roughened thigh was over both of hers keeping them from wildly thrashing.

"Now, I can understand how waking to find me in bed with you upsets you, but we are going to raise you up in the bed and then we are going to have a talk without you hurting yourself. Understood?"

"Yes," Winter gritted out between clenched teeth.

"Good." Viper slowly released her to sit up then helped her to maneuver into a sitting position with pillows supporting her back from behind. Once she was sitting up, Viper climbed out of bed, unconcerned with his nudity,

"You slept with me naked!" she screeched.

"Yes." He went into the bathroom, cutting off further comments. She had to bite back words because no one was listening. She heard the toilet flush then water running in the sink, which didn't help her full bladder. When Viper came out of the bathroom he casually began to get dressed, ignoring her furious glare. Winter was so mad she was beyond speech until he came to the side of the bed, yanking the covers away from her body before lifting her into his arms.

"What are you doing?"

"Taking you to use the restroom," he answered factually.

"Take me back to bed." He ignored her, carrying her into the large bathroom and sitting her on the toilet where he simply sat her down.

"Can you manage?"

"Yes. Get out."

"You have two minutes." She hurriedly used it then flushed the toilet and adjusted her gown with barely a second to spare before he was back, lifting her again. Winter was beginning to feel like a sack of potatoes. He lay her back down on the bed, making sure her back was up against the pillows before he stepped away, folding his arms across his chest.

"Evie will be here in a few minutes and I want us to get a few things settled before she arrives."

Winter opened her mouth to speak.

"Be quiet. I am going to talk, something that you have given me no opportunity to do the last two months. When we were dating, I was very careful to maintain a platonic relationship with you. I, at no time, led you to believe that we were more than friends, whether you want to accept it or not. I was going to find my brother's killer, regardless of who got hurt. I owed that to Gavin and Ton.

"I was determined to bring my brother home. To do that, I had to use you. I am not happy or proud about my behavior, but I did try to limit our relationship so that it wouldn't be as hurtful to you. I didn't succeed. You were hurt and I am sorry. I can't turn back time and do things differently. I sincerely doubt I would if I could. I was finally able, after three years, to bury my brother and give Ton, as well as myself, closure."

"I am glad everything is wrapped up in a tiny pink bow of happiness for you, Viper." Winter glared at him.

"Actually, you conned me, too, Winter. This fiery woman with a temper and a smart mouth, where was she all the time we were together?" Winter's lips tightened, she folded her arms over her chest and turned her head away from him.

"It's okay. I've always liked a woman who's able to speak for herself."

"Go to Hell."

Viper burst out laughing. "I've gotten off track. Despite my best intentions, I began to care about you and was very attracted to you."

At that Winter rolled her eyes, refusing to speak.

"I was, whether you believe me or not. That night after the football game, I almost went home with you, but one thing held me back. I knew you wouldn't be able to handle my life. You had worked hard to achieve your professional goals and succeeded in becoming a principal at a young age. I was worried that any association with a motorcycle club would cause negative reactions towards your career. And would you want to get to know me when you found out I was president of The Last Riders?

"I was going to come clean after Bedford was arrested, but you found out before I was able to do so and have refused to listen to me since. You need to get stronger before you will be able to care for yourself. The best place for you to do so is here. I have told the sheriff that this is where you will be staying and he also agrees."

"Why would he care where I stay?"

"He thinks that Jake's family won't be happy you're back in town."

"Jake is in prison."

Viper nodded his head. "His family wants him out, and they are mistakenly blaming everything on you. They refuse to admit Jake is violent."

"Surely Carmen has admitted to him hurting her?"

"No. She still refuses to believe it was him."

"But what about the fire? He would still be in jail for that and there was a witness to him running from the house."

"A witness that is refusing to testify," Viper informed her.

Winter knew Jake had an older brother that was almost as violent as him. Perhaps it would be safer to find another place until after the trial, but this wasn't it.

"I don't want to stay here."

"I know that, but you really have no option. Let me do this for you. If nothing else, we were friends, Winter."

"How could we be friends? I didn't even know who you were."

He turned his back to her, his face stark. Winter pushed down the regret within her at speaking so harshly to him, yet she didn't know what to do. She couldn't stay here close to him. Forget that he had deceived her. All she had to protect her against the hurt he had inflicted was the barrier she had put up against him.

Before she could think about anything further, a knock sounded on the door.

"Come in," Viper answered, moving away from the bed.

Evie came in, easily tuning into the tense vibe in the room and sought to lighten it.

"We need to get you dressed and downstairs for breakfast. Your therapist will be here in an hour."

"Call me when you need me to help get her downstairs." Viper left the room abruptly.

It was evident that Evie was a trained professional when she had Winter dressed and sitting in her wheelchair twenty minutes later. She then took out her cell phone to call Viper, telling him they were ready. Winter was self-conscious, wearing a pair of small shorts with a t-shirt worn over her sports bra.

Viper came in, easily carrying her downstairs to a massive kitchen teaming with a group of people fighting for breakfast. He sat her down at the round table.

"I'll fix you a plate," Viper offered. Razer, Knox and some tattooed guy that Viper had called Shade were also sitting at the table with large plates before them.

"Hello," Winter muttered.

She got nods in return.

Viper sat a plate down in front of her before sitting down next to her. Evie also sat down at the table with a plate full of smaller portions, which made Winter's plate look as if it would feed six people.

"I need a plate like hers. I can't eat all this," Winter protested.

"Eat," Viper told her then ignored her for the rest of the meal as he talked to the others at the table about deliveries and supplies. Winter was completely lost as to what they were discussing.

"They are talking about a big order going out tomorrow. That's why everyone is up today, working an extra shift at the factory next door." Winter remembered something about them running a survivalist company, but had not paid attention. It had been too painful to hear about Viper's alter life.

She had barely managed to finish half her food when she slid the plate away. Viper didn't take his attention away from the men, but pulled the plate to him finishing what remained.

"You need to use the restroom?" Evie asked. Winter blushed bright red and shook her head when she saw everyone had stopped talking.

The doorbell rang, producing a huge smile from Evie. "That must be your therapist."

She left the room to answer the door, returning within minutes with a mischievous look on her face.

"Winter this is Conner Stevens, your physical

therapist," Evie introduced.

Lord have mercy. Winter and every woman in the room could only stare in awe at the male specimen before them. Beth had promised to make it up to her and she had with the handsome blond standing before her.

She managed to tear her eyes away from Conner to see that Razer and the other males were not happy.

"Tell Beth she kept her promise. I forgive her," she whispered to Evie.

Viper's lips tightened and he gave her a look that she had no intention of interpreting.

"Are you ready to get started?"

"Yes," Winter replied, lifting her arms. Conner laughed, coming to her side and lifting her easily.

"I'll show you the way." Evie guided them through a doorway in the kitchen which led down a flight of steps. The narrow stairs opened to a large room that had been turned into a gym that held several of the machines that Winter had become familiar with during her therapy.

"The hot tub is through that door, and the sauna is through that one, she pointed at the wooden door. The restroom is next door to the hot tub room. Evie indicated where each room was before going to a closet and pulling out two folded mats, laying them on the floor together.

"Beth purchased the mats you requested." Conner sat Winter down on one.

"Today I am just going to see where you're at in your recovery and show Evie some exercises for you to do in the morning and at night. From now on, I will make my regular time around one. Sound good?"

Both women nodded in agreement. An hour later, Winter wasn't so sure. She had ditched her t-shirt and was sitting on the matt after the session was over, covered in sweat.

"Ready for the hot tub?" Connor asked.

"Yes," Winter groaned her reply.

"I have a swimsuit for you." Going to the closet Evie

took out a small package, following behind as Conner carried Winter into the downstairs restroom. It didn't take long for her to get changed.

"Who picked out this suit?"

"I did. Don't you like it?" Evie smiled.

"There is nothing to it, it's a thong. I don't wear thongs and the top is too small," Winter protested.

"You look great. Besides, no one is going to see it besides me and Conner.

She had a point. Giving in gracefully because she didn't want to keep Conner waiting, Evie opened the door to the bathroom. Winter tried not to be embarrassed as he slowly lifted her into the hot tub where they sat relaxing for ten minutes before Conner called time. Evie helped her into a robe afterwards then guided Conner upstairs to Viper's room. Winter was already falling asleep when he laid her on the bed.

Conner left with a wave at Evie, who waited until Conner left before untying Winter's robe, not wanting her to get the bed damp, when Viper appeared in the doorway.

"I'll take care of it." Evie left as he was pulling the robe off and removing the damp bikini. He took a t-shirt from his drawer and pulled it over her head, noticing her nipples had tightened in the cool room. Covering her with a blanket, he turned the heat up slightly before lying down next to her on the bed.

CHAPTER SIX

The next two days were physically hard for Winter, yet she did begin to feel stronger. She wouldn't let Evie help her unless she needed it when using her wheelchair to get into the bathroom. Thankfully, the doorway and room were large enough. The evenings were spent upstairs in Viper's room where either Evie or Beth would join her for dinner. Viper would only come in when she was asleep. Winter had learned to share the bed with Viper at night; it was hard to argue with someone when they waited for you to be in a medically induced sleep.

She had learned that he didn't have a shy bone in his body. He refused to wear anything to bed, and would flash his body as he got out of bed or after a shower. Winter would look away, but somehow she had managed to ingrain his image in her mind and it would strike when she was quietly reading or relaxing on the couch watching television. Thankfully, the attraction he held for her, she had managed to convince herself was gone. She would never give him another opening to hurt her.

She allowed herself a casual flirtation with Conner. She could tell he was attracted to her, and he made her feel something that she hadn't felt in a long time. He helped her feel normal again. Despite the wheelchair, she was beginning to do things on her own. Winter didn't feel like an invalid anymore.

Every morning Viper would carry her downstairs before Connor arrived and would show up at the end of her therapy to pack her back upstairs. Conner and Viper didn't talk, merely giving each other the bare minimum acknowledgement.

It was now Friday night and Winter was becoming stir crazy. The book she was reading was unable to divert her attention. Sighing, she closed the book, knowing that it was almost dinnertime and she would have Evie's company for a few hours. When Evie brought her tray, though, she was dressed in booty shorts and a laced, red leather top with nothing underneath. Winter looked at her in surprise.

Evie gave her a smile. "It's Friday night. We always have a party downstairs to unwind."

Winter tried to keep her expression neutral so that Evie wouldn't know her feelings were hurt.

"Maybe next week, Winter, when you're stronger," Evie said, sensing Winter's emotions.

Winter smiled hesitantly and then picked up her fork. She could tell Evie was in a rush to leave, so she chased her away, picking up her book to read after she left. She could hear the music as well as the laughter from the men and giggles from the women coming from downstairs.

Finally, unable to focus on her book, she got herself ready for bed. Sliding into the cool sheets, she turned the light off and went to sleep.

Sometime during the middle of the night a hard bang against the wall startled her awake with a small scream of fright, which escaped before she could prevent it. A warm hand circled her nape, bringing her back down to Viper's chest.

"Shh... go back to sleep," he murmured.

"What was that?' she asked sleepily.

"Nothing, go back to sleep." His hand rubbed her back until he felt her go back to sleep.

Saturday, Winter woke early and dressed before Viper. She was sitting in her chair by the window, reading, when he stretched lazily awake.

"How long have you been awake?"

"Not long. I thought I would read until you woke."

"I won't be a minute." True to his word, he was quick and Winter was downstairs eating breakfast before most of the others had dragged themselves out of bed. Evie came in with her hair pulled back in a ponytail, wearing sweats and a t-shirt, followed by Jewell and Ember, who also took a seat at the table, all with dark circles under their eyes.

"I take it you all had fun," Winter said with a smile.

"You could say that." Evie smiled as Beth and Razer entered the kitchen. They fixed their plates then joined Winter at the table.

"We were just telling Winter we had a good time last night," Evie said while Beth took a bite of her eggs.

Beth blushed, refusing to take her eyes off the plate. Winter looked at her curiously.

"I told her she could come next week if she's stronger," Evie said, watching for everyone's reaction.

Beth and the others simply looked at Viper to see his response.

Hastily, Winter cut in, "That's all right, I don't want to intrude. I've already taken over so—"

"I think it's a good idea," Viper inserted, taking the bacon she had left uneaten off her plate.

"Good, I have just the outfit you can borrow." Evie was practically jumping with excitement.

"Oh, no, you don't." Beth shook her head. "She can borrow one of mine, and I will have a discussion with her beforehand. I will not allow a repeat of my first experience."

Winter was getting the message this was no simple party. "Perhaps I may give it a pass. Thanks, anyway."

"I think you would enjoy it. It won't be as crowded as it usually is. Some of the members will be leaving Wednesday to go home for Thanksgiving. We always have a dinner here where everyone pitches in, but some members go home," Jewell replied. Her dark hair hung loose around her face, and combined with her green eyes, gave Jewell a sultry appearance that made Winter feel plain and washed-out.

"I'll think about it," Winter said while playing with her food.

"Let's get to your morning exercises."

Evie worked her hard that morning and Winter was happy with the results she was seeing. She had quit taking her pain meds, preferring to deal with the tolerable pain versus staying on the medication for longer than necessary. After therapy was finished, they decided to forgo the hot tub, choosing to sit at the kitchen table and drink a cold beer instead, so Evie enlisted Razor—who had been working out—to carry Winter upstairs to the kitchen. They sat talking, enjoying their beers for a while and then Evie ordered Train to carry her to the living room sofa; he politely did as he was told before returning to the kitchen for his meal. Winter was still wearing her shorts and pink sports bra, but as no one was in the room, she didn't let the exposure bother her.

Beth and Razer joined Evie and Winter in the sofa area as Rider came in with Natasha and sat at the bar laughing and talking. Evie left to get them another round of beers. As she did, she noticed Rider and Natasha glance her way before getting up and going up the stairs. Winter lowered her eyes, hurt that they had left because she was in the room.

She didn't have long to feel bad, though, because Viper came in the front door with an angry stride not long after. Seeing everyone seated, he sat down on the sofa next to Winter, throwing his arm over the back.

"Want a beer or whiskey?" Razer asked.

"I just came from seeing Sam," Viper snapped.

"Whiskey it is."

Winter hadn't asked any questions before, when she had thought they were friends. She would have quizzed him now, but decided to stay out of the discussion. However she didn't close her ears to their discussion, either.

Razer handed him his drink and then sat back down next to Beth.

"She still insists that Gavin is the father of her baby. I told her I would help locate the kid no matter what, but she won't change her story. I know Gavin didn't touch the little bitch; she was underage and that was a rule he wouldn't break."

"I agree with you. I don't believe he did, either," Razer said, taking a drink of his beer.

Winter bit her lip, trying to stay out of the conversation, but she couldn't help herself.

"Perhaps he didn't have time to tell you before he was murdered," Winter suggested. Samantha was Vincent Bedford's daughter, Winter's cousin. Evie had explained that Sam had told everyone that Viper's brother had fathered her child before his death, wanting Viper to help her find the child that Vincent had hidden from her. Winter hadn't even been aware that the girl had been pregnant.

Viper took a swallow of his drink and stood up. "I would expect you to take up for your family, but it's because of them I don't have my brother." Viper picked up his glass, going into the kitchen, while Winter paled, feeling as if he had struck her.

"Razer, could I impose on you to help me to the bedroom?" Winter made sure her voice didn't wobble. "Evie, I think I'll lie down for a nap. If I could borrow a phone, I can give you a call when I want to take a shower." For safety, Evie always waited in the bedroom in case Winter needed her help.

"That's fine. We're going to be eating lunch in thirty minutes. Want me to bring you something?" Evie asked, concern evident in her voice.

"No, I'll wait for dinner." Avoiding Beth's compassionate gaze as Razer lifted her into his arms. Winter held herself stiffly as he carried her to Viper's room. Razer sat her on the side of the bed, making sure her wheelchair was within reach.

"Need anything?"

Winter dared to reach out and touch his arm as he turned to leave. "No, I have everything I need. Thanks for all of your and Beth's help, Razer."

He nodded, giving her a funny look as he left. As soon as the door closed, Winter opened the phone and searched for the number she needed. It didn't take long to find it and make the call. Hurriedly, she maneuvered herself into the wheelchair before getting herself dressed.

Throwing her medications into her purse, she put the strap around her neck and shoulder. She carefully opened the door, just cracking it to peep out into the hallway. If everyone was already in the kitchen and dining rooms eating lunch, she should have just enough time.

Opening the door wide, she rolled her chair quietly down the hall. When she got to the head of the stairs, she tried to look as best she could to see if anyone was sitting in the living room. Seeing no one, she glanced down to lock the wheelchair in place before gingerly sliding out of her chair. For a moment, she almost lost her balance then her butt landed hard on the floor. A small whimper escaped her lips as she slid her hips forward about to go down the top step, butt first. When she looked down the step, she would have fallen in surprise if she already didn't have a death grip on the rail.

Viper was at the bottom of the steps, his foot frozen in place on the first step, and from the expression on his face, he was furious. Even the night he had gotten in a fight at the bar with the other motorcycle club he had held careful check on his emotions.

Winter was afraid of him. She did not know the man staring up at her. She tried to scoot backwards with pain shooting through her back, but the chair blocked her, so she tried to scramble into it when the doorbell rang, pausing her. She glanced back down towards the door.

Evie, who had come to the bottom of the steps, took in with a glance what was going on and went to answer the door with Viper watching.

"Someone call for a cab?" The cab driver waited expectedly.

Viper turned back to her.

Winter saw her chance for escape. Her mouth opened to yell, but she found a hard hand covering her mouth while another went around her waist, lifting her up and backwards into muscled arms. Wildly, Winter tried to shake herself loose, however she was held immobile as they backed silently away from the steps. Jewell followed, unlocking then rolling the wheelchair.

Winter could hear Evie telling the cab driver it was a mistake and offering him a twenty for his trouble before she was placed on the bed. Her mouth was released as Jewell closed the bedroom door. Rider stood staring down at her, shirtless with his pants half zipped while Jewell didn't look much better. Her top was on inside out and she just had on panties.

"What were you thinking? You almost killed yourself?" Jewell whispered.

Before Winter could answer, the door slammed open.

"Get out."

"Viper…" Jewell tried to calm him.

"Now!" Rider and Jewell left immediately. Evie tried to come into the room, but backed out quickly when Viper told her to go also.

"Do you know how close you came to falling and breaking your neck? What the fuck were you going to do?"

"I want to go home!" Winter yelled back. "You're an

asshole. I hate. Hate. Hate you!" Winter rolled to her side of the bed and started crying. She hadn't cried when her mother died, when she had lost Loker or even when Jake had beaten her half to death. Other than a weak tear here or there, she had stayed strong. However, after months of being confined and feeling dehumanized, the look of contempt on Viper's face for her had broken what little spirit she had left.

"I know you do." Sliding into bed with her, he took her into his arms, holding her close. "I'm sorry. I shouldn't have talked to you the way I did downstairs. I didn't mean it. I was just so angry with Sam and her father that I couldn't hold it in any longer. Will you forgive me?"

Winter was silent a long time. "I don't know." She sniffed, liking this soft Viper.

"Did anyone tell you that you know how to hold a grudge?"

"Yes, my mom told me that all the time."

"I liked your mom." Winter stiffened, but admitted the truth.

"She liked you, too."

"Still want to take that nap?"

"Yes."

Viper tugged off his boots and lay back down next to her, tugging her to him until her head laid on his shoulder. "Don't do that maneuver again, Winter; you almost fell. The next time I yell at you, just throw something at me instead."

"Okay," she said, already half-asleep.

CHAPTER SEVEN

She woke from her nap to find Viper working at his desk, restlessly running his hands through his hair. He had began bringing her dinner and joining her before working on his paperwork while she read. She had noticed that with Beth and Razer gone to spend the holiday with Lily that he was doing even more paperwork. Beth was an accountant and usually helped Viper with the paperwork in the evenings.

Winter pulled her chair close and hoisted herself into it. Viper turned to watch as she went into the bathroom without offering to help. They were giving her more independence and she appreciated it. When she came out of the bathroom, she rolled to the desk.

"Need any help?" she offered.

He sat back in his chair. "I wish, but..."

"I am an expert at paperwork. Plus, I enjoy it. I also know accounting. In case you have forgotten, I had to budget a whole school for the year and keep the figures straight. At least let me try."

He slid the books to her, explaining the various columns. It wasn't hard, mainly tedious. Viper was only having a difficult time with it because he hated to sit still. It didn't take long before Winter had caught on and began making headway in the mess he had created. He watched her chew on her pencil as her fingers flew nimbly over the calculator.

When Evie called on the phone to say that dinner was ready, Viper left her working until he returned with their food. They then spent the evening catching him up through the holidays. Winter smiled when he gave a sigh of relief as he closed the ledger and shut down the computer.

"Thanks. That took a load of work off both Beth and myself." Viper moved to turn the television on and sat watching as he took a beer out of the mini fridge he always kept stocked. "Want to join me?"

A closed expression came over her face. "No thanks, I think I'll take a shower then lie on the bed and read awhile." Viper stared at her thoughtfully as she rolled herself into the bathroom, taking her nightclothes with her. He was well aware that he had brought back memories of the many times they had sat and watched television together, and that she wasn't going to allow herself to get that close to him again.

The show flashed across the screen unnoticed as he realized she wasn't ever going to let him in her heart again. He had hurt her too badly for him to regain her trust. He had been lied to and cheated on once in his life when he was still in college before he joined the military, and he could remember the pain of betrayal well.

What he had done was much worse. She would never trust Loker James again. What he had to do, he decided, was to teach her to trust Viper, the man he had hidden from her. To do that, he was going to have to show her the real man in the true environment he lived in, and let her make her choice. The choice of whether they had a future together was in her hands, but Viper was going to use every trick he knew to get her to make the decision he wanted.

* * *

"One more. Come on, Winter, you can do better than that."

"I'm tired, Conner."

"One more, and I will give you an extra five minutes in the hot tub."

"Deal." Winter forced her tired legs to do one more stretch upwards. Her belly quivered as the muscles pulled taut.

"That a girl. Get changed, and I'll meet you at the hot tub." Conner helped her into the wheelchair before leaving to go to the hot tub. Winter rolled herself to the bathroom and changed into the tiny bikini.

She put on the robe she had brought with her when Viper had carried her down. He and Cash had stayed to work out. She rolled herself to the hot tub without glancing in Viper's direction and Conner helped her inside.

"You're getting much stronger, Winter. Next week we'll try and let you start walking more than a few steps."

"Really?" She couldn't keep the excitement out of her voice.

"Really. The house seems much quieter today." Winter knew he wondered where his fan club was. Several of the women made a point to be around when he was there.

Winter nodded, sinking lower in the water. "Some of the people who live here left to visit their families. Where does your family live?"

"Texas. It's too long of a trip for Thanksgiving, but I am planning on going home for Christmas," he said with regret.

She frowned. "What are you going to do for Thanksgiving dinner?"

"Probably eat at the diner." He shrugged.

"I would invite you to dinner here, but I am a guest myself," she said apologetically.

"That's all right; the food at the diner is good.

"That's long enough, Winter, we need to get you out."

69

Conner stood in the tub and helped her to sit on the edge then he stood between her legs until she had her balance. As he began to move away, Winter's leg began cramping and she almost slid off.

Conner jumped out of the hot tub and then sat her on the floor, massaging her calf and thighs. His hands were massaging her inner thigh when the cramp finally eased.

"Thank you. I don't know what I would have done if you hadn't been here."

"Don't go in the tub by yourself, Winter. Your muscles are still recovering from the trauma."

"I won't. I promise." She gave him a shaky smile when the door opened and Viper walked in, his eyes landing on Conner's hands that had continued resting on the inside of her thigh near her crotch. His eyes became glacial. Before he could say anything, though, Winter jumped in with an explanation.

"I had a leg cramp. He was massaging it for me."

"Glad to know. For a minute there, I thought he was being unprofessional."

The smile died on Conner's mouth as he removed his hands, helping Winter into her wheelchair.

"Thanks again, Conner," Winter said before deciding to go for it and ask Viper for a favor.

"Viper, would it be all right for Conner to come to dinner tomorrow? He has to eat at the diner."

Winter looked pleadingly at Viper. "I am afraid that's not possible. Tomorrow is for members of the club only." He gave a smile, which Winter didn't quite trust. "But I will tell you what I can do. Friday is our party day and I am sure there will be plenty of leftovers. We allow non-members to participate with an invitation. Will that work?"

Winter looked hopefully at Conner.

"I will look forward to it, Winter. Thanks, Viper."

"My pleasure."

Winter smiled at Viper when he asked if she was ready to go upstairs.

"Yes, please."

Viper rolled her in the wheelchair to the bottom of the steps before picking her up and carrying her upstairs. Connor followed as far as the front door before saying goodbye.

He continued up the steps to their room, setting her down in her other wheelchair. They had rented an extra one, after packing the wheelchair up and down the steps had gotten old, quick.

"I will make some calls while you grab a shower, in case you have another cramp," he said snidely.

Winter decided to ignore it. "Thanks, I won't be long. I was lucky he was there. He is a really nice guy. You know? You can tell he is lonely with his relatives being in Texas." She kept a running monologue as she gathered her clothes.

Finally, she went into the restroom. Viper heard the shower running, his hands clenched as he heard her singing in the shower. She had treated him like her fucking BFF, talking about a guy she was crushing on.

Viper had recognized the look on Conner's face when he had walked into the hot tub room. The man was only biding his time to make his move. Viper had every intention of preempting his strike. Winter was about to find out how he got his nickname.

CHAPTER EIGHT

The kitchen was crowded with those wanting to cook while Winter sat at the table with a cup of coffee, sipping it with enjoyment as she watched Rider and Evie argue over the best way to make sweet potatoes. When Evie made gagging noises after Rider mentioned marshmallows, Winter couldn't hold back her giggles.

"They are like this every holiday," Bliss said, taking a sip of her own coffee.

She watched the perky blonde take a bite of her toast and smile. The woman was sweet and quirky. At first Winter had talked to her less than the other women, but they had continually run into each other in the gym or hot tub room; so they had slowly gotten to know each other and Winter had developed a friendship with her.

It was mid-afternoon before they were ready to eat. Razer and Beth were the last to show, coming in just as everyone sat down at the table. Beth slid into a chair at the table next to her.

"I thought you would have dinner with Lily?" Winter couldn't keep the surprise out of her voice.

Beth smiled. "This is the first Thanksgiving we have spent apart, but a friend from college invited her to spend the holiday with them and she accepted."

Winter raised a brow. "As overprotective as you are, I am surprised you let her go."

Beth laughed, turning red. "Lily is old enough to make her own decisions now, that was the whole point of her going away to college, but I did ask Razer to check them out for me. He assured me it was safe," Beth confessed.

Beth was facing Winter so she saw the unguarded look on Razer's face as he stared at Shade across the table. Shade kept his face expressionless, aware Winter was watching.

"How long has she known this girl?" Winter questioned Beth.

"They met at the first of the school year. Next year they are thinking about being roommates. It's great for Lily. I was about to break and let her come home, but I didn't want her driving back and forth to the nearest college. This girl has made college life bearable for her. We'll have to invite her one weekend."

Winter had her confirmation when she saw Razer's face at Beth's words. Shade stayed expressionless as usual, continuing to eat his meal.

"I would wait awhile. Finals will be coming up, then Christmas. Besides, you have a wedding to plan after Christmas. I'm sure Lily can explain that it will be several months before you can return the favor."

"Perhaps you're right. I'm going dress shopping in Lexington after Christmas. We could make a weekend of it, just us girls."

"That sounds like a good plan," Winter agreed, seeing the relief on both of the male's faces.

The food was delicious. Both the turkey and ham were demolished. Winter made sure she tried both Rider's and Evie's sweet potatoes, gushing over both of them. Viper, sitting across from her, admired her as she deftly stroked each of his club members' egos.

Everyone helped with the cleanup. The men voluntarily

cleaned the table as the women loaded the dishwasher. Beers were opened and the men crowded into the room off the kitchen to watch the game while the women sat at the kitchen table, planning Beth's bachelorette party.

"I think we should have it at the Pink Slipper," Beth said.

"That won't work," Evie said in response.

"Why not?"

"Because they won't let us in the door," Evie explained.

"Oh," Beth said unhappily.

"How about Rosie's?" Evie suggested instead.

"That sounds good," Beth agreed.

"I'll talk to Mick about us renting the bar for the night."

"Hell, yeah." Natasha and Jewell high-fived each other.

While the men were yelling at the game, Bliss and Natasha got up to give everyone refills on their beer before sitting back down.

"That's settled then." Beth leaned back, taking a drink of her beer. "Winter, I bought an outfit for you to wear to tomorrow's party. I hung it in your closet before coming downstairs."

"That was sweet of you, but I'm sure I had something that would have been fine."

Beth stared at her a minute before replying, "I seriously doubt that. I want to explain about the parties, Winter. The first one was a shock for me."

Winter began getting worried. "I have been to several parties, Beth. I am not a social butterfly, but I don't think I'll embarrass myself."

"That's not what I mean, Winter. What I meant is that the parties can get a little carried away; you may see some things that will shock you."

As the women talked, the men's voices steadily grew lower as they unashamedly listened. Viper was about to interrupt—he had every intention of talking with Winter to give her an idea of what to expect tomorrow night—but he was enjoying listening to Beth beat around the bush. Several of the men were hiding their smiles.

"For Heaven's sake, Beth, I think she's seen a naked man before. Hell, she dated Viper for two years," Jewell interrupted exasperated.

"I never saw Viper naked when we dated. We never had sex," Winter confessed to the women.

Rider yelled out at a touchdown, and Knox elbowed him in the ribs so they could hear.

"You dated Viper for two years and never fucked him?" Evie asked in astonishment.

Winter had felt herself becoming more laid back since they had brought her to the clubhouse, since she wasn't under constant public scrutiny. Her new mellow attitude was brought out further by the wine she had for dinner and the two beers she had drank afterwards had her confiding in the women.

"No. At first, my mom was sick, so I thought he was being understanding, then mom died and I still thought the same thing. That excuse lasted about a year," she said, opening another beer. All the women at the table watched the movement.

"What about the other year?" Bliss asked with wide eyes.

Winter picked at the label on her beer with her fingertips, a blush staining her cheeks. "We went to church together," Winter said. The women looked at each other, not understanding.

"Yeah, so?" Jewell asked what everyone was thinking.

Winter looked at Beth. "Oh, I understand." Beth nodded.

"Well, fucking explain it to us."

"It's our Christian belief not to share sex before marriage. Many couples in our church don't even kiss before their wedding day." Beth was now as red as Winter.

"So you thought…" At this point Jewell had difficulty holding back her laughter. "…that Viper shared your

Christian values?"

When Winter nodded, none of the women could hold back their laughter, more than one had to wipe tears away.

"What about the last months you were together?" Stori asked.

"I thought he was gay."

Viper choked on his beer and started to jump off the couch, but Knox and Shade held him down. The women turned at the shuffle.

"What happened?" Winter asked, seeing the men in a scuffle.

"I think the other team got the ball," Evie said, laughing.

"Oh, then, I was at a football game and saw you guys walk by, and I realized he wasn't gay," Winter went on explaining.

"How did that make you realize he wasn't gay?" Bliss asked.

"I saw him look at you. No man who is gay looks at a woman's ass like that."

The whole table got quiet and the men listening got even quieter.

"That's when I realized he just saw me as a friend." Each woman at the table knew that had hurt, watching as Winter took another long drink of her beer.

"Damn." All the women threw dirty looks at the men while Bliss looked upset and started to get up from the table. She remembered the very incident that Winter was talking about. A hand grabbed hers and tugged her back down with a heartwarming smile. Bliss saw no jealousy in Winter's smile.

"Back to tomorrow's party." Winter wanted to divert the attention away from Bliss. "I am sure I am a big girl and if I see anything I can't handle, I can get Viper to take me to my room."

"I am sure that won't be a problem," Beth agreed with a smile then thought of something else. "Uh, maybe you should stay away from Rider and Knox tomorrow night, to be on the safe side."

"Why? Do they drink too much?"

Beth didn't know how to answer, now realizing Razer's dilemma. She decided to hope for the best. Halftime must have been over because the men started yelling again. Winter's back started hurting from being up all day and she caught herself almost falling asleep when warm arms picked her up.

"Time for bed." Viper carried her to bed. She would have fallen asleep dressed, but he helped her into a t-shirt and pulled the covers over her. She didn't even care that he was dressing her.

Frowning, he went downstairs to talk to Evie and Beth in private only to halt when he heard the women talking.

"I have seen it happen with people who have been critically injured. They become almost asexual from being in a hospital and the recuperative period. Once she starts becoming more independent, she will regain her sexuality," Evie explained.

"I don't think it's only that. She was having her feminism challenged before the accident. What woman's ego wouldn't take a hit with an attractive man keeping you at arm's length for two years? It had to be confusing for her. I do agree that once she becomes more mobile, she will become more confident in herself. I thought Conner will help with that, but he called me yesterday, asking to be replaced as Winter's physical therapist."

Fuck, Viper was going to fire him for his unprofessional behavior, yet the man had done the right thing. Viper sat back in his chair, drinking his whiskey.

Some of the members had gone on to bed. Razer, tired of waiting, came for Beth, leading her away. Cash sat down at the table next to Evie, his hand going to her top, unbuttoning several buttons. Natasha came up behind Viper, her arms going around his neck then sliding her hands down his chest. Viper's hand caught hers.

77

"Not tonight." Viper didn't know which woman was behind him, it didn't matter.

Standing up, he put his glass in the sink. The woman he wanted was waiting in his bed.

CHAPTER NINE

Excitement and nervousness stirred within Winter all the next day. It was almost anticlimactic to open the closet and see the outfit that Beth had bought for her. Disappointment hit her, but she hid it, not wanting Evie to see.

The simple black skirt came to her knees and buttoned up the front. The top was a plain blue, both being something that she could have worn to work. Winter was expecting at least a frilly top.

Evie tried to hide her own disappointment, almost offering to go find another outfit, but also not wanting to hurt Beth's feelings.

"You look great." She tried to sound enthusiastic.

"Thanks." Winter shrugged. It didn't matter. It wasn't like she was going to be the belle of the ball anyway when she was tied to her wheelchair.

Viper came in as Evie finished brushing her hair. At least it was beginning to look healthier. Her hand shook as she placed the brush down. He was wearing a pair of black jeans with a black t-shirt.

"Ready?"

"Yes."

"Evie, can I have a minute with Winter?"

"Sure thing. I need to get changed. See you downstairs." She left, closing the door behind her.

Viper sat on the side of the bed, guiding Winter's wheelchair close to him.

"Winter, I think the women may have given you a warning that the parties aren't what you would usually expect."

"I think I understand, Viper. All the women have stopped by to give me a heads up." He looked down to see her twisting her hands in her lap.

"Whenever you get uncomfortable, let me know and I will bring you back upstairs."

"I'll be fine. Conner will be there, remember? I wouldn't want to bother you."

Viper reached out to stroke her soft cheek. "You could never be a bother, Winter, except when you're trying to kill yourself on the steps." Winter turned her face away from his touch.

"Can we go? Connor will be here any minute."

"Of course." He lifted her into his arms, carrying her downstairs. From the time that he turned with her in his arms at the bottom of the steps and she was given a clear view, Winter realized the warnings hadn't been strong enough.

"I am ready to go back upstairs," she said wide-eyed. She had expected the varying stages of undress. She thought they were warning her about that, not what she was actually witnessing.

The room was crowded with club members, but several faces were unfamiliar. "I don't recognize some…"

"I told you, non-members can come on Fridays if they have been invited. Some enjoy the thrill of hanging around motorcycle clubs. A few want to become members and use this as an opportunity to get their foot in the door. They are not allowed alcohol. All 'hangers' have to be out by two. We don't sleep with strangers in the house. We like to party, but we aren't stupid."

"That would be wise," she said, watching a woman she had never seen before give Cash a blowjob.

"I'm really, really ready to go back upstairs."

"Sit down and relax. Remember Conner will be here."

"Conner can't come in here and see this. He'll think I—"

"I don't think when he sees you he will think that at all." In fact, he was counting on it.

"You're sure?"

"Positive."

"I am going to get you a drink. Do you want bottled water?"

"Yes," Winter managed to get the word out. She was watching Jewell dance with Rider. The woman was wearing a pair of leather shorts and a white corset left unlaced to show her breasts as she moved provocatively to the drumming music. Rider was playing with her nipple as they danced.

Viper returned with her water, setting it down in front of her before sitting down close to her on the couch. Winter tried not to be obvious about observing the members, but it was hard. Shocked, she saw Evie sitting on Crash's lap, his hand obviously under her short skirt.

Winter tore her eyes away, determined to make Viper take her to her room, when she saw a shocked Conner coming in the room with Natasha and a grinning red head she didn't know.

"Winter, your friend is here," Natasha said.

"Hi, Conner." Winter tried not to be self-conscious of her appearance. She was dressed unattractively compared to the scantily clad women in the room.

He sat down in the chair next to the couch, which was as close as Viper intended to allow him to be near Winter.

"I wasn't expecting this. I should go," he said, trying to keep his eyes on Winter.

"This is a little more than I was expecting also, Conner.

I understand." Winter was embarrassed.

"No, you have to stay. The girls have wanted a piece of you since we laid eyes on you. Winter doesn't mind sharing. She's had you to herself long enough." Natasha broke in, sitting down on the arm of his chair, which placed his eyes level with her breasts.

Natasha was wearing a leather skirt and a black lace corset, obviously wearing no bra, as her nipples teased the lace while the other woman hadn't even bothered with clothes. She was wearing a red bra and she just had on a tiny skirt that barely covered her ass, certainly not the thong she was wearing. Ember set down a beer in front of Conner, sitting down between his legs.

Winter was about to call a halt and get Conner to pack her upstairs when she saw the look in his eyes. She had lost again. Natasha's hand had gone to Conner's jeans and her tongue touched her lips. All it took was a promise and he lost whatever attraction he felt for Winter.

Viper took mercy on Winter, not wanting to torture her longer than necessary. He had accomplished his goal of getting Conner out of the picture.

"Natasha, I believe the second bedroom is open." Eagerly the women jumped up, taking Conner's hands. His eyes glazed over when the women surrounded him in a mass.

"Winter…" He turned towards her.

Viper stiffened beside Winter when Conner held out his hands to Winter. "I'm sorry, Conner. I don't share." She pasted an artificial smile on her face. "Go have fun. I'll see you later." There was no way she could compete with the young, healthy women. Her body wasn't up to the vigorous sex that she could see he had planned for the waiting women.

Dropping his hands, he frowned for a second then he turned to Natasha taking her hand in his.

"I noticed you the first day. I heard how wild biker women are…." Winter watched as the women led him up the stairway.

"Well, that was fun," Winter said gloomily. "Can I go back upstairs now?"

"Come on, Winter, don't let him spoil your fun."

Winter was about to scream in frustration when she saw Natasha and Ember come back into the room, going to sit next to Knox on the other couch.

"I don't understand. I thought…"

Viper shrugged. "I guess they changed their mind."

"You set him up."

"Of course, he was your physical therapist. I paid him to get you stronger, not fuck you."

"You pay him? I have insurance."

"Your insurance only pays for a limited amount of therapy a week, then only a limited amount overall. You would never return to normal with those limitations."

"This is ridiculous. I can pay. I have money saved up. I can pay for my own therapy."

"Yes, you can, but you're going to be out of a job for a while. You're certainly not going to be recovered enough to go back this school term, if ever."

"I can go back. My back is healing. You're right, probably not this school term, but next."

"We both know the damage to your back. You're not going to be able to stand on your feet for long hours. What about when the kids get physical. If a fight broke out, you wouldn't even be able to step between them for fear of damaging your back again."

"That's what security is for."

Viper lifted a brow, knowing they both knew the score of her physical limitations.

"It's nothing that we have to worry about tonight. We are going to relax and maybe have a little fun."

"I am not in a 'having fun' kind of mood. You made sure the first man I have been interested in for months is in bed with another woman then tell me I am no longer fit to do a job I love. You're making it hard for me to have fun." Winter looked down at her hands.

"I'll just have to do better, won't I? Everyone else seems to be having a good time, don't they?"

Winter kept her eyes away from the various members. Some were having a very good time.

"Let's dance and see if we can't put you in a better mood."

"This is ridiculous. I can't dance."

Rider and Jewell walked off the dance floor. Her mouth opened to ask him to help her upstairs, but then she thought better of it, remembering Beth's warning.

"Chicken?" Viper taunted when he saw her change her mind about asking Rider.

"Kiss my ass," she said, looking frantically around the room, about to interrupt Evie's orgasm when she saw two women that Winter assumed had been invited to the party approach the seating area where Viper and her were sitting. If she wasn't feeling frustrated with her body before, these two just made it worse, dressed skimpily with curvy bodies that Winter couldn't compete with in the best of health. Next to them, her body was a bag of bones.

"Hey, Viper." One cuddled up next to him on the arm of the couch while the other slid seductively to her knees in front of him, her hands going to his thighs.

Winter stiffened as she watched the women's familiarity with him.

"Tara, Stacy, you two having fun tonight?" Both women nodded their heads, gazing at him, leaving no doubt as to what was on their minds.

"Have you thought any more about letting us join The Last Riders?"

"I have told you no several times. My answer hasn't changed."

"Come on, Viper, why not?"

"We only take on one or two new recruits a year, both slots are filled.

They pouted in unison. "Where are they?"

"One is in Ohio, the other is right here." Viper pulled Winter closer to his side.

Winter was going to deny it until their expressions made her angry. Her mouth tightened into a grim line.

"Her? You're joking, right?" Stacy asked.

"No," Viper said, trying not to laugh. Winter was about to explode.

Winter sat with her mouth closed. If he was going to use her to get the twin bimbos off his back, she wasn't going to interfere after the derogatory looks they were giving out.

"Whatever, Viper. I bet she can't do what we did for you the last time we were here."

"That was back in the summer, months ago, but it did give a lasting impression. I think you girls should go find Knox."

Disappointment filled both their faces. "Can we do something for you first?" The one on her knees covered his jean-covered cock with her hand, rubbing him. Viper's hand caught hers.

"You're going to need all your energy for Knox," Viper said in a tone not to be ignored. They left reluctantly, giving Viper wistful glances.

"Knox already has..." Winter said, watching them approach Knox.

"The more the merrier with Knox. He can handle them."

Winter turned her head, not even wanting to talk anymore. Viper rose, picking her up into his arms.

"What are you doing?"

"I feel like dancing."

"I can't dance," Winter protested.

"Yes, you can."

Viper stood on the edge of the floor, letting her feet slip to the floor. Turning her to face him, he slid his arms around her slowly, swaying back and forth. Although he used to love to go out on the weekend just to dance when she was in college, Winter hadn't danced in years; when they had dated, he never took her. She allowed herself to soften against him, swaying to the music. The beat was too fast for how they were moving, but it felt so good to be on her own two legs and doing something normal again. Winter began enjoying herself for the first time in a long time.

The next song was slower and someone turned the overhead lights off, just leaving the lights on at the side tables, giving the room a soft glow. After another slow dance, Viper lifted her and carried her to an ottoman that was placed at the back of the room. Winter was surprised no one was sitting on it even though the room was crowded.

"Do you want a drink?"

"No, thank you."

Viper sat down next to her. As she glanced around the room, Winter noticed that Cash was standing and talking to Stori while Bliss and Dawn were sitting on each side of Train.

"Thank you, Viper. I enjoyed that." Winter's cheeks were flushed.

"Does your back hurt?"

"Just a little, no more than usual," she admitted.

"Let me make you more comfortable," Viper offered, his voice lowering.

"That's not necessary." Ignoring her, Viper's hands slid around her waist, sliding her sideways with one hand maneuvering her legs until, within seconds, she was lying flat on the large ottoman.

"That better?"

"Viper, I don't need to lie down. I'm fine. Everybody is looking. I am not a total invalid."

"No one can see anything. The crowd and couch are blocking off most of the room. Relax. Cash and Train have been in bike wrecks and know how hard it is to heal. It can't bother you that Dawn and Bliss see you lying down, either. Does it?

Winter shook her head.

"I don't want you to put any strain on your back." He leaned down, taking her mouth in a way she used to dream of him doing for so long. The slight taste of whiskey on his tongue was heady, making her want more. Her soft lips parted wider, allowing him to deepen the kiss.

The ottoman, while in the middle of the floor, was blocked off from view, but she still didn't want to kiss Viper in front of the others. Her hands went to his chest to push him away, however Viper's hand went to her skirt, unbuttoning it to her thighs. Winter started to protest.

"I am just making you more comfortable," he reassured her.

"By undressing me?" she asked. "That's not making me more comfortable, it's creeping me out."

Viper leaned over her, kissing her neck. "I don't think so. I think it's making you wet. Let me see." His hand slid higher under her skirt, going unerringly to her pussy.

The upper part of the skirt hid from the others in the room what he was doing to her. A smile was on his lips as his fingers teased her wetness and a tiny whimper escaped as his finger found her clit. His mouth moved caressingly across her flesh, coming to stop at the top button of her blouse. His knuckles grazed her tender flesh as he released several buttons, sliding the material until it fell to the sides of her quivering breasts, which remained covered only by her lacy white bra.

His tongue found the swell of her breast as his finger entered her pussy. Winter's hips arched as his thumb rubbed her clit. When his hand tugged her bra aside to expose her breast, a gasp escaped her as he took the nipple in his warm mouth.

"For two years, I wanted to taste these little morsels, to know if they were pink like bubble gum or red like strawberries. I'm good with strawberries." He bared her other breast, unsnapping the front clasp of her bra. Winter gasped, catching the cups of the bra, holding them in place. The dark blue top slid silkily down, providing a dark background for her creamy skin.

Reality intruded into the seduction. He was carefully weaving around her when he had unsnapped her bra. She blinked up at him, trying to turn her head away from the mesmerizing gaze of the predator studying the meal he was determined to have. It was the same look he had given Bliss months ago. Winter remembered she had wished he would look at her that way, now her stomach clenched in fright at being the focus of such sexual intent. She was unable to turn away from the spell he was using to lure her into losing control.

Viper swirled his thumb against her clit as he added another finger to her warm pussy, his thumb pressing harder against the sensitive bud as his large fingers stroked her faster.

His mouth nipped her flesh above her breast, while Winter's hand left her loosened bra to press against his jaw. Viper struck in an instant, sliding the bra cup away and sucking her nipple into his mouth. His hand started squeezing it from the bottom up, forcing the blood to the tip he had in his mouth.

The sensations of pleasure were overwhelming to someone who had become adapt at ignoring her body's desires. She had felt so ugly lately, trapped in an all but useless body. Viper was making her feel desires that were turning into a burning need that had her moving her hand from his jaw to the back of his neck to press him closer to her tormented flesh.

"Are you shy, pretty girl? You're so pretty with your little strawberry nipples and your pussy. Girl, your little pussy is tight and hot." His fingers found the spot he was searching for deep within her.

"I bet you taste like strawberries, too. If you weren't so shy I would unbutton this skirt the rest of the way and see if this pussy is as wet as it feels."

"Viper..." Winter moaned.

"But you are shy, so I will restrain myself, even though my cock is as hard as a rock." Taking her hand in his, he laid her hand on his cock over his jeans. Winter tried to remember that Bliss and Dawn were nearby, but she couldn't catch a thought as Viper stroked her pussy until she couldn't help herself from forgetting their existence.

It had been years since she'd had an orgasm. Well, before she had dated Viper, she had only had sex a few times with a boy she'd dated in college. Only once had he managed to make her come. She had been so self-conscious of her body, and he had been rushing to get his, that he hadn't really cared if she was satisfied or not. Winter had later found out from her roommate, who had laughingly told her, that he was only fucking her to keep her occupied so her roommate and his friend could have the room.

Viper was no inexperienced boy, though. His fingers within her wet sheathe knew exactly what they were doing, scrambling her thoughts and driving her to an orgasm that was building in intensity until a soft moan drew Winter from her sexually-induced haze.

Opening her eyes, she was shocked to see that Cash had Dawn over the back of the chair, fucking her, while Train had Bliss bent over his lap as he thrust hard into her mouth. Winter wanted to die of shame.

Her hand moved down to stop Viper, yet he caught it with his own that wasn't driving her crazy. Circling her wrist in a hard grip, he pulled it up to lay by her head.

"Don't stop me now, pretty girl," Viper's dark voice tempted her. "I can tell you're about to come; your little pussy is squeezing my fingers tight just like it's going to be squeezing my cock soon... real soon." Using the hand by her head, he turned her to face Cash and Train again, both men's eyes were trained on her, their expressions tight.

"Let them finish. Look at their faces, you have them ready to explode from watching you." Winter blushed and tried to turn her face into Viper's shoulder.

"Imagine what they're thinking. How Cash's cock is buried in Dawn's pussy, but I bet he's thinking it's buried in you. Train is thinking you're the one sucking him off."

Winter moaned as his thumb against her clit stroked even faster. She couldn't prevent the knot of desire from exploding into an orgasm. She watched helplessly as both Cash and Train pounded their own release into the moaning women.

Winter tried to jerk Viper's hand from her, but he simply rose up, pulling his hand away and began buttoning her skirt.

"Relax, they didn't see anything other than that pretty face of yours." He finished buttoning up her skirt and then he snapped the front clasp of her bra before buttoning her blouse. "That and those perfect little nipples."

Winter blushed in shame, not believing that she had allowed things to get so out of hand.

Viper stood with Winter in his arms, carrying her from the room and up the steps while she refused to look around her, turning her head into his shoulder. Back in the bedroom, he carried her through to the shower and placed her inside.

"Hold onto the bar." Winter grabbed onto the metal bar in the shower, trembling in reaction to her actions downstairs. She started crying and was trying desperately not to become hysterical.

Angrily, she ignored Viper as he removed his clothes, throwing them into the laundry basket in the corner before stepping into the shower with her.

"I hate you."

"I know."

He turned the water on warm, easing her body under the gentle spray. She wanted to jerk away from his touch, but was afraid she would fall in the slippery shower. He put shower gel in his hands and began washing her, despite her protests.

"Get out!"

"You're angry that you liked it, whether you admit it or not. And you did like it, a lot. *I* liked it, a lot. You're going to have to get over it." His hands slid down her slippery belly to find her cunt with his soapy hand, washing her thoroughly.

"No, I won't." She smacked his hands away from her.

"Yes, you will. I like to fuck and play. And when I do, I don't care if anybody is around watching. Most of us don't. Everyone has been walking on eggshells around you. That ended tonight," he informed her with a ruthless edge to his voice.

"I am not a recruit for your little club. I'm not like those women wanting to join The Last Riders Motorcycle Club. Unlike them, I would not fuck everyone," she screeched at the man everyone knew to be terrified of. He held complete control over a motorcycle club that was strong and brutal enough to remove any threat they faced.

Viper laughed. "Pretty girl, you got Cash's and Train's votes tonight. And you don't have to fuck everyone."

Ignoring her curses, he turned the water spray on, rinsing her body of the soap. He stepped out of the shower and then lifted her out. Taking a towel from the side, he dried her off then carried her to bed where he laid her down. Getting in next to her, he pulled the covers over both of them.

"What are you doing? I want my gown."

"From now on, you sleep naked next to me, unless you're on your period, then you can have a pair of panties," he conceded the last.

"Go to hell," she snapped.

Viper smiled at her temper, pulling her close. "I take it you don't want to earn my vote tonight?"

She tried to hit him, but he grabbed her hand, carefully turning her until he was plastered against her back.

"I'll take that as a no. Go to sleep."

Winter wanted to yell at him, but exhaustion from her

long day had drained her body while the shower had relaxed her muscles so she was able to lay comfortably against him.

She would deal with him in the morning, she promised herself.

CHAPTER TEN

As the morning sun woke her, Winter lay still, not wanting to wake Viper. Carefully, she edged to the side of the bed and maneuvered herself into her wheelchair. Grabbing some clothes, she went to the nightstand, glancing at the bed to make sure Viper was still sleeping as she snagged his phone. Then, going into the bathroom, she made a quick phone call. Dressing herself and brushing her hair into a ponytail, she rolled her chair to the bathroom door, peeping out to make sure once more that he was still sleeping.

She moved slowly so no squeaking floorboards would raise an alert. Creeping across the bedroom until she reached the door where she peered out into the hallway, and seeing no one, she rolled her chair out into the hall before shutting the door quietly behind her. She hoped everyone was still sleeping after their late night as she then rolled the chair down the hallway, sure this time she would be able to make her escape. When she got to the head of the stairs, she unintentionally let a small scream of fright escape her.

Shade was leaning casually against the wall, hidden from view from the hallway. He looked tired and cranky, which on him wasn't a good look, it was a scary one.

"Going someplace?" he asked casually.

"Breakfast?" Winter tried not to appear guilty.

"No one is up yet."

"I can make my own."

"How were you going to get down the steps?" he asked coldly.

Winter didn't answer his question.

"What are you doing here?" Winter asked impatiently.

"Viper had a feeling you would try to make a run for it after last night." Shade shrugged. "Seems he was right."

"He asked you to stand here all night?" she asked in disbelief.

"Yes, need a lift downstairs or do you want to go back to bed?"

"Downstairs, please." She needed to be downstairs for her plan to work. The doorbell rang just as he was about to lift her.

"Your accomplice?"

"Who is it?" Viper asked from behind her.

Winter stiffened, he was wearing faded jeans that hung low on his hips and no shirt. He wasn't even wearing shoes. She almost did not answer him, but knowing all he had to do was open the door to find out the answer to his question, she decided it would be stupid to argue.

"Pastor Dean."

Viper grinned. "Could be worse. Shade answer the door while I get Houdini."

Expecting Viper to pack her back into their room, she was surprised when he lifted her into his arms and carried her downstairs.

Pastor Dean was walking in the door as Viper reached the bottom of the steps.

"Viper, Shade, Winter; it's good to see you all again." Pastor Dean smiled at each of them as Winter was merely embarrassed that the handsome minister saw her in Viper's arms.

"Want some coffee?" Viper asked, not waiting for a reply while he carried Winter to the kitchen and sat her at the table, leaving to start a pot of coffee.

"Sounds good to me." Pastor Dean sat down at the table next to Winter, giving her a reassuring smile.

"Going to bed, Viper."

"Thanks, Shade." He left without a word to her or Pastor Dean while Winter's angry glare followed him out the door.

"So what brought you out so early in the morning, Dean?"

"I called him."

Viper leaned against the counter with his arms folded against his chest. His eyes pinned her to the chair before he moved to get cups and filled each with coffee. Setting them down on the table, he took a seat.

"Why?"

"I asked him to take me home."

"In that case, he has wasted a trip. You're not ready to be on your own yet. Give it a couple more weeks; if you still want to go home, then I will take you myself," he said, lifting his cup to his lips.

"I want to go now."

"That's not possible."

"Why?"

"I think that is self-evident," he replied.

"No, it's not. I can get myself in and out of the wheelchair. I can get dressed and cook. There are people in worse shape than I am who stay by themselves."

"That's true, but do you have a gym with all the equipment you need? Do you have a hot tub to relax your muscles, or someone to massage those cramps out of your legs that you still have to take medication for? I actually think you could be on your own, but it would drastically slow your recovery." Viper's hard reminder of the club's resources that had benefited her recuperation began to make Winter feel ungrateful.

Winter hated to admit it, however he was right. Besides, he hadn't even mentioned that Evie worked with her in the mornings and evenings.

"I still want to go home." Winter wasn't wanting to give up.

"What you want to do is escape because of last night."

"What happened last night?" Pastor Dean asked when Winter remained silent. "It's all right, Winter; I can guess. The first time Beth went to one of their Friday nights, she stopped seeing Razer and started dating me. Let me ask you a question and I want you to be truthful. Did they force you to do anything you did not want to do?" His serious expression left no doubt of his concern for her.

"No."

"She let me finger fuck her in front of Train and Cash," Viper informed her pastor without remorse.

"Viper!"

He shrugged and looked at Winter. "You're the one that dragged him into this. I'm not embarrassed."

Winter, however, was mortified.

"You wouldn't be. You probably do it every Friday night," Winter snapped, hating him.

"Pretty girl, I usually do more than that on Fridays. I restrained myself for you." Winter stared at him in stunned surprise. The asshole thought he had actually done her a favor.

"Don't do me any favors, you jerk!" she yelled at him.

"Be careful how you talk to me or next time, I won't. I am not bashful. I don't care who sees me fucking you," he warned.

Winter wanted to melt into the floor. She could not believe he was talking this way in front of a pastor.

"I am sure you are feeling embarrassed, but I have to agree with Viper. I hate for you to delay your recovery because you're regretting your actions of last night. If you don't want to attend the parties, I am sure Viper has no intention of forcing you to do so, nor into doing anything else that you're uncomfortable with."

"Of course not. She can stay in the bedroom. I will even keep her company," Viper agreed with a smile of intent.

"Good, then it's settled." Pastor Dean stood up, preparing to leave. "Winter, I hope to see you back in church soon."

"Wait." Both men ignored her. What was happening here? A man of the cloth should have been shocked at what he had heard; instead, he was shaking Viper's hand and walking out the door.

Viper walked back into the kitchen after seeing the Pastor out, and all Winter could do was stare in bewilderment at losing the opportunity to escape from his grasp, again.

"If you want to exercise while I make breakfast for us, I can carry you downstairs."

Winter was smart enough to know when she had lost the battle.

"Thank you, I have some venting I need to do, so I think a few minutes with the punching bag is just what I need."

Viper lifted her easily into his arms, carrying her down to the gym where Winter changed into her workout clothes and did exactly what she had told Viper she would do; worked all the aggravation he was putting her through out of her system.

When the food was ready, Viper came and took her back upstairs. Everyone slowly began coming in as they ate their breakfast. Viper had made a lot of food, and while a few ate what he had prepared, many stuck with toast and coffee.

At first she felt self-conscious around them, especially when Cash and Train entered and found a place at the table to drink their coffee. Gradually, she relaxed when neither man paid any attention to her. Viper, who was sitting next to her, placed his hand on her thigh, giving it a squeeze. Winter stiffened, but when he didn't move it, she reached down, intending to do so herself, only to have him take it in his hand and link his fingers through hers. Winter gave up trying to get her hand back and simply let it lie within his grasp.

"What's everybody doing today?" Beth asked after Razer and she finished eating. Winter wasn't surprised when the general consensus was sleep.

"Winter, Lily and I are going into town to get an early start on our Christmas shopping. Anyone else want to go?"

"I've been looking forward to shopping, but are you sure I won't be intruding?" Winter asked, eager to get out and go shopping. She hadn't been out since before her accident and wasn't sure if she really wanted to be seen around town in her chair, though; no matter how tired she was of being cooped up.

"Not at all. Lily is dying to see you. Her friend is dropping her off at noon. We can be here to pick you up at one."

"Thanks, Beth. I can hardly wait."

"Don't worry about picking her up. We can meet you in town. I promised Ton that I would take him to the grocery store. We can all meet up at the Buy/Low market," Viper said.

With that settled, Viper packed Winter upstairs to get showered and changed. He went to his desk, sorting through scattered paperwork as he waited for her to get dressed.

She was going into the bathroom when she stopped. "Viper, thank you for helping me recover. I also appreciate you hauling my ass up and down the steps."

Viper gave her a sexy grin. "It is a very sexy ass; I don't mind at all. Now, go get changed."

* * *

Beth and Lily met them in the parking lot of the Buy/Low Market where Viper and Winter had stopped on the way to pick up his father, Ton, at his home. When Viper and Winter had been dating, she hadn't really gotten to know Ton well. Viper had never encouraged any invitations she had wanted to extend. Looking back now, that should have been a big warning for her. She had obviously missed a lot of those signs.

"Ready?" Both sisters were patiently waiting.

"Yes, Winter answered Beth after Viper had helped her into the wheelchair.

"Let's roll," Lily joked, taking the wheelchair handle.

"Let's meet up at the diner in two hours," Viper suggested.

They all agreed, going their separate ways. The girls hit all the stores, laughing and giggling at some of their choices of gifts for the members of The Last Riders. Beth commissioned a handcrafted, long-handled razor knife for Razer, boots for Evie and then took the time to get each member a gift.

Winter didn't know the women as well, so she picked up several gift cards when Beth assured her the women loved to shop. She drew a blank as to what to buy for Viper, however when Beth fell in love with a hot red leather jacket, Winter purchased it as an early Christmas present despite her protests.

As they roamed, Winter stopped to look through a tray of bracelets, sliding different ones on and off her wrist; Lily and Beth strolled over to watch. They were so pretty, Beth even started trying them on, admiring how they looked on her own wrist. One in particular caught Winter's eye. It was a beautiful, handcrafted, wide bangle bracelet with little dangling charms that had designs engraved into the purplish silver. It was truly a piece of art.

"Lily, this would look fantastic on you with your coloring." She held it out to the women, unsnapping it so Lily could slide her wrist inside. When she didn't move, Winter raised her eyes to Lily's face. A look of pure terror was frozen on her ashen face.

"Are you all right? What's wrong, Lily?" Winter didn't know what to do as she looked towards Beth.

Beth looked up at her words, seeing what was in Winter's hand and quickly took it away.

"She's allergic to silver."

"I'm sorry. I did not realize or I wouldn't have shown it to her."

"That's all right. I shouldn't have been a baby about it." Lily smiled at her, but the look of terror still lingered in her beautiful eyes.

"It's time we met Viper and Ton at the diner," Beth said, changing the subject. The women paid for their purchases before walking down the street to the diner.

Ton was walking across the parking lot when several motorbikes came roaring down the street. The women turned, thinking it was The Last Riders, only to stare in amazement at another group of five bikers with a lone woman on the back of one.

Easily recognizing Sam, Winter was amazed at the woman's boldness at taking up with another group of bikers as they parked in the diner's parking lot with Ton staring them down.

"This is going to be bad," Beth predicted, hurrying off to reach Ton before the crazy man picked a fight. Winter and Lily took off after her with Lily pushing the chair as fast as she could. Winter was sure they appeared ridiculous barging towards the group of bikers.

"Move out of my way, old man," Samantha ordered.

"I want to talk to you and you're not going to be able to ignore me this time." Winter saw Beth try to tug Ton away from the group of bikers, but he wasn't budging. Giving up, Beth took a step back while searching in her large purse for a phone. Winter heard her calling someone when the argument between Ton and Sam got even more heated.

"I have nothing to say to you because you don't want to hear the truth. Whether you want to believe it or not,

Gavin is the father of my baby."

"Gavin wouldn't have touched an underage girl."

"Oh, he did all right; several times as a matter of fact," Sam taunted.

Winter could only sit in her chair and watch, powerless as the two argued, slowly coming to the realization of some dangerous undercurrents coming from the bikers. The Last Riders were often scruffy and wore faded clothes, yet they never had the appearance of these scumbags that Sam had attached herself to.

These bikers were dirty, and she could smell the alcohol and weed on them from where she was sitting. Their eyes were glued onto Lily and Beth as they spread out around them. Winter was about to warn them when one slid his arm around Lily, jerking her to his chest while two others maneuvered Beth towards the back of the diner's parking lot. Lily's scream was cut off as the biker put his hand in her hair, jerking her neck back at an awkward angle, his head lowering to hers. Winter tried to ram him with her wheelchair, but he struck the wheel violently with his heel, sending it careening in circles before she could manage to stop spinning.

"Ton!" Winter screamed, watching in horror as Lily fought frantically to get away from the biker who was determined to thrust his tongue down her throat. Beth started screaming and so did Winter, trying to find help.

Ton, realizing what was happening, hurried to Beth, trying to get her away from the men, but another guy that had been standing behind Sam blocked his path. Ton tried to hit him, but the biker punched him hard in the stomach and Ton dropped to his knees. The biker that had Lily grabbed her ass, lifting her against him until her feet were off the ground, carrying her in the same direction as the two men were taking Beth.

"Stop! Sam, you have to make them stop," Winter pleaded to the woman watching impassively.

"I don't have to do a fucking thing other than to go in

that diner and get me a hamburger. We were minding our own business." Sam shrugged. "These guys aren't pussies like The Last Riders." She walked to Winter, taking the handlebars of the wheelchair, and tried to give it a shove to send it careening, but this time Winter was prepared, grabbing the wheels to hold the chair steady.

Sam, angry she had been unsuccessful, tried to tip the chair over and almost threw Winter out, but was thrust away by Viper, who sent her tumbling to the pavement. People were finally coming out of the dinner, yet no one made a move to help.

"You bitch! I will kill you if you touch her again," Viper promised.

"I am not afraid of you, Viper. This time I have somebody to back me up that isn't afraid of your pussy club."

Viper moved to go to Lily and Beth. This time the two remaining bikers blocked his path.

"What are you going to do, Viper. Take them all on?" Sam jeered.

Viper answered by hitting one in the face. The sound of crunching bone made Winter nauseous. The man staggered backwards as the other one came forward and the fighting turned ugly. Winter watched as Viper took on one and then the other man as he fought to help his buddy. It was useless; the two were ineffective against Viper's assault.

The sound of motors racing down the street did not stop the fighting or the men who had Beth and Lily. The last Riders pulled into the lot and surrounded the fighters. Razer gunned his bike towards Beth and Lily, startling the men into letting Beth go, however the one that had Lily tightened his grip around her waist, turning her to face the group of angry bikers.

A released Beth ran to Razer as he climbed off his bike. He pulled her close for a second then told her to go stand next to Winter. Winter could tell she wanted to argue, but she didn't, coming to stand next to her, using the chair to steady her weak knees.

Viper was still fighting the men. One took a step towards him and was met by Viper's fist then the ground. Razer and Knox threw themselves at the ones who had touched Beth. The four fought dirty, and Winter couldn't bear to watch. Her eyes caught on Lily who stood in frozen terror as the biker held her in a tight grip around the waist with her pretty dress torn off one shoulder.

Winter then saw Shade and Rider get off their bikes. Rider moved forward, but Shade gave a hand signal and Rider backed off. Shade did not rush the man as Razer had his victim. Instead, he took off his sunglasses and jacket, leaving him in his long sleeve black t-shirt. You would think that the man holding Lily would let her go since they were outnumbered, but no, now he held onto her for dear life. His life.

Winter was scared of Shade when he was in a good mood, even more when he was steadily maneuvering himself closer towards a target, the man holding Lily hostage.

"Let her go." Shade's voice was deadly.

One of the men Viper was holding yelled out, "Slot, let her go."

The man ignored his biker buddy; smart enough, at least, not to take his eyes off Shade.

"Let me get on my bike and get out of here, then I will let her go. She your bitch?"

"She is no man's bitch."

"She's yours. Just let me go. No trouble."

"You had trouble the second you looked at her." Shade motioned to Rider, who was sneaking forward to move back. Slot looked at him, but Shade did not take advantage of the man's lack of attention; instead, drawing his attention back towards him, which wasn't easy.

"Have you heard of The Last Riders?"

"Yeah, but I ain't afraid of you. You guys fuck more

than you fight."

Almost casually, Shade replied, "That's because the other motorcycle clubs have learned not to mess with us, which gives us more time to fuck. Did they tell you how we got our name?"

"No." The conversation was making the man more nervous; you could practically see him shaking. Winter couldn't blame him. Shade was dressed in black. What skin you could see, he had covered in tattoos except his face, which was filled with menace and determination.

"See that wheelchair over there with the woman sitting in it?" The man was beginning to look more terrified than Lily.

"Yeah."

"I'm going to give you one just like it. They call us The Last Riders because, if you fuck with us, we fuck you up so bad that you will never be able to ride again. Slot, you have taken your last ride." Shade finished his sentence between gritted teeth then, before Slot could take another breath, Lily was out of his reach and Shade was beating the shit out of him.

The sheriff and his deputies were now swarming the parking lot. Someone from the restaurant ran across the street to get them. None of The Last Rider members made a move to stop Shade, though. It took two deputies and the sheriff to pull him off the whimpering biker. With a one last kick to the man's face, Shade let himself finally be pulled away.

As soon as Lily was freed from Slot, Razer had led her immediately to Beth. Winter frowned; through the whole ordeal Lily had stood frozen as a statue. It hadn't changed with her release, either.

Beth enfolded her into her arms, speaking quietly into her ear. Winter couldn't hear what she was saying, but she could tell it had no effect.

"Does she need to go to the hospital?" Winter asked, concerned.

"No, I need to get her out of here and go home," Beth answered.

"The sheriff will give us a ride home and we can come back tomorrow for your car," Razer said, moving close to Beth and Lily protectively. The whole time, Lily still did not move. The sheriff's car pulled next to them and the sheriff got out to open the car door for the three of them.

"You all right?" Viper moved to stand next to her.

"Yes."

"I will be back in a minute to get you and Ton. I am going to go get my car."

"Okay." Winter didn't know what else to say, giving his hand a tight squeeze and a nod to his father who immediately moved to her side as Viper jogged off.

"I'm sorry, Winter. I should have left when Beth tried to get me to," Ton apologized.

"It would have been wise, but I understand your frustration with Sam. She's had Viper just as angry, Ton."

It didn't take Viper long to return with his car and get Winter as well as Ton settled inside it. They dropped a quiet Ton off before returning to the clubhouse. He was packing her back inside when the other members began returning, yet he never broke his stride to look or even speak to anyone. He merely kept walking into the house and took Winter upstairs to their room where Viper sat her down on the bed.

"Do you need me to get your pain medicine?" Viper asked in concern.

"No, my back doesn't hurt."

"I need to go downstairs, you all right?"

"I'm fine. I think I'm going to lie down for a while."

"I'll bring our dinner up when it's ready."

"Sounds good."

Winter watched silently as he went into the bathroom and washed his hands and face before going downstairs. She could tell he was still furious. She just hoped the sheriff was smart enough not to release the bikers anytime soon.

Viper went downstairs where the members were waiting for him. The women were sitting in the living room while the men were off in the kitchen.

"Cash?" Viper wanted information.

"The sheriff arrested all the bikers. Sam was let go as you requested. Rider is trailing her. Seems she has taken up with the club across the state line."

"Blue Horsemen?" Viper asked, surprised. Until now, they had been smart enough to keep a respectful distance.

"Yes."

"Confirm this then we will make our move." Cash nodded in agreement.

"Where is Shade?" Viper asked.

"Same place Razer is," Cash answered.

Viper nodded. "Knox, Train, make sure when this goes down they leave some of them breathing. I want someone left alive to spread the message not to fuck with us."

"It's going to take more than me and Train to accomplish that job. We could contain Razer, if we're lucky, but Shade…" They both shook their head. "You know how he is when he's pissed and that doesn't even begin to describe the mood he's in now."

Viper nodded his head in agreement. "Cash, when we're ready to make our move, send for back-up from Ohio. Not enough to make us weak there, but enough that we can take care of the Blue Horsemen while we keep Razer and Shade from wiping out the whole club."

Viper turned to Train. "Get Evie," he ordered.

Train left to go into the other room. Moments later, Train returned with Evie by his side.

Viper gave her his instructions. "I need you to take the shopping bags in my car to Beth. Let her pick out her stuff then you can bring the rest back here for Winter. Check on Lily and ask if they need you for anything."

"I'll leave now." Viper tossed her his keys.

As soon as she left the room, Cash asked the question

that was going through all the member's minds. "What about Sam?"

"I am done asking for information from her. She is never going to tell the fucking truth. Evie and the women can deal with her." The other members nodded in agreement.

"When do you want to hit the Blue Horsemen?"

"We don't go in blind. Let Shade do the recon then we'll make the decision. I want the brothers from Ohio here a few days before we hit their club. When I give the word, I want to be ready to ride."

The Last Riders sat grim-faced, each preparing for the battle ahead. The Blue Horsemen club would pay for what just a few had done. By the time they were done with them, they would no longer exist.

CHAPTER ELEVEN

Monday morning dawned with the members quietly getting ready to work their shifts in the factory. Winter rose early, letting Viper sleep. After she dressed, Winter rolled her wheelchair to the desk and began tending to Viper's never ending paperwork. The amount was staggering. If she hadn't been working on the paperwork during her free time, it would have been even worse.

After an hour, she took a break, grabbed a drink from the small refrigerator Viper kept in his room, and opened a granola bar to snack on. Viper lay on his stomach on the bed, the sheet tangled around him, barely covering his firm ass.

He hadn't come to bed last night until late. He had eaten dinner with her then told her he had to return downstairs, so she had watched television until drifting off to sleep.

He had not touched her since Friday night at the party. Winter couldn't help questioning if he was still hooking up with the female members. Jealousy tore at her, but she forced those feelings out of her head, refusing to go down that road with Viper again. He had misled her once, so this time she had to be wary while she kept her eyes open and her heart detached.

"What has you looking so gloomy?" Winter had been so lost in her thoughts, she hadn't been aware that he was awake and staring at her.

"I was wondering how Lily was doing. Have you heard?"

"Yes, Evie said she's doing better."

"Good, I was worried about her."

"You know Beth and Lily well, don't you?"

Winter was hesitant to answer, but answered truthfully. "As well as they let me. They are pretty tight, never fought or tried to steal each other's boyfriends the way some sisters do. I don't know if Beth even dated anyone before Razer. Lily has always been with Charles. Everyone in town knows he has loved her for years."

Viper nodded, adjusting himself so that he sat up in the bed, leaning back against the headboard. The sheet barely covered his cock, which Winter noticed had a morning erection.

"She return the feeling?"

Winter didn't know how to answer. She was a hundred percent sure that Razer would get zip out of Beth about Lily. She knew them better than anyone in town and they expected her to maintain their privacy.

"I don't know." Winter decided to plead ignorance. Going back to the desk, she returned to his mound of paperwork.

"Why are you being so evasive?"

"Why do you want to know so much about them? You want to know something, ask Razer, or better yet, Beth. She will tell you herself if she wants you to know," Winter snapped in return.

Viper moved to the side of the bed before standing and stretching lazily. Winter didn't turn her eyes from the ledgers, trying to keep her eyes off his impressive body. The tattoos on his chest, abdomen and arms—she hated to admit—pushed her buttons. Thankfully, she had never known he had a tattoo when they dated or it would have driven her crazy.

Winter determinedly returned to the paperwork, ignoring the warmth flooding her body. She heard him go into the bathroom then the shower running. Several minutes later, she heard him come out and get dressed. The whole time refusing to even glance in his direction.

"You have a new therapist starting today," he interrupted her wayward fantasy.

"What happened to Connor?"

"He quit Friday."

"Before or after the party?"

"Before."

"Why didn't you tell me?"

"Didn't want you changing his mind," he answered, pulling on his shirt. "He needed to concentrate on your recuperation, not getting inside your pussy. You ready for some breakfast?"

"Yes," she said through gritted teeth.

Viper gave her a sexy grin, picking her up. Minutes later, she was seated at the table with a plate of food in front of her. Winter had just finished when the doorbell rang. Train escorted an older woman into the kitchen.

"Winter, this is Donna; the new physical therapist," Viper briefly introduced the two women.

Viper carried her downstairs where she changed out of her clothes. She had developed the habit of leaving extra workout gear in the laundry room off the gym. It saved several trips up the stairs for Evie. Donna put her through her paces. Tired, Winter started to roll her chair towards the showers.

"Where are you going?"

"I was going to get a shower?" Winter asked, confused.

"I am not done with you yet."

"You're not?"

"No," Donna said firmly. "See this."

Beth saw her walk to a piece of equipment that was

covered up. She had thought the men had purchased a new piece of equipment for themselves. It wasn't, it was for her; a set off parallel bars for her to start walking longer distances. Winter felt tears of happiness try to break through.

"You ready?"

"Oh, yes."

"Let's get started then." It was the hardest thing Winter had ever done. Before, Conner was just having her take a few steps, now she was walking back and forth along the length of the bars. Donna wouldn't let her push it and brought it to a stop after a few attempts.

"We'll work on it again tomorrow," Donna promised.

The hot tub was heaven on her muscles. She was relaxing against the side of the tub when Viper came into the room.

"How did it go?" Viper asked Donna, but it was Winter who answered.

"Great." Happiness shone out of her face, removing the sadness that always seemed to cling to her.

"I need to get to my next client. You got her?" Donna asked.

"Yes."

Donna left, telling Winter she would see her tomorrow.

"I am ready to get out." Winter moved to stand by the side of the tub, waiting for him to help her out.

"The hot water help your back?"

"Yes, it relaxes the muscles in my back and legs."

Viper nodded, his eyes tracing a drop of water rolling down the skin between her breasts. Winter felt self-conscious for the first time, standing before him in the tiny bikini.

"Viper?" His dark eyes came back to hers, reluctantly leaving the expanse of exposed flesh.

He lifted her out of the hot water before reaching out and handing her a towel. He waited patiently as she dried off then picked her up and carried her to their room.

111

"I really like my new therapist. I got to walk again today, Viper." He had sat her in her chair and was watching as she gathered her clothes to wear. Winter looked back at him before entering the bathroom to get dressed. "I am hoping I will be out of your hair in a couple of weeks."

Viper nodded, not saying anything. He simply stood, staring out the window. For the first time in his life, he was confused at how to reach a woman. Winter refused to see his interest in her, ignoring the messages he was sending her at every opportunity. She had turned the tables against him. Now he knew how she had felt for those two years, trying to attract his attention while being constantly rebuffed.

He heard the shower stop and the sounds of her getting dressed. She was still fragile and would be for quite a while. She wasn't strong enough yet to deal with the full force of his desire, but she was healing. When he thought she was capable of dealing with him, then all the restraints he had placed on himself would be removed. He was giving her the time her body needed to heal, but also to repair the mind fuck he had done for those two years.

Viper's hands clenched into fists, forcing his body to relax, and to get his cock back under control. The sight of her in the bikini had almost sent him over the edge, wanting to grab her, but he had been able to gain control.

He hadn't fucked anyone since the night she had been attacked and it was beginning to get to him. When she had thought he was faithful to her for those two years, he had fucked anything that crossed his path, working his desire for her out on numerous willing female bodies. Now, when she could care less about him, he found himself unable to bring himself to touch another woman.

Winter had her revenge and she didn't even know or care.

* * *

Winter was walking by Christmas. She was slow and

hesitant, but gradually becoming stronger.

Without saying anything to Viper, she called the school board and told them she would be able to return to work in the upcoming semester. Thankfully, the school would be closed until the second week of January. She would still need the cane she was using, but she felt more than capable of dealing with the workload. The physical part of her job, she could delegate to her vice-principal while regaining the final stages of her strength.

Christmas was quiet around the house with just a few of The Last Riders remaining. Even Shade had disappeared for the holiday. Beth and Razer had spent the holiday with Lily, who had seemed recovered from the biker grabbing her.

Beth told Winter that she had finally convinced Lily to see a psychologist. The women had never shared with her what demons tormented Lily, and Winter wasn't sure she wanted to know what had damaged the sweet girl so badly. Some things in life were better left undisturbed.

Christmas dinner had been good with just Viper, Rider, Knox and Evie. This time, Winter had pitched in to cook and was rewarded with the compliments given. Smiling, she shrugged off the compliments and they settled down to a night of watching television.

Two days later, the crew was back and it was Friday; a combination that Winter could tell would lead to a wild night. She hadn't attended another party and wasn't about to. She planned on returning to her home at the end of next week, giving herself one more week of therapy, and though she adamantly refused to admit it to herself, a last week with Viper.

CHAPTER TWELVE

"That will do it. I don't want to overwork those muscles."

Winter relaxed, leaning down to catch her breath.

"You're looking much healthier, Winter," Donna complimented her.

"Thanks. I actually feel pretty good. I don't take pain meds anymore and I don't have as many muscle spasms."

"That shows they are almost healed. What does your doctor say?"

"To take it easy and not run before I can walk." The doctor had made the joke, but Winter hadn't found humor in the pun.

Donna laughed. "Don't worry. You're handling the workouts well and I think in a couple of months you'll even be able to ditch the cane."

Winter grinned back. "I am planning on it. I'm already scheduled to return to work the week after next."

Donna frowned. "Are you sure you're ready? There is a big difference walking around a house, staying on your feet for short periods versus standing for hours at a time. What did the doctor say?"

"I didn't tell him," Winter confessed. "I'll do fine,

though. I have staff at school. When I get tired, my vice-principal can handle things."

"I would think about it seriously, Winter. I think the next school year would be a more realistic option."

"I need to get back to work. I don't want them to replace me permanently. There is just the one high school in Treepoint. If I lose my job, I would have to find another school district."

Donna stopped arguing, knowing good jobs in Treepoint were hard to come by. "Let's get you in the hot tub."

Winter changed into her swimsuit and met Donna in the hot tub room. Sinking into the warm water, she was beginning to relax when Donna's phone rang. Listening unashamedly and seeing Donna's concerned look, she came to the conclusion one of her patients had an accident.

"I'm afraid we need to get you out of the tub," she said after disconnecting her call. "One of my patients has had a bad fall and they need me to help get her back in the bed." Winter got out of the hot tub with her help. Donna normally would have stayed while Winter got dressed, but she urged her to leave.

"I can handle it from here by myself. You go on; I'll be fine. I can get dressed then call someone to help me up the stairs. While Winter refused to let herself be packed around any longer, for safety reasons, someone always stood close by as she went up and down the steps.

"Are you sure?" Donna asked, her mind on the other patient.

"Go." Finally convincing the woman to leave, Winter went inside the restroom to get changed. When she was almost dressed, she heard voices enter the hot tub area then splashing as they obviously entered the water.

Winter hurried, not wanting to remain there without anyone's knowledge. Quickly opening the door, she went out and started towards the hot tub room. The door was half closed, blocking her from view. She was about to make her presence known when she heard voices and stopped.

"Leave that alone." Winter recognized Bliss's voice and Rider's when he replied.

"Take it off."

"No, I don't know where Winter is."

"We saw her therapist leave so she obviously isn't down here. She has to be in her room. Lose the top," Rider demanded with a voice full of frustration.

Winter frowned. Why would Bliss be concerned about her whereabouts before she took off her top? The other women in the club had no problem baring their breasts, regardless of who was around. But thinking back, Winter realized Bliss had never exposed more than the bare minimum of her upper body. Although she had no shame when it came to walking around in skimpy underwear.

"Damn shame to hide such a pretty tattoo," Rider murmured. Through the crack of the door, Winter could see him playing with the woman's breast. Feeling uncomfortable with the situation she had found herself in, Winter was determined to leave as unnoticed as possible.

"Be glad when everything gets back to normal, when she goes home. Viper said it won't be much longer."

"I think he's starting to care for her, Rider."

"Same way he always has, as a piece to a puzzle, not a piece of ass."

"What does that mean? Vincent Bedford is in prison, what information does Viper need Winter for?"

"He won't cut ties with her completely until he finds that kid. Once he does, then she won't matter to him anymore."

"I think you're wrong," Bliss argued.

"Yeah? Hell, Bliss, you have been around long enough to know how Viper likes to fuck. You fucked him yourself. Think her body, as broken as it is, can take a pounding the way Viper likes to give it?"

116

This time Winter noticed Bliss didn't interrupt Rider. She couldn't, the man had his tongue down her throat and wasn't giving her time to talk about anything anymore.

Unobtrusively, Winter edged quietly by the door, making her way into the gym before going upstairs. Thankfully, nobody saw her come up from downstairs. She got herself a drink, sat at the table and waited. It wasn't long before Evie came in, and Winter asked her to watch her up the steps.

Once in her room, she thanked her.

"No problem. I was coming up anyway to get dressed. You coming down tonight or staying in the room."

"I think I will come down for dinner," Winter said, coming to a decision.

"See you then." Evie grinned before leaving, unaware of the hurt Winter was hiding.

She made her way to the chair by the window and looked out without actually seeing anything. The day was unseasonably warm, making one think spring was officially here. It hadn't been a warm winter, so the men took advantage of the weather and fired up the grill in the huge backyard.

It took several minutes before she could gather her thoughts enough to realize she was actually watching Viper and Shade putting steaks and burgers on the grill while the women sat around the two large picnic tables, talking. Winter didn't need to see the scene below to realize she didn't belong.

She was about to turn from the window when she saw Evie approaching the men with a seductive walk. Both men turned and watched as she approached. Winter's stomach clenched, and she was sick at what she knew was about to happen. Evie leaned into Viper, who put a casual arm around her waist, laughing at something she said. Evie wiggled closer and reached out a hand to trace down a particular path on Shade's arm. Winter felt eyes on her; Shade was watching her watch them.

He turned back to the grill, turning the steaks, moving beyond Evie's touch. When Viper and Evie looked up, she realized he had used the motion to warn the other two that she was watching.

Stepping away from the window, she went into the bathroom, locking the door and turning on the shower. Winter was not surprised to hear the bedroom door open and Viper knock on the bathroom door.

"Do you need some help downstairs? The food will be ready soon."

"No thanks. I'll get something later. I think I'll take a short nap first."

"You sure?"

"Yes." Winter cut off the water, not wanting to raise his suspicions, and was relieved when she heard the bedroom door open and close.

She waited a few minutes more before opening the door, making sure he wasn't coming back. She went to the closet and dragged out her suitcases. Packing her things took little time, mainly jeans and shirts. Putting everything by the bedroom door, she changed into jeans and a loose fitting emerald sweater. Brushing her hair out, Winter took a long look at herself. This time she was determined to get out of the house. He wouldn't be able to throw up her helpless condition when she looked healthy.

For the first time in a long time, she stared at herself, shocked at the changes. Her hair had grown out, now brushing the top of her shoulders, curling softly and gleaming the chestnut color that suited her pale complexion. The green sweater matched her emerald colored eyes. She had lost weight after the attack, but the workouts had tightened and toned her body. She was still underweight, yet she had gained muscle mass. She would never be as pretty as the other women, however at least she no longer looked helpless.

Winter reached out and grabbed the dresser as she fought to regain control of her emotions.

When she had first found out the severity of the damage that had been done to her body, she didn't see an end to her misery. Winter feared she would never fully recover, not only from the attack, but also from her love for Loker. Now she could see that she was almost there. To do the rest, she had to accomplish two things. First, keep strengthening her body with the therapy and workouts, and two, put an end to Viper's games.

With that in mind, she used the phone to call the one person she knew would enable her to walk away from the man she was determined to cut from her life for good.

Carefully going down the stairs, Winter focused intensely on making it on her own. Everyone was outside, leaving the house strangely quiet, however every creak made Winter's hear skip a beat. After finally making it to the bottom, she let out a huge sigh of relief and headed towards the backyard.

Their Friday night was in full swing as she made her way to the picnic table where Evie, Bliss, Dawn, Rider, Viper and Shade where sitting and eating.

Finding an empty seat at the end of the table next to Dawn with Bliss across the table, she gave everyone a fake smile as they greeted her.

"Let me get you a plate," Viper offered as he started to get up.

"No thanks, but I will take one of those beers. She pointed to the cooler at the end of the table. Shade reached in and pulled one out, passing it down the table until it reached her. Opening it, she took a long drink as the conversation returned to normal. She sat and listened as they talked, watching as several members from the other table got up and began dancing or sitting around on the patio furniture. The music was a nice touch, and for a second, Winter regretted not being there for the spring and summer, imagining the yard was very nice during the warmer months.

"Bliss, I like your top; the color suits you," Winter

complemented the woman during a lull in conversation.

"Thank you. I got it with the gift certificate you gave me for Christmas."

"I'm glad you were able to find something you liked," Winter said sincerely.

"I was wondering something; I noticed all the women members have tattoos with different numbers on them." Evie's and Dawn's tops were barely there, and had tats that were easily seen on the curve of their breasts.

"Yes, we can pick which tattoo we want and put the date on it," Evie explained. "Some, like me, just have the date tatted."

"I see." Beth took another sip of her beer, aware of the conversation at the table.

"Does everyone have the same date?" Winter wanted to know why Bliss was hiding her tattoo from her and she was determined to find out before she left.

"No," Evie spoke cautiously now, beginning to suspect the trap that was waiting.

Viper stiffened in surprise at the turn of the conversation. He turned to look at Winter and saw the intention in her expression.

"What determines the date that goes on the tattoo?"

"It's the date we become a member of The Last Riders," Evie explained slowly.

"I see. How do the women become members?" Winter asked, knowing instinctively that the information was going to hurt.

Evie looked around the table, willing someone to jump in and take over the discussion. Thankfully, Viper did with a grim look.

"Ask what you want to know, Winter."

"I just did. What's the big secret?"

"No secret, it's just club business. Only the members or potential members need to know, but I will tell you. The women become members by fucking or causing six of the eight members to have an orgasm."

Winter's hands tightened on the beer bottle, disgusted that she could ever care about the man staring coldly back at her.

"Well, doesn't that make it nice for the male members? How do they become members? By fucking a certain number of women? What is it, a hundred?" she said snidely.

"No, the recruit that wants to become a member and join us must pick four of the original members."

"Male members to fuck?" Winter asked in surprise. The angry glares from the men around the table answered her question.

"No, they pick four of the eight members to beat the hell out of them then, if they fight well and aren't hurt too bad, they become members."

Winter didn't know which was worse. The ones she was pretty sure were the original members were definitely men that she wouldn't want to take on, one on one, much less four of them.

"You guys have a thing for numbers, don't you?" Winter said sarcastically.

"We have to know that a man we are making our brother can handle himself and have our back. Going on beer runs and dumb shit like that won't be of any help to us when another club wants our cut."

Winter could kind of see his point-of-view on that scenario.

"Well, your club has worked out all the details. So the women get the tattoo after they fuck their sixth original member?" Winter still didn't understand what Bliss's tattoo had to do with her.

"Basically, yes." Viper's firm voice held no apology.

"I can see by the women's tattoos that they are very proud of their accomplishment." The women at the table stiffened. Evie was the first to speak.

"We don't deserve that attitude. You might think that is a large number of men to sleep with, but we happen to think we are very selective. I have girlfriends who aren't in The Last Rider's that go out to party every weekend, and fuck a couple of different guys a month, knowing shit about them. I know everything about these men, who I might add, have lugged your ass around for the last month and been nothing except polite to you.

"I agree. I apologize for any affront I may have caused. All of you have been more than kind to me and I shouldn't repay your kindness by being a bitch." The women relaxed at the table, but Winter could tell they were still angry and so were the men.

"I don't see your tattoo, Bliss? May I see it?" Bliss stiffened in her seat, looking at Viper.

"Show her," Viper ordered.

Bliss reached out and pulled her top back, leaving the curve of her breast bare, giving a clear view of the tattoo. It was very pretty. Winter swallowed the nausea rising in her stomach as she saw the date. It was the day she had been attacked, surrounded by a daisy chain of four flowers.

"Who gave you the last vote you needed?" Winter sat, staring at the striking tattoo with images of her attack replaying through her mind.

"I did," Viper admitted.

Winter knew that the daisy chain had significance and it was only when the word chain came to mind a second time that the realization hit her.

Winter forced herself with an iron will to remain calm and not let anyone see the hurt screaming through her body. She fought herself to stay seated and finish her beer. Those at the table wanted to leave, but it was like a train wreck everyone was waiting to happen. Winter wasn't going to let them see how devastated she was, however she couldn't leave, letting Viper get away with his games.

"Now I understand why you said what you did to Bliss today, Rider." Everyone looked at the two members who sat in confusion, not understanding yet what she was referring to, but Winter was about to remind them. "I heard you tell Bliss that you guys could get back to normal after I leave like Viper told you. If that is any example," she pointed to Bliss's tattoo, "I bet you can hardly wait until I am gone. Viper told you two weeks; I am not going to cramp your style. I am leaving tonight. My bags are packed and my ride should be here any minute. I would like to thank each of you for your help this last month," Winter said proudly.

She turned to Viper, who stared at her impassively except for the burning fury in his eyes. "You put yourself out for nothing. They said that you were still playing me, hoping Vincent would tell me something about the baby. You were way off base. Sorry, I couldn't have been more help, but at least this time you didn't have to waste two years of your life."

"I see that Rider and Bliss were a fountain of information for you." Both of them sat still as statues while Bliss had fear on her face.

"They didn't know I was even there. I was in the hallway and they were in the hot tub."

"But they were discussing my business?"

Winter shut up. She hadn't wanted to get Bliss in trouble. She didn't know Rider well, but he had always been helpful and kind to her. She was beginning to regret her plan, especially now that she was afraid she had gotten Bliss in trouble. She had made friends with the woman and she hadn't wanted to hurt her. Bliss had covered herself for the last month, something she was proud of, just to spare her feelings.

"Bliss and Rider didn't do anything wrong, I was the one eavesdropping."

Viper ignored her defense of the members. "So who did you call to come get you this time?" he huffed.

"The sheriff." Winter knew she had made a terrible mistake when Viper motioned to Shade, who immediately stood, pulling his phone out of his pocket before going indoors.

"He will still come," Winter said bravely. This had gone so wrong. She was supposed to have made everyone angry enough to throw her out.

"Will he?" Viper mocked her.

"It doesn't matter; I'll just call someone else. I can take care of myself. I don't need to stay here anymore."

"So you feel fully recovered?"

Why do I feel like that's a trick question? Winter thought frantically.

Definitely not liking the look in his eyes, Winter clutched her cane and began walking backwards away from him. She didn't know where she was going. She just knew Viper was in front of her and Shade was inside the house. The only option left was to put a little space between them until Viper calmed down. He was furious with her. That night in the Pink slipper, he didn't lose his temper fighting with the other motorcycle club members ganging up on him. Viper had handled them with calm control. Winter wished she could see a little of that control now.

Viper stalked her as she went backwards, edging her towards the side of the yard where there was a gazebo with a swing. Frantically, Winter looked for an escape route, but couldn't find one.

"Aren't you going to make a run for it?" Winter threw a dirty look at his question. He was throwing back to her that she wasn't a hundred percent healed yet.

"You're being ridiculous. I am the one with the right to be angry."

"What have you got a right to be angry about? You don't wear my ring. I have never told you that I am in an exclusive relationship with you. Have I ever once told you that you were mine? Did I ever, in all the time I have known you, let you believe that I was yours?"

The questions beat at her with each step she took.

"No," Winter answered truthfully, finding herself cornered against the side of the gazebo and swing. When she tried to step around the swing, Viper blocked her path, pinning her against the gazebo wall.

"When I would go out of town, and you tried to make me jealous by going out with every single father in the fucking PTA, what did I tell you?"

"Have a good time." Winter turned her head away, unable to stare in his face as he mocked her.

"I could have fucked you silly as Loker James, but I wanted you to know who I really was before I put my dick in you. I won't always be so nice. I am not a nice person. Never was, don't want to be. Nice people get fucked over. My brother was an example of that."

Winter started to argue, but Viper talked over her. "You're a nice person. I fucked you over, deal with it because I am done trying to make amends. I never led you to believe there was more to us than there actually was, and until you come to grips with that, you are going to stay pissed at me. But I can deal with pissed; actually, it makes me want to fuck."

Winter stared at him in shock as his hand went to her breast, pulling down her sweater and bra, leaving her breasts bare. Looking around in embarrassment, she tried to tug her top back up dropping her cane in the process. The other members were now dancing or engaging in their own sexual activities, ignoring them. Winter knew no one could see anything with Viper and the gazebo blocking their view.

He dragged her attention back to him when he caught her hands in his and lifted them above her head, knotting a soft cord around her wrists that she hadn't seen nailed into the side of the gazebo.

"You guys are prepared for everything." Winter struggled against him tying her hands.

Viper laughed. "We try." Before Winter could tell him to let her go, he captured her mouth in a kiss so full of heat, her brain almost exploded.

Tearing her mouth away from him this time, more determined she hoped. Her top was lowered again and this time he took her nipple in his mouth, teasing it with his teeth, his other hand uncovered her other breast, squeezing it from bottom to the top, forcing the blood to the nipple. Winter's head fell back against the gazebo.

"Do you know how many times I imagined you like this? With your breasts just waiting for my mouth, your nipples for me to suck them until you scream for mercy? I fucked every woman here the last two years pretending it was your pussy I was inside."

"You fucking liar. I bet you didn't think of me that night with Bliss once. There were four daisies. Does that mean she fucked four members that night?"

"Yes; Cash, Evie and me. We fucked all night long." After making that admission, his hands unbuckled her jeans, spreading them open before sliding his hand inside. Winter kicked out at him, but he stepped between her legs, making her attempt useless.

"Careful, I don't want you to hurt your back. More importantly, I don't want you hurting something of mine I plan to be using in a few minutes."

"You go to hell, if you think tying me up—"

Viper cut her off. "You don't like it? That's all you had to say," with a twist of his hand the cord around her wrist was loosened before giving away. "We don't need safe words, a simple no will do, but your wet pussy is telling me no isn't on your mind." His hand had been playing with her clit the whole time. He knew exactly how excited he was making her. A finger slid deep inside, making her brace against the gazebo to steady herself.

Viper lowered his head once again, finding her nipple and sucking it into the wet heat of his mouth. A whimper escaped her as another finger joined the one inside her.

"I did think of you that night, but as tight as her pussy was, it can't compare to yours." His fingers began sliding in and out of her as one of her legs shifted to wrap around his legs between hers. "You got even wetter imaging me fucking another woman? Or that there were four of us giving it to her?"

"You said Evie, Cash and you; that is only three."
Winter didn't care how many people Bliss fucked that
night, as long as Viper kept building her orgasm.

"There was someone else, but he doesn't like his
business talked about anymore than I do." The reminder
almost saved her from him, but he didn't give her time to
build her defenses. "I never told Rider fuck about when
you were leaving because you are staying right where you
are, in my fucking bed." With that, he lifted her up into his
arms, packing her into the house.

Carrying her up the steps, Winter tried to remember
when she lost control of the situation.

When they entered his room, Viper sat her gently on
the floor before starting to remove his clothes. She stood
there and watched as his clothes fell to the floor. For the
last few months she had lain next to his body, forcing
herself to pretend that she wasn't attracted to him any
longer. But as he stood before her naked, she finally
admitted to herself that she had lied.

She wanted him badly. His body was a piece of art and
she wasn't talking about his ink. His sculpted muscles and
obvious strength were a turn on for her. She had waited
for him for so long, she could take her chance tonight and
be the woman with memories of him or someone who
could hold onto a grudge in a lonely bed.

Viper reached out and pulled her shirt over her head,
unclasping the bra before he let it drop to the floor. He
then sank to his knees as he drew her jeans off after
removing her shoes. His mouth found her pussy as soon
as the jeans hit the floor at the same time his hands held
her hips as he licked the tiny button, finding her wet.

Winter's hands sank into his thick hair as he brought
her near orgasm. Using his tongue, he pressed her clit flat,
stopping her climax. Her hips shifted as she tried to bring
herself over, but he held steady, denying her.

Standing to his feet, he turned her to the bed before

127

lifting her up and placing her in the middle.

"Viper..."

"Spread your legs." Viper reached inside his nightstand and pulled out a condom. Tearing the package open, he carefully rolled it on as he stared at her sprawled on the bed. "I am going to be careful, so I don't hurt your back. If you feel any pain, you tell me and we can change positions."

Winter lowered her lashes, feeling inferior for a second; sure he had never worried how he fucked other women. She remembered what Rider had said earlier about her not being able to handle Viper and she was beginning to realize that he was right. She didn't compare to the women in looks and now her body even let her down when it came to sex.

Viper grabbed a handful of her hair, dragging her attention back to him. "I don't care about your back other than I don't want to hurt you. I better not see that look on your face again tonight. The only thing you need to worry about is how I am going to teach you exactly what I like then, from now on, you're going to give it to me when and where I want it."

Winter's mouth opened to protest as his cock teased her clit before entering her in one sure stroke. Her back arched at the unbelievable pleasure of him entering her.

"Stay still; let me do all the work." He smiled into her neck as his lips traced a path downwards to her breast, pulling it upwards to his waiting mouth. Surrounding the nipple, he took the tip of it between his teeth, sucking strongly. Stroking inside her, he raised her leg to his hip as his cock drove deep inside her pulsating sheath and his thrusts escalated.

Winter reached out, touching his smooth chest as he moved above her. She had fantasized so many times of having sex with him that it seemed almost unreal that she was lying beneath him as he moved forcefully above her.

Viper caught her eyes with his as his hand went to her

pussy. "This is mine."

Winter could only stare at him in return, trying to douse the hope building deep within her soul. Was he telling her that now he considered them in a relationship? She was afraid to believe what his face and words were telling her.

Swiftly, he twisted his hips, hitting the spot deep within her, pushing her into a climax that rippled through her entire body. Viper stroked her, extending her orgasm until she begged him to stop. With a grin, he rose on his arms above her, moving his hips in a series of thrusts that had her grabbing the rails above her head before he came inside her.

Rolling off her, Viper went into the bathroom before coming back and lifting her into his arms. Turning the shower on until the water steamed, he pulled her inside, turning her until the spray hit her back.

Swallowing nervously at the tenderness he was showing her, she searched his face to find him staring down at her with an unreadable look. Winter dropped her head, hiding her face against his chest. She was sure she had, again, read too much into his actions, making more out of him than just having sex with her; she was nothing more than a fuck to him.

Viper stared down at the woman he had wanted to fuck for the last two years, making himself wait until she could see the real man she was with. From her expression, he could see the doubt and fear in her eyes that he was still using her for whatever messed up reason she had come up with. He didn't need her for information or as a fucking partner. He had his pick of several women, in and out of the club.

A grin passed his lips. When she realized just how much he expected of her, she was going to run. She wasn't going to be happy to find herself as the newest recruit.

CHAPTER THIRTEEN

Winter scooted to the edge of the bed, trying not to wake Viper.

"Where are you going?"

"I have to go to the bathroom. Then I am getting out of this bed. If I stay here much longer, I will be paralyzed again."

Viper laughed, gripping her hip as he rolled closer to her, his chest to her back. Winter closed her eyes while enjoying the feel of him at her back. His mouth nuzzled her neck, his teeth grazing the sensitive skin.

"You sore?"

"Which part of my body isn't?"

"You need one of your pain pills?"

"No, if I need anything, I will take a couple of ibuprofen. At least I don't have to do my exercises this morning. You took care of that last night," Winter groaned.

"I am trying to build up your stamina."

Winter laughed. "You're crazy if you think a night like that can be repeated."

"Welcome to your new normal," Viper told her with a straight face.

"I will never survive." She turned to look back at him.

Viper's arm slid around her waist, pulling her back down on the bed. He then slid his leg between hers, pulling her body back to his own.

"You are going to crave my dick in your pussy."

A movement at her head made her realize he was reaching for yet another condom. She groaned as his hand slid downward to her mound, easily renewing the fire that had just died down.

Releasing her, he rolled the condom on before she felt his cock sliding in deep from behind. Her pussy was slightly sore from the night, and each time he stroked inward, the smooth flesh set off a sensation of tugging at the swollen flesh.

Winter couldn't prevent the whimpers escaping. "Fucked you so much and your pussy is still tighter than a fist," Viper groaned.

"Viper…" Winter's hand gripped the arm around her waist.

"You're gripping my cock…"

Both came together, lying content until finally Winter had no choice other than to get up.

Viper rose from the bed, going to the bathroom and coming back before she could manage to make it halfway across the floor. Glaring at him when he came back out, he swept her off her feet without pause and carried her to the bathroom. He set her down to turn the shower on, letting the steam fill the room before joining her.

"I think you are going to put me back in my wheelchair," Winter accused him.

"We keep fucking like that I will need one for myself."

* * *

They were sitting at the table eating cold cereal when the other members began coming into the kitchen. Beth and Ember began cooking breakfast for everyone.

"Couldn't manage to fix yourselves something decent?" Jewell asked, sitting down with a glass of juice.

Winter turned bright red. Viper sat back in his chair with his arm casually over the back of her chair. Razer and Shade sat down at the table as Beth served Razer his breakfast. The smell of bacon had Winter eyeing his plate of food enviously. Smiling, Beth slid one just like it in front of her.

"I love you," Winter said fervently.

Beth smiled before taking a seat with her own plate. Shade and Viper eyed her before getting up to fix their own plates. The women smiled at each other as they ate their food.

"How is Lily doing?" Winter asked.

"Good. She goes back to school in two weeks. Her and her friend are planning on going to spring break together."

"Where are they planning on going?" Winter asked before taking a bite of toast.

"They're having trouble making their minds up. Penni wants to go on a mini cruise, says it the perfect place to meet guys without the party atmosphere of the beaches on spring break."

Winter tried to keep her lips from smiling at Shade's frown. "Does Lily want to go?"

"Actually, she wants to go to Arizona." Shade's frown changed to a smile.

"To see the Grand Canyon?" Winter asked, thinking that was a strange choice for a spring break vacation.

"I asked the same thing." Beth laughed.

"What did she say?"

"She said Arizona has cowboys. Seems she has this thing for them; has the impression they are all macho, protective and are gentlemen. She thinks they are sexy." The women laughed good-naturedly at the young girl's fantasy.

Shade's smile had disappeared.

"Doesn't Arizona have tornados?" Winter asked casually.

Beth's laughter stopped. "Really?"

Shade and all the men nodded.

"Spring break is right in the middle of tornado season," Winter confirmed.

"I'll have to tell them. Maybe a cruise would be better." Shade didn't seem any happier.

"Perhaps you might convince them to stay a few days in Lexington. Spring meet will be on at Keeneland then you could bring Lily back with you and we could have your bachelorette party on that Friday."

Beth considered it for several minutes. "I think that's a great idea. Thanks, Winter."

Winter smiled at Beth, ignoring the narrowed stare of Shade.

The arm around her shoulders moved to cup her neck, Viper's thumb sliding against her sensitive flesh. She looked at Viper to see him smiling in appreciation at her maneuvering.

"I'm looking forward to the bachelorette party. Evie talked to Mick; he said to let him know the date and we could have the bar for the night. It's going to be nice just us, no men," Jewell said.

"Well, us and a few of my other friends," Beth clarified, hesitantly.

"Like who?" Evie asked, suspiciously sitting down at the table with her food.

"Crazy Bitch, Sex Piston, Killyama…"

Evie raised her hand "You have got to be shitting me. Tell me you're not seriously considering inviting them to your party."

"I have to invite them. It will hurt their feelings if I don't."

"Those bitches don't have any feelings. Not normal ones anyway," Shade butted into the conversation.

Beth sent Shade a reproachful look.

"There is a problem with them coming," Evie reminded Beth. All eyes turned to Bliss who was unashamedly listening from the kitchen counter.

Beth shook her head. "No, that is all forgotten. They'll be cool, they promised."

Everyone looked at her doubtfully.

Winter remembered the fight at the Pink Slipper and how the biker bitches wanted Bliss badly. She doubted those feelings had disappeared. Especially the crazy one; she didn't seem like she would forget a thing.

"May I make a suggestion? Suppose we have the party at eight until two. Tell your biker friends it starts at eleven. If Bliss wouldn't mind, she could leave a few minutes earlier than when they would arrive."

Bliss smiled in relief. "That works for me."

Beth not so much. Winter loved Beth; she was a truly kind person who didn't want to intentionally hurt anyone. Winter swallowed a lump in her throat when she saw Razer's gaze fixed on Beth. It was obvious he loved her; he knew she wasn't happy with the solution, but didn't have another one.

"Okay, if that makes everyone more comfortable," Beth conceded. The whole room nodded their heads.

CHAPTER FOURTEEN

Winter borrowed Evie's car to drive herself to the doctor on Monday. Satisfied with her progress, he agreed to sign her work release. Winter wanted to celebrate, but she was by herself, all the members were hard at work at the factory.

A big order was due to go out on Thursday and many had to work overtime. She frowned, realizing suddenly that her world had narrowed down to The Last Riders. She had never had an overabundance of friends, yet there were a few she could have called at a moment's notice for lunch.

Winter decided to go to the diner for lunch by herself. The diner wasn't very busy with only a few customers occupying the tables. Pastor Dean was sitting at one by himself.

"Mind if I join you?" Winter asked.

He rose and pulled out a chair at the table. "Not at all."

Pastor Dean sat back down as the waitress came to take her order. Winter appreciated his gentlemanly manners. He was an extremely good-looking man, who was also an excellent Pastor. Winter had sought his guidance several times after her mother's death.

"You seem to be recovering well."

"Other than the cane and that I move as slow as a turtle, I am," Winter agreed happily.

"Now that you're better, I am hoping to see you in church again. The children in your class miss you."

"I miss them." Her class of preschoolers was small, but she was eager to see them again. "I'll be back this Sunday."

"I'll count on it." They discussed how several of the older church parishioners were doing until their food arrived. They were drinking coffee when Mrs. Langley came in from her beauty shop appointment to meet her friend.

Mrs. Langley was Winter's aunt and Samantha's grandmother. The woman was as kind as Samantha was cruel. She sat down at their table to wait for her friend's arrival.

After both assured each other that they were doing well. Mrs. Langley brought up the uncomfortable situation herself.

"Winter, I heard at the beauty shop what happened with Samantha. I am deeply ashamed at her actions."

"Aunt Shay, you're not responsible for her actions, you have nothing to be embarrassed about," Winter reassured her there were no hard feelings.

"First Vincent, then Samantha. My daughter would be heartbroken if she were still alive." Mrs. Langley's daughter had died three years ago. Samantha, who had always stayed in trouble, had become even wilder without her mother's guidance.

A sudden thought struck Winter, she didn't want to hurt the woman, but the truth needed to be brought out.

"Aunt Shay, has anyone told you that Samantha had a baby three years ago? It was right around the time of Samantha's mother's death." Mrs. Langley's expression became cautious. Winter knew then she was right, everyone had been so cautious of protecting the woman's feelings, they were ignoring the only source of information they had. Even Pastor Dean was giving the older woman a concerned look.

"She told Loker James that it was his brother's child. He is devastated. He loved his brother and the thought of his murdered brother's child out there with no family caring for it is hard for him to accept," Winter explained gently.

Mrs. Langley stared at Pastor Dean several minutes before answering in a quiet voice. "She told him it was Gavin's?"

Winter heard Pastor Dean break into the conversation. "You knew Gavin?" Surprised at the familiarity of the name coming from Pastor Dean, it was only Mrs. Langley's answer that made her forget to question him.

"He stayed at my home while they were building the factory. Vincent invested in the business and as my home was so large, he asked if Gavin could stay there. Of course I accepted. I didn't know Vincent was planning on killing him." Her frail hand shook as she sat her tea glass back on the table. "It probably made it easier to make him disappear." A tear ran down her withered cheek. Pastor Dean handed her a handkerchief.

"You couldn't have known, please don't blame yourself."

It took several minutes before the older woman could get herself back under control.

"I couldn't help him, but at least I can help Loker. I knew Sam was pregnant. She came to me when she first found out because she wanted to have an abortion. She was too far along and she stayed with me until she had the baby. When she went into labor, she called Vincent and he came to the house to pick her up. Afterwards, when I asked about the baby, they told me Samantha had given it up for adoption. I would have cared for the child, but they told me no. I have no idea where my great grandchild is and they won't tell me." Anguish filled the old woman's eyes.

"Do you know if the baby was Gavin's?" Winter

pushed gently, knowing her aunt had to understand Viper's predicament.

"It wasn't. She never told me who the father of the child was, but I know for a fact it wasn't Gavin's."

"How?"

"Because I was the one who drove her to the doctor's appointments when she was pregnant. She became pregnant *after* Gavin disappeared."

Winter sat back, disappointed. "Samantha gave Loker the baby's date of birth. He was still in town when she conceived." Pastor Dean looked as disappointed as Winter.

Mrs. Langley shook her head, saddened by her granddaughter's treachery. "The baby was premature. Doctors said that it was because Samantha was so young and she didn't take care of herself."

"Will you give me the name of the doctor you took her to?" Winter asked.

"Yes." Opening her purse, she took out a pad of paper and pen, writing down the doctor's name and address.

"The doctor is in Jamestown." The town next to Treepoint was thirty miles away, which was a distance that would enable Vincent to keep his daughter's pregnancy a secret.

"Yes. Vincent was afraid of the gossip in town, so he had me take her there. That was where she had the baby."

Winter stood up from the table and hugged her aunt tightly. "Thank you, Aunt Shay. Loker has been upset that his brother was accused of getting an underage girl pregnant. Then having that child missing was hard on him."

"I am glad I could help." Winter could see a tiny bit of the burden on the woman lightening.

Her aunt's friend entered the restaurant, so with a hug and promises to see her soon, she left to join her.

"No one thought to ask her. Samantha never went to visit her grandmother," Pastor Dean remarked.

"That's how I can tell you're not from a small town," Winter answered. A closed expression came over his handsome face.

"What do you mean?"

"If you were from a small town, especially Treepoint, you would know however many problems you have with your family that you always turn to them when you're in trouble."

"Good to know." Pastor Dean gave her a wry smile.

"Beth wouldn't think to ask because that woman is incapable of hurting anyone's feelings. She would have avoided upsetting Aunt Shay."

"Yes, she would," Pastor Dean agreed.

"You should know, you dated her for a while," Winter probed.

"Beth is very kind hearted." His expression became closed.

"Yes, she is." She reached out and gripped his hand, his turned and held hers.

The waitress brought their ticket. When she would have paid, Pastor Dean wouldn't let her.

"My treat."

They walked out together. Pastor Dean followed beside her as she walked to her car and held the door open for her. She was about to get in when he spoke.

"Winter, it was a nice thing you did today, Loker wouldn't have stopped until he found that child, he wouldn't have been able to."

"I know. Viper is stubborn."

Pastor Dean's head tilted to the side in question. "You call him Viper?"

Winter paused, finally admitting to herself what she had known all along. "Loker was imaginary. A disguise he surrounded himself with, he's Viper to me now." She confessed something to him that she hadn't been able to do to herself, "I never had Loker; he was a mirage."

Pastor Dean shook his head in disagreement. It seemed

as if he was about to say something, but changed his mind. "See you this Sunday."

Winter watched him walk away before getting into the car and driving back to the clubhouse. She was getting out of her car before she realized something and stopped in her tracks, turning back to the car she bumped into Shade.

"I'm sorry I wasn't watching were I was going," she apologized.

"It's all right. I was coming out of the factory when I saw that you were upset about something." Winter took a step back, being close to Shade made her nervous.

He was wearing loose jeans that clung to his hips, black biker boots and a black t-shirt. His arms and neck that were visible gave a menacing air to the man, and combined with the vibes he put off, anyone would be afraid of him. When they were surrounded by the other members, it slightly muted the effect, yet alone it was overwhelming.

Winter was upset. "I just realized that I have been trying to get back to my home since I returned to Treepoint then the first time I actually have the opportunity, I don't even go by to check on my house."

Shade laughed, taking her arm as they walked to the flight of steps to the house.

"Well, it's too late now." With a swift movement he had her up in his arms, packing her up the large flight of steps.

"I could have done it."

"There are seventy-five steps, everyone has counted them. Twice. There is no need to put that kind of pressure on your back." Winter gripped the cane as he effortlessly carried her inside the house before setting her down on her feet inside the doorway.

"Thanks. I appreciate the lift."

"Anytime," he said before going back out the door. No one could say Shade was a man of words. Winter laughed to herself, excited about telling Viper the good news. She went into the kitchen to see if anyone knew where he was and found him sitting at the table with Knox and Jewell finishing lunch.

Not wanting to interrupt their lunch, she went to sit in a chair next to Viper.

"Doctor's appointment go okay?" he questioned.

"Yes, he signed my work release. I'll take it by the business office tomorrow."

"I still think it's a little soon, but I know you're bored around the house all day."

"Not really, I have all your paperwork to keep me busy. I think you need to hire someone fulltime to do the paperwork and keep the ordering on schedule."

"Nope. It is a club business, only a member is allowed access," Viper said firmly.

"I'm not a member." Confused at his words, Winter was surprised he had allowed her to do the paperwork for him.

"That's a different situation," he said, getting up from the table to get himself another bottled water and handing one to her before sitting back down at the table.

"Why, because I'm sleeping with you?" Winter started to get angry, she was still upset with herself for not going by her house. She had thought earlier that The Last Riders were taking over her life when in fact she wasn't ready to admit that she was letting herself become too attached to Viper.

"We don't do much sleeping anymore, plenty of fucking going on, though," Viper teased her.

Winter flushed with Knox and Jewell listening closely.

"But that is not why," he continued.

"Well?" Winter asked.

After taking a drink of water, Viper answered, "Because you are a probate, that allows you access to almost anything."

Winter gave him a glare. "I thought you were joking when you said that to Tara and Stacy."

"Tara and Stacy?" Jewell butted in, enthralled with the

argument going on in front of her.

"The fuck twins," Knox answered.

"Oh." Jewell nodded her head.

"You know them?" Winter asked, surprised.

"Yes. Everyone does," Jewell answered, not knowing she was walking into quicksand.

"Is there anyone that walks through the door you guys haven't fucked?" The three members at the table wisely remained quiet.

"Winter," Viper tried to head off the eruption that he could see coming towards them.

"Don't 'Winter' me, you man-whore. I told you that I wasn't going to become a member and I meant it. I am not going to fuck any members and I am certainly not getting a tattoo branding me as your club's whore. I have no idea how Beth allowed herself to fuck eight different men," Winter said angrily.

A gasp from the doorway had Winter turning in her chair to see Beth and Razer standing in the doorway. Her face was pale and she looked like she was about to cry.

"Beth, I am sorry. I didn't mean anything. I was just angry at Viper. I let my tongue run away from me," Winter apologized.

Beth turned and left the room and with an angry glare Razer followed her.

"Winter."

Winter turned to look at Viper who gave her an angry stare.

"I'm sorry." Winter wanted to cry. She felt terrible at what she had said.

"That won't do this time. You insulted not only Beth, but also every member of the club. You have to make amends or you need to leave," Viper said sharply.

Winter's heart sank. She had let her mouth run away from her, insulting everyone that had helped her through recovery. They hadn't deserved the judgmental attitude she had been throwing at them since the day she had arrived.

"Both. I'll do what I have to do to make amends then I will leave." Winter didn't know why it felt as if her heart was ripping in two. She had wanted to leave since the day she had arrived.

Viper held his emotions in check, angry with himself for pushing her in front of the others, but being President meant he had to hold everyone responsible for their actions. "We are giving out punishments Thursday."

Today was only Monday. That gave her three more days with Viper, if he even still wanted anything to do with her after the way she had acted.

"Okay, there is something I want to tell you. I don't expect it to make a difference as to my punishment, though."

Viper nodded his head, his anger unrelenting.

Winter swallowed down the tears threatening to fall. Opening her purse, she took out the slip of paper that her Aunt Shay had given her and handed it to him.

"That's the doctor who Sam went to when she was pregnant. Aunt Shay confirmed Gavin wasn't the father. Sam didn't become pregnant until after Gavin had been killed. Both Sam and her father knew the truth."

Viper sat stunned, no one had even thought to question Sam's grandmother, thinking she would have hidden it from her. It had been a stupid mistake. If not for Winter, it would have taken them much longer to figure out the truth.

"This won't take away the punishment, but it will lessen the severity. You're welcome to stay as long as you want. Thank you, Winter. It was eating me alive thinking that Gavin's child was out there somewhere."

Viper never had any intention of letting her leave, but this way he was able to relent without showing favoritism. Everyone in the club was held to the same rules, even himself. Winter had to learn that in public he was the President of The Last Riders. That only in their bedroom could she have more leeway.

"I know," Winter said softly.

"Did she say who the father was?" Jewell asked.

"No, but I didn't ask. I was afraid to push for too much information."

"I'm going to call and tell Ton then the sheriff. Maybe now that we have a doctor's name there is hope of finding the kid."

"You're going to keep looking even though the child isn't Gavin's?" Winter asked in surprise.

"It's someone's child and we have a responsibility to make sure that the child is safe and cared for," Viper said.

"How is it your responsibility? The baby isn't Gavin's; you have no connection to the child." Winter had planned on beginning to search for the child herself. However, distant the child was, it was a relative of hers.

"I do as a human being. There is a child out there who has disappeared and no one but a bitch of a mother and a murderous grandfather knows what happened. I think we all have a responsibility to make sure the kid's in a safe environment."

"Me, too." Winter lowered her head in shame. She had misunderstood this group of people from the beginning. She deserved whatever punishment they gave her.

Winter went upstairs while Viper made his calls. She thought he might come upstairs when he was done, but he was conspicuously absent until dinner. Winter went downstairs to the kitchen and wasn't surprised when the conversation quieted as she entered. Fixing a plate of food, she went to sit at the table with Evie and Knox, but they threw her a dirty look before taking their plates and moving to another table.

She sat down at the empty table, forcing the food down her throat so that she could escape, when she felt a chair pulled out beside her and someone sat down next to her. Winter looked up to find Beth staring back at her. A chair scraping had Razer sitting down in tight-lipped anger. Winter couldn't blame him.

"I am so sorry, Beth. I was angry at Viper and took it out on the club, you in particular," Winter apologized.

Beth picked up her fork. "Don't worry about it, Winter. It was only a few months ago that I believed the same thing. I have become very close to The Last Riders and now I can't imagine my life without them. When Razer and I get married, we still plan on going back and forth between my house and the club until Lily graduates. Then, I plan on giving her the house. Razer and I want to build a house for us behind this one. They are his family and they have become mine. If you let them in, they can be the very best thing that could happen to you," Beth advised.

"I already know that, Beth. When I went out today, I didn't even think of going by my house to check on it or consider moving back. Then when I came here and Viper said what he did, I lost my temper. It's no excuse, but I just wanted you to know I didn't mean to be a bitch," Winter said miserably.

"You could never be a bitch," Beth lied.

"You're too nice for your own good." They laughed and even Razer relaxed as they ate their dinner.

Afterwards she went back upstairs to find it still empty. Too early for bed, she turned the television on and watched a movie until she knew Viper wasn't coming back that night.

Holding back hurt tears, she took a shower and climbed into the bed. Trying not to think about where he was sleeping or with whom, she slept restlessly until she felt the bed depress and Viper pull her close. A tiny sob escaped.

"Go to sleep," he murmured.

She nodded her head while sinking into the soft mattress, finally letting a deep sleep take her.

CHAPTER FIFTEEN

The rest of the week passed quickly.

Each night Viper didn't come to bed until well after she had gone to sleep. Her eyes had circles underneath from imagining him with the different women. It was hurting her so much that she couldn't sleep. She would have moved back home if not for the punishment the club would give her that night. Winter was determined to face the music and accept whatever punishment they gave her to make amends for her harsh words.

It was midday before she remembered that she needed to take her doctor's release to the Administration office. Beth waited outside when she went inside; they were going to go to Winter's house afterwards to pick up her own car.

The secretary took the paperwork from her before going into the Superintendent's office next door. Seconds later, Tom Murphy came out. Winter had never liked him—he was the classic example of a pretentious prick—however he was technically her boss, so she had hidden her dislike and appeared respectful in his presence.

"Winter, I am glad to see you're doing better," Tom greeted her with his usual plastic smile.

"Thank you, I would like to get back to work. As you

can see, I have the doctor's release that states I am able to perform my job." Winter nodded at the release form in his hand.

"Please come into my office."

Holding the door open for her, Winter went in, sitting down reluctantly in the chair he offered. As he sat down behind his desk, she noticed he was no longer smiling.

"Winter, I think perhaps it would be better for everyone involved if instead of returning to work you turned in your resignation," he intimidated.

Stunned, Winter didn't know how to respond. She had missed months of work recuperating, but it had never entered her mind that she would not have a job to return to when the time came.

"Why? I am aware I have had to miss—"

"It has nothing to do with your injuries," Mr. Murphy quickly interrupted.

"It doesn't?" At his nod, she said, "Then I don't understand. Exactly why am I being fired?"

"You're not being fired; I wanted to give you the choice so that it wouldn't go on your record. You can find another job in another more lenient school system." Again the plastic smile was pasted on his face.

"Perhaps you need to explain exactly why the school system wants my resignation."

"Very well, I didn't want to embarrass you, but it has come to the attention of several of the school board members that you have not been acting in a professional manner that is required of those who work for our school system."

"How have I been acting unprofessional? I have been in a wheelchair the last few months. It has only been the last few weeks that I was able to start walking again. I have certainly not been the party girl you are trying to insinuate that I am," Winter argued.

"It has become common knowledge around town that you are living with one of The Last Riders. In fact, the president of the club. Is that true?" he asked.

Winter's stomach sank. "Yes, but I lived there while I recuperated. I am moving back into my home tomorrow." Winter's flesh crawled at the look he gave her, barely hiding his contempt.

"You just admitted that you have been able to walk for a few weeks. Certainly there was no reason that you could not have maintained your own residence." Winter remained silent. "Are you involved in a relationship with the one they call Viper?" This time he made no attempt to hide his contempt.

Winter remained silent. She didn't even know the answer to that question herself anymore. Each morning Viper was gone before she woke and didn't come to bed until she was asleep.

"Yes, well, the school board thinks it's best that you resign and find a position elsewhere. We cannot have a high school principal over hundreds of children living with a motorcycle club."

"I have a contract. I won't resign. I have done nothing to be ashamed of."

"That remains to be seen, Winter. You certainly are within your rights to try to save your job, just as we are to terminate you as an employee. I am sorry." She could tell that he wasn't in the least sorry.

Winter didn't say another word as she left his office with her head held high. If Murphy and the school board thought she would slink into the background, well, they didn't know her, not at all.

* * *

Winter didn't say a word to Beth after briefly explaining she had been fired. Beth kept giving her concerned glances while Winter's face remained impassive, not wanting her to know exactly how devastated she was. When Beth parked in her driveway it was with a feeling of relief that she would have some privacy.

"Thanks, Beth. I will be all right from here."

148

"You sure? I can wait around for a while if you need me. I'm just taking Ton to the store for Viper then I am free for the day."

"I'm sure," Winter assured her hastily.

Getting out of the car with the use of her cane took a little time, though Beth waited until she had her front door open before pulling out.

The inside smelled of must and everything needed a good dusting. Winter sat on her couch and let everything that had happened over the last few months go through her mind. How her whole world had changed within the last months. She had gone from a professional to a woman living with a motorcycle club with no responsibilities other than to help with paperwork that no one had asked her to do anyway.

She had worked hard for her degree, had been proud of becoming a principal of the high school, more importantly, so had her mother. Now everything was gone. Even the house she had shared with her no longer seemed like a home.

Winter felt lost. Sighing, she got to her feet. She was never the type to feel sorry for herself and she was determined to take the life back she had lost since she had been attacked.

Jake was in prison for the arson of Carmen's parents' home and Winter's attack. She wondered how Carmen was doing.

She was straightening her kitchen when she heard a knock on the door. Confused, as no one knew she was there, she went to open the door. Surprise filled her when she saw the women from the club waiting to be asked in. Winter opened the door wider for them to come inside.

"Whew, you need to open a window." Dawn was already moving as she talked.

"Why is everyone here?" Winter looked at Evie as she was the one who usually spoke for the women.

"We got the big order out and were sitting around

bored so we decided to come and see if there was anything to do here," Evie answered as she moved around the room.

"Oh." They were probably so excited to get rid of her that they would probably build her a new house to move into.

Evie's eyes narrowed at her hurt expression. Sighing, she continued, "You and Beth have one thing in common. Your emotional baggage. We're trying to be nice to help you, not because we want to get rid of you. Beth called me and told me you got fired. We wanted to cheer you up. There, are we good now?"

Winter nodded, relieved, and then went to Evie, giving her a hug.

"There is something you need to know about me," she said, pulling away. "I don't hug."

Laughing, Winter turned away to see the rest of the women smiling at her.

"I do," Natasha said, moving to put her arm around Winter's shoulders.

"It sucks that asshole fired you," Dawn said as she rolled her sleeves up.

"I should have seen it coming. Treepoint is a small town and they don't want their children influenced by a bad example. My contract does have a clause about moral turpitude."

"What in the fuck is that?" Ember asked.

"Basically, my morals aren't up to the community's standards."

"Why in the hell would you sign a contract with that in it?" Evie asked.

"Some professions require them," Winter said in defense.

All the women were giving her pitying looks.

"Anyway, the teachers' union will give me a lawyer, but it will take several months to look into the case, which means I won't be returning to school this year." Winter was saddened by the thought.

"That means you can stay with us. No sense in moving back just to be by yourself," Natasha said.

"I don't think that's what Winter wants," Evie told Natasha, again the women turned to Winter.

She looked around the house. If she was honest with herself, no, she didn't want to come back to the empty house. The clubhouse had become a home to her. The thought of coming back here to live by herself had her blinking back tears. The only thing holding her back was the distance Viper had put between them the last few days.

"I told you she doesn't want to be here," Natasha whispered to the other women. Each of the women had been in Winter's position when it had come time to make the decision to become a member of The Last Rider's. It wasn't easy and it required a soul searching within oneself to find the decision that would be life altering.

"Well, she doesn't have to decide today. Let's get busy so we can get back to the club before the meeting," Evie said decisively.

The women split up into groups. Winter and Evie did the kitchen, cleaning the refrigerator and freezer out, and then began tackling the cabinets, throwing away the items that had gone out of date. Winter made a box of food items to take to the church on Sunday for a food donation. The other women dusted and mopped the house for her. When Natasha was done vacuuming, the women packed the box of food and extra suitcase of clothes she had prepared to Winter's car.

"You okay?" Evie asked.

"Yes." Actually she was; the women's camaraderie had made her feel better after the way Murphy had treated her. She didn't deserve their help after the way she had put them down for the lifestyle they chose to live, especially since she was finally admitting to herself that she didn't want to leave them.

"Let's get back. I don't want anyone thinking I'm

dodging my punishment." Winter's car started with no problem When she looked at the window that Jake had smashed her face into, she paused for a second, remembering the pain and fear of that night.

Evie came to her side, opening the car door. "Let's go." Evie's words dragged her from the nightmare of that night.

The women followed behind her, both cars pulling into the parking lot of the clubhouse at the same time. The women helped with her suitcase, putting it in her room for her while she waited tensely in the kitchen for the meeting to begin.

Bliss sat a beer in front of her before sitting down next to her.

Winter smiled at her. The woman really was beautiful. She was wearing a tiny purple top left unbuttoned and short, blue jean cutoffs. Whenever Winter sat next to the blond woman she felt plain and boyish. Bliss put out sexual vibes that a blind man would see. She no longer tried to hide her tattoo and it looked very pretty against the purple of her top. Winter would hate her if they hadn't become friends, she was too freaking nice to dislike.

"You look pretty tonight," Winter complimented Bliss.

"Thanks, I love the material of this top." *I can see why*, she thought glumly. All the men coming in were giving lustful glances at her.

Winter swallowed, she didn't know how she would take it when Viper saw her.

"Don't look so worried, I have a punishment coming tonight, too. I was late three shifts this week. We're not supposed to let our play affect our work, but…" Bliss leaned towards Winter, lowering her voice so no one could overhear.

"Trying to earn another punishment?" Razer sat down at the table, interrupting her words. Bliss closed her mouth on the rest of the sentence. Winter stared at the embarrassed woman, not sure what was going on.

Obviously she was not supposed to talk about whomever was making her late for work, but why would that matter to Razer? A sick feeling hit Winter. Unless it was Viper or Razer himself. Winter truly didn't believe that it was Razer.

Razer leaned across the table. "Don't want to know what you're thinking because it's wrong whatever it is. I haven't touched Bliss. I won't have you getting Beth upset, so you need to get that straight in your head." A clear warning was in his eyes.

Winter nodded, getting his message loud and clear.

"Cool it, Razer," Viper said from behind her back. She hadn't even seen him come in the door, too frightened at Razer's reaction.

Razer leaned back in his chair. "We're straight, aren't we, Winter?"

Winter nodded her head, ignoring Viper. If Winter had any real concern that Razer was cheating, even badass as he was, Winter would still tell Beth. The fact was, though, Winter never saw him act any way other than in a friendly manner with the women.

Worried now more than ever that Viper was the reason Bliss had been late to work, Winter started to get angry. He was responsible for not one, but two women getting punishments. If he hadn't been aggravating her, she wouldn't have mouthed off, and now Bliss was getting in trouble for obviously letting him wear her out at night.

Bliss and everyone at the table could tell that Winter was ready to lose her temper, but before she could open her mouth, she was lifted from her chair and packed outside into the cold backyard.

"What are you doing? It's freezing out here," Winter asked angrily.

"I could tell you were about to bust my balls for something. I thought I would save you the hassle of another punishment. From now on, when you want to argue with me, do it in private," Viper informed her.

"I can do that. This private enough for you?"

"Yes." Viper folded his arms across his chest. He could tell she was about to rip into him about something.

"I don't think it's fair Bliss and I have to take a punishment when it's your fault that we both got into trouble."

"How in the fuck is it my fault Bliss got in trouble?" Viper's confusion was obvious and truthfully, she didn't know how she had jumped to that conclusion other than she had been worried sick about Viper messing around on her this last week.

"Well?"

"Give me a minute, I'm thinking," she snapped.

"I am freezing my balls off and you're thinking?" Viper asked, giving her a look that doubted her intelligence.

"I may have been wrong about Bliss," she admitted. "Bliss was telling me she was taking a punishment for being late to work. Razer stopped her from telling me who, so naturally I just assumed—"

"You assumed it was me fucking her all night, making her late for work?" His expression had her crossing her arms in front of her as she stood her ground against the furious biker.

"Why would he care who she told me she was with?"

"Probably because it was none of your fucking business," Viper snapped back.

Winter swallowed her reply.

"Bliss has been late the last two weeks. Whose pussy was my dick in last week?"

"Mine." Then, becoming brave, she brought up the subject she had avoided all week. "This week, though, you didn't come to bed until late and were gone before I woke up."

"Have you missed that we had a huge order going out?"

"No." Winter's arms dropped to her sides.

"You want to know if I've put my dick in someone else?"

Winter's head dropped, biting her lip. "Yes."

Viper's hand went into her hair, tugging her head back until she was staring into his face.

"I haven't fucked another woman since the night you had the hell beat out of you."

"You haven't?" Winter hid her shock.

"No, I haven't. Satisfied?" She believed him.

Winter gave him a smile that lit her face.

"Yes," she answered. Viper smiled at her being sweet.

It didn't last long. "Now, about me being responsible for your punishment. Was it me being a smartass, calling the women whores, and hurting Beth?"

Reluctantly, Winter admitted, "No, but you made me so mad, I lost my temper."

"Then the punishment will make sure that you don't open your mouth when you lose your temper again."

Winter's lips tightened. He was being a hard-ass.

Unfortunately, that mood lasted longer than his sweet one. "We done?"

"Yes." She was more than ready, it was freezing outside.

"Good." Viper took her arm, leading her back inside.

Winter sat back down at the table, watching as Viper went into the large room connected off the kitchen. Cash handed him something. Winter saw it was a red cloth bag.

"Bliss," Viper called.

Bliss got up from the table, going to Viper. He held the bag out to her. Bliss put her hand out and dug inside the bag. When her hand came out, she was holding a folded piece of paper. She returned to her seat.

"Rider." Rider, who was leaning on the kitchen counter, walked to Viper. He also pulled a piece of paper from the bag.

Viper repeated the procedure five more times. Winter was surprised when Shade's name was called, although no one else seemed surprised in the room.

"Winter." Winter got up from the table, walking to

Viper. Hesitantly, she reached inside the cloth bag where there were several pieces of paper left in the bag. Winter picked the first piece she touched and hoped for the best. She walked back to her chair self-consciously because everyone's eyes were on her.

"Natasha." Natasha grinned as she picked her punishment. Winter liked Natasha; she was always upbeat and was ready to do anything anyone needed help with around the club. She came to the table and sat down across from her.

"That's everyone." Viper handed the bag back to Cash before going to the counter to grab himself a beer.

Winter watched as those that picked a punishment opened their slips of paper. Tentatively, Winter opened hers. Relief washed through her.

"I got the worst one," Bliss complained.

"What did you get?" Natasha asked.

"Laundry for two weeks." She pouted.

"That's not bad. I got dishes for three weeks. Want to switch? I don't mind the laundry if it's for two weeks," Natasha bargained.

"I don't want to pack everyone's laundry up and down the stairs for two weeks, I may be willing to switch." Both women stared at Winter. Belatedly getting the message, Winter opened her paper and read out loud. "Seed inventory."

Natasha and Bliss switched papers.

"Mine seems the easiest." She was actually glad that they didn't want to switch. She would get it done in a few hours and put the punishment behind her. Neither woman answered, drinking their beer.

"Dinner's ready," Evie called.

Winter waited until the line died down before getting her plate. Viper sat down next to her with a huge plate of food.

"What did you pull?" he asked curiously.

"Seed inventory; seems simple enough," Winter said,

concentrating on her dinner and missing his conniving grin.

"You going to stay until you finish the inventory?"

Winter didn't tell him that she had brought another suitcase full of clothes and had already decided to stay for a while longer.

"Of course," she said, staring down at her food.

Viper leaned back in his chair after he was done eating. Winter noticed how tired he looked. He always seemed so invincible, yet Winter knew how well their business was doing and knew that he was going to have to be realistic.

"You're going to have to hire some more help, Viper. You can't keep up this pace. Sooner or later, you're going to get orders that you will have to turn down until there are more people to help fill the orders."

"I know. We've been talking about it. Right now we're trying to figure out how many and which positions to hire for. Once we come to a decision, I'll put a notice in the newspaper."

"The jobs are going to be a big help to the community. Even if you offer twenty jobs, that's twenty families that will have a decent income coming in."

"We aren't taking it lightly, Winter. We're trying to figure out whether to offer more jobs at a slightly lower rate or fewer jobs at a higher wage. We're going to give them a benefit package also," Viper said ruminatively.

Winter smiled at him. Many of her student's parents desperately needed jobs. The Last Riders were really going to provide an economic boost for the area.

Shade and Rider came to the table.

"What punishment did you get?" Rider asked. It was obvious what the two had in mind.

"What did you get?" she asked first. Winter was a fast learner.

"Cooking, two weeks," Rider answered. Winter looked at Shade.

"Cleaning the stove, fridge and pantry."

"I got seed inventory." Both men turned and walked away. Winter was beginning to get a bad feeling that the job was not going to be as easy as it sounded.

Viper was trying to keep a straight face. Winter took their plates to the sink where Bliss was already doing the dishes, then followed Viper into the television room where someone had started a movie. Most of the members sat and watched the movie before going to bed. It had been a long week for everyone and it showed on their tired faces.

Bliss was curled between Rider and Train, her purple top gaped open, revealing her breasts, which Train took advantage of by yanking it aside and raising one of her pert breasts to his mouth. Rider's hand unbuttoned her cutoffs, his hand sliding inside the parted material.

Winter tore her gaze away and back to the television. She was about to make an excuse to leave when Viper forestalled her by gripping the back of her neck and raising her head. His mouth fastened onto hers, drawing her body closer to his with a hand gripping her ass. She tore her mouth from his, uncomfortable with spectators in the room. The room was almost empty except for her, Viper, Bliss and the two men, however that didn't make her any more comfortable.

Winter jumped up from the couch when Bliss started pulling Train's cock out. Viper relentlessly pulled her back down onto his lap, though.

"Relax," he murmured. When Bliss had Train's cock out she went down on him with her mouth, bending over him, her knees on the couch. With her ass in the air, Rider jerked her shorts down, leaving her bare.

Viper sucked on her neck as his hand moved from her belly to her breast. Train's hands buried in Bliss's hair as she sucked on his cock while Rider pulled a condom out of his pocket and rolled it over his hard dick.

Winter had seen much more than she wanted to see, yet couldn't tear her eyes away from the erotic tableau.

Rider sank his cock into Bliss's pussy with a loud

groan. Then Bliss wiggled her ass back, taking more of him
as Train thrust steadily into her mouth.

Viper used his leg to spread Winter's thighs. She was
lost watching a sight that she had previously only heard
about, but was now taking place a few feet away. There
was no doubt about the pleasure the three were
experiencing, either.

Viper's finger's slid inside her loose jeans to find her
wet. "You like watching Bliss get fucked, or watching them
give it to her?"

Winter's head fell back against his chest as his fingers
stroked her creamy slit. His fingers stopped when she
didn't answer, though.

"Both," she reluctantly admitted, relieved when his
fingers resumed their stroking.

Rider gripped Bliss's hips before his thrusts increased
in speed. The slapping of their bodies filled the room.
Train groaned as he lifted his hips while his hand pushed
Bliss down on him driving more of his cock down her
throat as he climaxed. When he was done, Bliss lifted her
upper body slamming her hips back into Rider.

"Fuck me hard, Rider!" Bliss was lost in ecstasy as she
came with Rider slamming his hips against hers. Train
leaned forward to play with her clit as Rider fucked her,
sucking a pink nipple into his mouth. The woman's
screaming almost pushed Winter into her own climax, but
Viper stopped, lifted her up and carried her upstairs.

She could hear her whimpers of need, unable to stop
herself, her body needing his desperately. She desired
Viper so badly she wanted to scream at him to hurry. She
didn't know if she would have had the strength to deny
him if he had lain her on the couch and fucked her in the
television room in front of the others.

He slammed the bedroom door closed behind them
before jerking her clothes off and removing his own then
positioned her over the bed. Thinking he wanted her to get
on the bed, she started to crawl forward, but he smacked

her ass with a hard hand.

"Stay still," he snarled at her.

He held her still with a hand on her hip as he pulled on a condom he hastily grabbed from his nightstand.

Winter heard the package tearing then his cock was nudging at her pussy before sliding in with a hard thrust.

"Your pussy is burning me alive." The slick sound of his cock sliding in and out of her had her gripping the blankets on their bed.

"I'm going to fuck you so hard that you're going to beg me to stop," he forewarned her.

Winter was almost ready to come. His cock was stretching her, pushing high inside her pussy, sending lightning through her system. At the same time, Viper leaned over her, grasping her breasts tightly, using them to pull her back harder against his thrusting hips.

"You want gentle, then you need to find another man that can give you that. I want you to push that tight pussy back at me," Viper ordered. Winter's moans were now smothered in the blankets her face was buried in. When he surged forward, pounding his hips against her quivering ass, Winter came, seeing white lights in her mind as the explosion tore through her body.

Viper groaned behind her as his cock jerked inside of her, sending her into another orgasm. She didn't know if she could handle it. When he pulled his cock out of her, Winter sank to the floor on her knees, leaning against the bed.

Picking her up from the floor, Viper gently laid Winter on the mattress, pulling the blanket over her to her shoulders. Bending down, he kissed her cheek, trailing his lips to her mouth to give her a lingering kiss.

"You okay?"

Winter nodded her head in response.

"Back?"

"Fine."

Viper left her to go to the bathroom. When he came

back, he lifted the blankets to slide underneath, moving her closer to him until she lay on his chest.

"Evie told me about your job. What are you plans?" he asked.

"Go to sleep," Winter murmured.

Viper rose until he was leaning back against his headboard, arranging her so that she was staring into his face.

"You're not going to let them get away with taking your job, are you?" he asked angrily.

"Viper, this is a small town; they only started selling alcohol within the last few years. I would have been stupid not to have expected them to try to break my contract," she said wryly.

"Can they do that?"

"I honestly don't know. I read my contract pretty thoroughly before signing, I'm just going to have wait and see what my lawyer advises. The teachers union will provide me with one," she explained.

Viper ran his fingers through her tumbled hair. "I have plenty of job openings, take your pick, but I hope you pick the one with the paperwork because Beth and I are having a hell of a time keeping up." His head fell back against the headboard; he did look exhausted.

"I can do that until the school gives me my job back or I make my mind up about what to do next."

"Good." Viper closed his eyes, his hand lazily stroking her back.

Winter's finger traced over his tattoo, it was a piece of art the way it had been designed. All the men had the same exact tattoo; you couldn't miss it with many of them going around shirtless whenever they wanted.

"It's beautiful."

"My chest?"

Winter smiled at his joking. "Your tattoo, though your chest isn't bad, either." Viper smiled, still keeping his eyes closed as she traced the defined lines. "Each symbol stands for an original member?" Winter asked as she gazed at the tattoo closely.

"Yes."

Winter studied the tattoo; the center was a Navy seal insignia with a snake wrapped around it from the bottom up, leaving the face of the snake glaring back. Objects surrounded the insignia, which were two revolvers with a metal chain wrapped around the barrels of the gun linking them together, brass knuckles, a hand of cards, and a razor knife. The whole tattoo had a layer of shadows giving it a smoky effect. It made a chill go down Winter's back just staring at the intricate designs of the large tat.

Winter touched the razor knife. "Razer, that's an obvious one as well as your own wrapped around the seal insignia."

"I never did have much imagination. You might as well give up. No one has figured out all of the symbols."

"I bet I can," Winter boasted." "I have become an expert at puzzles from a couple of months in a wheelchair with nothing to do with my time except several magazines of puzzle solvers. Let's see how I do."

"Go for it." Viper put his hands behind his head, giving her a full view of the tat.

"The revolvers are Knox and Rider."

"That's good. Everyone has a hard time with that one."

"I don't know why; those two go everywhere together." Her finger touched the chain wrapped around the revolvers. "The chain is Train, that one is a little obvious," Winter said.

Viper looked down at her in surprise. "How do you know?"

"He has a chain wrapped around the handlebars of his motorcycle." Winter had seen him washing his bike the day she had gone to the doctor.

Winter didn't understand the unfathomable look he gave her. "Am I right?" she asked, gloating at her deductive skills.

"Yes," he finally answered, amusement in his voice, so Winter continued on with her game.

"The brass knuckles are Cash."

"How did you know that one?"

Winter gave him another gloating smile. "I live in Treepoint remember? I know a couple of the men he's been in fights with. He doesn't believe in playing fair."

"No, he believes in winning," Viper said with respect in his voice.

"The shadows are obviously Shade."

"Usually people think he is the cards or the chain." Winter could tell this time she had surprised him with her deductive reasoning.

"Then they don't know Shade," she said wryly. "Is the navy insignia a member?" She asked.

"He isn't anymore, the insignia stands for Gavin." Viper's voice had thickened.

Winter tried to slide off Viper, but he held her still. "I am so sorry about your brother," Winter said softly.

"Rider, Knox and Gavin were tight. They wanted to come up to Treepoint with him, but I wouldn't let them. I didn't want to scare everyone off before the deal went through and the house was ready for us to move into."

Tears filled Winter's eyes as she saw he held the guilt of his brother's murder inside.

"It wasn't your fault, Viper. It was no one's fault except my greedy cousin." She lowered her head to his chest as his hand moved to stroke the back of her neck.

"There is one more you haven't told me yet who it is," Viper redirected her attention.

Winter raised her head, staring into his eyes, seeing that he held no ill will towards her because of Vincent's actions. Her attention returned to the tattoo gazing at the last symbol. She was almost sure the cards themselves were a clue but she was stumped.

"Joker?" Viper shook his head. "Ace? Poker?" At that, a laugh rumbled through his chest.

"No."

Winter gave it one more try. "Luck or Lucky?"

Viper's laughter stopped and he looked at her in surprise.

"You are good. Congrats."

"Is he in your Ohio house?"

"No, he's still in the Seals. Lucky came out of the service for a while, during the time we started the club, but he missed the service."

"Were you close?"

"All eight of us are close, but yes, Lucky and I were close. He is a good brother, one of the luckiest bastards I know." His finger touched the hand of cards on his chest. "They call this hand of cards a Deadman's hand. Lucky is one of the most lethal sons of a bitch to ever be in the service and they give him the jobs men usually don't walk away from."

"I thought that went to Shade."

"What do you mean?"

"His symbol covers the whole tattoo. He is the protector of the club, isn't he?"

"He is our enforcer, yes," Viper said carefully.

"I saw him lay out several of you during the picnic. All together it took four men to hold him back." Winter didn't try to hide the admiration in her voice.

"You saw that?"

"I could hardly miss it. I thought he was going to rip poor Charles's head off."

"Charles, who?" Winter tried to hide her smile at Viper trying to dodge the truth without telling an outright lie.

"Lily's high school boyfriend. I've told you that before," she reminded him.

"What makes you think he was after that kid?" Again he tried evasion. This time it was her giving him a look that doubted his intelligence. *Does he not remember I'm the principal of high school males, where they learned the bro code in the first place?* Winter thought.

"Because Shade wants Lily?" Winter mused, smiling wryly,

"What's so funny?" Viper's eyes narrowed at her.

"Well, he is going to need Lucky's good luck to accomplish that feat."

"You don't think it would work out?" The bro code reappeared again when he thought Winter didn't think Shade and Lily would make a good match.

This time it was Winter who tried to dodge the question. Sliding off Viper, she got out of bed to go to the bathroom.

"Winter, he's a friend of mine. I want to know," he demanded when she came out. "Don't you think he is good enough for her?" A trace of anger could be heard in his voice.

Winter stopped, gazing back at him before going to the closet and pulling out a towel, needing time to think of how to answer his question. Wrapping the towel around herself, she walked back to the bed, sitting down beside his sprawled body.

"Lily is a beautiful woman." Winter tried to explain in a way that he would understand her hesitation at the possibility of a relationship between their two friends.

"She is attractive," he admitted slowly.

Winter gave him a smile to let him know that she could never be jealous of Lily's beauty. "She is beautiful inside and out."

"She's beautiful," Viper conceded.

"Has Razer discussed this with Beth?" Winter asked, curious.

"Beth refuses to discuss Lily." Viper at this point realized that Winter knew the whole club was aware of Shade's intentions for Lily.

"She is very protective of Lily. Beth is also a little oblivious where Shade is concerned." Viper lowered his lashes and his face went impassive at her words. Winter's voice turned hard. "I am not."

"Say what you are getting at."

Sighing, she continued, "Lily has a lot of issues, and I don't know Shade well enough to know if he will be able to handle her with the care she needs. If he screws up, he won't get a second chance."

Winter gave him the only warning she would give. Lily was her friend and she wasn't going to throw her to the wolves. The only reason she was giving him a heads up at all was because Shade was the one The Last Rider's depended on for their protection. Lily deserved someone strong enough to protect her. Winter had observed Lily's reactions to certain situations and she had a terrible feeling that Lily needed a protector.

"If Beth finds out he is as bad as I'm thinking he is, Shade won't get a chance. Lily will listen to Beth, even if she's crazy over a man. If Beth doesn't approve, she will walk away. They are that close. No one, not Razer or Shade, will come between those sisters. That being said, I think he's playing it smart by keeping his activities away from Beth, and me also because what I can't see I can't tell, can I? But if I get any inclination he's not the man I think he is, I will have a long chat with Beth and put a stop to it myself."

"Is that a threat?" Viper asked in a challenging tone.

"Yes, I love her, too. Lily is sweet and she has a side to her that really is mischievous and fun, yet she has temper that can get her in trouble. Beth and Lily are two of the best people I know or will ever know. Beth is laid-back and easy going, but Lily is not. Shade needs to decide if she is really what he wants before he makes a move because, if she gets hurt, it will affect Beth and it could hurt her relationship with Razer. I see how much she loves him and I don't want to see their relationship affected."

"That's fair," Viper conceded. "I'll have a talk with him. Are you going to give Beth a heads up?" Winter was aware he was in a difficult position. He had opened up to her in confidence. As head of The Last Riders, he needed someone to talk to about his brothers who he could trust to not betray his confidences.

Winter smiled. "There isn't really anything to tell. He hasn't made his attention to Lily obvious and I haven't seen anything I could tell her about. Now, I am going to go take a hot shower. Are you going to be awake when I get back?"

"Definitely."

"Good, because I need to check out that tat on your abdomen." Winter's finger traced the tribal tattoo on his arm. Admiring the sleeve, she was unaware she was provoking a response from Viper.

Before she could move out of reach, the towel slipped to the floor with his helping hand.

"Why wait…"

CHAPTER SIXTEEN

Saturday morning, Winter woke to an empty bed. Stretching lazily she smiled, remembering the night before. It took several seconds for something to work its way into her consciousness. Her body, while sore, wasn't in actual pain. She had noticed several times that the pain was lessening in intensity and duration, but it was the first time she had woke up not needing to reach for the ibuprofen.

Feeling as if her life was getting back on track, she took a shower, humming to herself as she shampooed her hair before rinsing it out. Carefully getting out of the shower and getting dressed, she made a list of things she needed to do during the coming week before her rumbling stomach reminded her that she was hungry. Glancing at the clock on the nightstand, she was surprised to see that it was lunchtime. Winter was amazed she had slept so long, usually her back would have woken her well before now.

Continuing to hum to herself, she left the bedroom, hoping there was still some food left. Winter was at the top of the staircase when the voices drew her attention down the stairs. A huge number of The Last Riders members that she hadn't met were filling the living room and doorway as they stood casually talking. Several glanced up to see her standing at the top of the steps before turning back to their conversations.

Winter carefully went down the steps, aware she had several curious eyes watching her cautious descent. Reaching the bottom of the steps, she maneuvered herself through the crowd of men. She lowered her eyes, blushing when she caught several intent gazes on her figure. Not wanting to appear like a blushing virgin, she nevertheless hurried through the men, consoling herself that she had her cane if one of the men reached out to touch.

Entering the kitchen, she found it almost as crowded. Giving a sigh of relief, Winter made her way to Beth's side.

Beth, standing beside the counter, gave her a welcoming smile as she approached.

"Good morning. Sleep late?" She gave Winter a knowing look.

Refusing to be embarrassed, Winter changed the topic. "Who are all the strangers?"

"Actually they aren't stranger's, they're members from the Ohio house. They showed up this morning. Razer said that Viper sent for them, but didn't tell me why."

Winter wondered why so many had been brought in from Ohio. She searched the room, not finding Viper. She knew her questions would have to wait.

"Hungry?" Beth asked.

"Starved," Winter admitted.

"Me, too. Let's grab a plate." Both women picked up a plate and went to the mounds of food that the members on kitchen duty had prepared.

Rider looked flushed and hot as he watched everyone load their plates. Winter hid her amusement at the rugged biker, covered in more food than what she was sure had made it to the buffet.

Loading her plate with eggs and fruit, Winter followed Beth to a table with a couple of empty chairs.

Once they managed to fill their stomachs, Winter questioned Beth. "Where is Razer?"

"He's in a meeting with Viper and Shade." A worried look crossed Beth's face.

Evie and Jewell, sitting at the same table, deliberately spooned more food into their mouths when they heard Winter's question. Winter had known deep down something was going on and she didn't think it was good. Evie and Jewell confirmed it with their silence. Winter didn't question them, not wanting to place them in an awkward position. She was just going to have to be patient.

A flash of red caught Winter's eye as a group of three women she had not seen before passed by their table. She had known that there were other male members here from the other house, but she hadn't realized that they had brought women as well. Truthfully, she hadn't thought that the other house would have even more women available to their members. Her hand tightened on her glass of juice.

Beth's eyes dropped to her plate. "That's Joy, Sunshine and K.O."

Winter's eyes tracked the women across the room as the male members talked familiarly with them as they filled their plates. Beth and Winter just stared at each other, their thoughts completely shared.

"Sunshine and K.O. have both been members for a couple of years. Joy has three votes Rider, Knox, and Cash's. Razer won't be giving her his vote," Beth explained, not taking her eyes off the woman.

"I see." With Razer unwilling to give his vote, that left Viper, Shade, Lucky and Train.

Viper didn't *have* to give her his vote; it came down to if he would or not. When they had gone out before her attack, he had obviously fucked around, but now that they were actually intimate, would he still be having sex with the other members? Winter was unsure of Viper and what they had going on between them. She knew what it meant to her—what it had always meant to her—but Viper guarded his emotions, which left her unsure of his feelings.

Winter took deep breaths, not wanting the other women to sense her distress. Obviously she was unsuccessful as Beth reached across the table, taking the glass out of her hand and held it tightly within her own grasp, giving her the strength she was desperately striving for.

"There is another way besides the sex to get their vote," Evie revealed, seeing they were upset.

Winter's eyes raised in surprise. "There is?"

Evie nodded. "That's how Beth became a member. You can earn their marker, but that's hard to do, so don't get your hopes up. Beth accomplished it by helping solve Gavin's murder and the club owed her a debt for the way we treated her. Joy will not go that route. She will fuck to get the votes." She dashed Winter's hopes.

Winter had never really believed that Beth had been with six of the members, but she was glad that her instincts had been proven right. On the other hand, it made her feel worse about the ugly comment that had resulted in her drawing a punishment.

Returning Beth's squeeze on her hand, Winter turned to her friend. "I'm really sorry for my remark. I shouldn't have let Viper goad my temper by trying to say I was a prospect."

"Whether you want to admit it or not, Winter, you are," Evie spoke, looking the other woman in the eyes. "You have to face facts, Beth did. If you want a relationship with Viper, and I can see you do by your reaction to the women from the other house, then your only option is to become a member. Viper will never turn his back on The Last Riders. He and his brother started the club and he enjoys the lifestyle. I know you care about Viper, so if you want a relationship, then girl, you have only one option."

"To become a member?" Winter knew Evie was right, even as her mind and morals fought against her decision.

"Yes." Evie had made it clear that unless she became a

member, a relationship with Viper wouldn't last. Becoming a member of The Last Riders made you a member of the family. If she didn't become a member, she would always be on the outside.

Sighing, she leaned back in her chair, knowing she was going to go for it. Fear filled her stomach. What if she went through with getting the votes and Viper didn't return her feelings? Surely she wasn't stupid enough to let him make a fool of her twice.

"Well, I guess I better start collecting markers."

The women laughed this time.

"Not many left to collect." Evie laughed. "I heard you already managed to get Train, Cash and Rider's vote. That wasn't so bad, was it?"

Winter blushed bright red, refusing to look at Beth who chimed in. "You have Viper's."

"That leaves two more. You're ahead of Joy, and she's been here longer, but I think she's determined to get her votes this weekend," Evie speculated as all the women at the table turned to gaze at the woman flirting with Train.

"She certainly is going after the man who can help her get the votes," Jewell said with envy. Winter sensed the women wanted their own piece of Train.

He came across as laid back and easy going until you actually studied his actions. He was always aware of where everyone in the room was. If something needed to be done, he was the first one there. He and Knox were always surrounded by the women and Winter figured that it was because they were probably the best at giving the women what they needed. But it was his grey eyes that set Train apart; they belied his easygoing nature and held a flash of turbulence whenever his temper was roused.

One day, Winter had been eating lunch when she had seen Rider accidently bump into Beth. He didn't apologize fast enough for Train, who clocked him for not being careful. He kept you guessing if he was going to react with a smile or his fist.

"I'll talk to Razer about giving you his marker," Beth promised, drawing Winter's attention back to her.

"Thanks, Beth."

"Geez, what is this club turning into? You guys are missing out on the best part," Jewell muttered.

"I am not missing out on anything," Beth gloated.

This time it was Beth receiving the envious looks. Winter and Beth laughed, and the topic switched to Beth's upcoming wedding.

"Next weekend I'm going to Lexington with Lily and her roommate to find my dress." She looked at Winter. "Would you be one my bridesmaids?"

Tears came to her eyes. "I would be honored."

Beth turned to Evie. "Will you be one of my bridesmaids? I also asked Sex Piston and Crazy Bitch." Being the peacemaker she was, she was picking two from each set of her friends.

Evie's voice wavered, "No, I don't deserve it."

Beth gave her a frown. "Don't talk like that again, that's all water under the bridge now. It happened months ago. Would you treat me like that again, truthfully?"

Evie was quiet several minutes before admitting, "No, I wouldn't. I would leave The Last Riders before I ever treated you that way again. Those biker bitches taught us all a hard lesson, Beth; one that we haven't forgotten."

"I knew that all along, Evie. Now I am not going to take no for an answer. I wish I could have everyone as a bridesmaid, but Razer drew the line at asking more than five brothers to be groomsmen. Said he was going to have to 'bribe a few of them'," Beth mimicked her fiancé.

"I can see that." Winter bet he used threats instead of money. The members wouldn't be anxious to be dressed in the tuxes that she was sure they were going to be forced to wear.

The outside door opened and Viper, Razer and Shade came in with grim expressions on their faces. The men glanced at their table and then Evie stood up at a signal from Viper.

"We have to go into the other room," she told the women at the table. All the women stood up without demur and headed to the living room. Winter and Beth moved more slowly, but did as they were told. Winter knew Beth was just as concerned as she was, but they were simply going to have to wait until later to find out what the meeting was about.

Viper went to the middle of the room while the members surrounded him.

"I want to thank everyone for being here. I know you put in a hard week at work and spent the night riding up here. First off, I would like to tell everyone that, with Winter's help, we were able to prove that Gavin didn't disrespect the club rules by fucking Sam. The bitch lied, just as we all knew she had. We still haven't been able to locate the baby, but the sheriff is continuing to investigate. We offered our assistance if he needs it. Evie and the women have been given permission to do what is necessary if Sam makes any further attacks on the club, but as of now, we are done with the bitch."

Murmurs of approval filled the air before they quieted down with Viper's next words.

"I wanted to handle this a few weeks ago, but Shade cautioned me to hold my hand. The group that Sam has attached herself to are one percenters, and he didn't want us to strike out before we were ready. We are now prepared and that's why I sent for you. We planned on hitting their club tonight, but they called for a meet this morning. My guess is they have someone watching the house and are aware that we are about to strike.

"I was not happy that they wanted a meet, but did so because Shade urged me to at least talk to them. I was glad I listened. The president of The Blue Horsemen informed me that the four men who attacked Beth and Lily were outlaws, no longer associated with their club. They have been trying to get their colors back, but they have been outrunning their enforcers. We offered our help and they accepted.

"Shade has put in motion a set up for tomorrow that they won't be able to resist. We won't need a show of force, but I am not an idiot. I won't send you back to Ohio until our business with them is complete.

"Enjoy yourselves tonight and we'll take care of business tomorrow morning. If everything goes as planned, you can be back home tomorrow night."

After the meeting broke up, Viper and Razer went in search of their women, finding them seated on the couch with worried frowns.

Winter saw that Viper and Razer now appeared more relaxed and her nerves settled instantly.

"Everything okay?" Winter asked, searching Viper's eyes.

"Everything is fine. We thought we had an issue with another club, turned out we were wrong." Viper shrugged. "The brothers are going to stay the night and head back tomorrow."

Relieved, Winter felt the tension Beth and she were feeling dissipate. Viper sank down onto the couch next to her, pulling her onto his lap at the same time Razer made the same maneuver with Beth. At first, Winter felt uncomfortable, aware of the eyes of the house on her, but gradually she relaxed as she and Beth discussed bridesmaid dresses. Curious, Winter asked Razer if he had chosen his groomsmen.

"Yeah, anyone that wouldn't black my eyes. They aren't too happy being dressed up as a penguin for the day." He cast Beth a reproachful look before he admitted defeat. The woman was determined to get her dream wedding, and Razer was all about giving her what she wanted. "Viper, Shade, Cash, Train and Rider."

"Not Knox?" Winter was surprised. Knox and Razer were constantly talking and cutting up with one another.

"Do you see Knox in a penguin suit?" Winter studied

the man in question. Knox definitely was the largest of the members. It would be hard to find a suit to fit him, but it wasn't his size alone that would have prevented Razer from asking. Knox was the bluntest of the group. If Razer asked Knox, he would in all likelihood tell him to fuck off. He had the shortest fuse, both with his temper and his sex drive. He was constantly with a woman, sometimes two. His muscled frame sometimes packed one on each shoulder as they went upstairs. He was the least handsome one in the group, yet he was the one your eyes were constantly drawn to.

He had a clean-shaven head and several piercings. The one on his tongue constantly caught your focus when he talked and his cock was constantly out with the women. She had even noticed what she would think would be several painful piercings on it. Even now, she watched the woman named K.O. press tightly against him as he leaned against the wall. Jewell walked over to them, and within seconds, the three were heading upstairs.

Winter caught Viper's gaze and blushed. He gave her a wicked grin and continued talking to Razer. She relaxed against him as the discussion turned to colors for the wedding. Beth was debating sage green and coral when she deciphered Winter's look of horror and decided on a peaches and cream theme. They had become so involved in their conversation that they hadn't noticed the men had stopped talking and begun listening. It was only when the topic turned to flowers that Viper tugged on her hair.

"Want to go for a ride?"

Winter had never ridden on a motorcycle. She was nervous, yet she didn't want to refuse to go.

"I haven't ridden on a motorcycle before." She glanced out the window and noticed it was beginning to get dark. "Maybe we should wait until tomorrow. It's getting dark outside."

"Nope, you don't want to miss a moonlight run," Beth urged, gazing up at Razer with a wistful look.

"Want to join them?" Razer asked Beth.

Her eager look said it all. Before Winter knew what was happening, she found herself upstairs in her room, getting changed into warmer clothes and a pair of boots that Viper had told her to grab from a pile in the closet. Going back down the steps carefully, she noticed that several other members had decided to tag along.

Viper was waiting for her at the bottom of the steps. When she walked to his side, he took her cane from her hand and leaned it against the bottom of the steps. Sweeping her up into his arms, he turned and went through the door that Razer was holding open with a grinning Beth by his side.

The club parking lot was filled with motorcycles, making Winter wonder which one was Viper's. Her question was quickly answered as he strode to an oversized monster on two wheels. Placing her on her feet by the bike, he left her to find a spare helmet.

"Be back in a second." As she stood waiting, the other members stopped and stared at Viper's bike. None said a word, but Winter could tell from their expressions that something was unusual about his bike to draw so much attention.

When Viper reappeared from the factory, even Winter could see the flush on his cheeks in the dark.

"What happened to your old bike? You loved that machine; you wouldn't even let me touch it. I know you said it needed some work, so you've borrowed my extra but let me take a look at it, maybe I can do something with it," Rider said, looking at Viper's new bike with an expression that was a mixture of repugnance and disgust.

"There is no fixing it, the engine is gone. I needed a new one anyway. It was breaking down all the time." He shrugged, helping Winter carefully onto the bike.

"It's a weekender's bike," Train said with revulsion.

Viper threw him a hard glare and the bikers scrambled to their own rides.

Winter hesitated. "What's a weekender's bike?"

"Put on your helmet," Viper ordered without answering her question.

Looking at the other bikes, she realized that none of them had a seat on the back like Viper's. It actually looked like a small leather chair. She put on her helmet, trying to keep the tears at bay. He'd obviously had one installed with her in mind, making the motorcycle comfortable for her to sit on. Winter leaned forward, holding Viper around the waist as he started the engine and pulled out in the lead. She glanced sideways to see Cash with Evie at his back. Evie was giving her a thumbs up.

Winter couldn't help enjoying the moonlight run through the mountains. It was a thing of beauty, seeing the light of the town down below and the stars above. With the wind blowing, it almost seemed as if you were flying through the sky. Viper was obviously an experienced rider, taking the twists and turns of the road as if it was second nature. Winter didn't want the ride to end and was unhappy when Viper made a signal to Cash, expecting them to turn back to the clubhouse. They continued on for another mile before their speed changed, slowly turning into a large empty lot surrounded by a group of huge trees.

The bikers all got off their bikes then a few of them pulled blankets from the bags and started to lay them on the ground. Cash went to a huge fire-pit built out of bricks. Removing a tarp covering the middle, he pulled a lighter from his pocket, and within a few minutes, a fire was steadily building strength.

As the fire built, something triggered and her memory finally kicked in. "This is Cash's homestead, isn't it?"

Cash, who was nearby, heard her. "You recognize it?"

"Everyone who drinks in Treepoint would recognize this spot." Winter turned to face Cash, who was standing with his arm around Evie. "When I was a little girl, my dad liked to take a drink every now and then." Everyone listened as Winter talked. Cash had never revealed much of himself to the other members and listening to someone that was associated with him before he became a member of The Last Riders gave them a revealing insight into their friend.

"Do you mind?" Winter questioned before continuing the story.

"No." Cash gave her a twisted smile as she recalled the memories of the place where they were standing.

"This would have been where your grandmother's house was and I'm betting that's her original fireplace."

Cash's nod confirmed her suspicions.

"Anyway, as I was saying, my father liked to drink, but Treepoint was dry during that time. Cash's grandmother was our local liquor store. A car would pull in front of her house and blow their horn, once for beer, two for whiskey, and so on. Cash would always bring it outside in a brown bag. The whole transaction took about a minute. Your grandmother had it down to a fine art," Winter said with true respect.

Cash's grandmother had been a respected woman in town, despite her bootlegging business. When the town finally went wet, she retired to a home closer to town. Winter had not seen her for the last couple of years; she had suffered a stroke, becoming paralyzed.

"How is your grandmother?" she asked.

"Feisty and mean as ever."

"I was sorry to hear about her stroke."

Cash's grin faded and his face became shrouded in the shadows of the trees as he took a step backwards. "Thanks, I'll tell her you were asking about her."

Winter heard Beth's soft laughter as she wrapped her legs around Razer's waist while he carried her into the darkness of the trees. Small groups of the members were sitting on their bikes, talking and drinking beer. Several couples were lying on the blankets that had been spread around the fire and were openly making out. When Cash dragged Evie down on one, Viper's arm went around her waist, lifting her off her feet. Her back to his chest, he walked with her into the dark woods. They didn't go far. Winter could still make out the members in the glow of the flames.

Viper leaned back against the tree, facing the fire so she could see the erotic sight of the members in the firelight. His hand buried itself in her hair and tilted her head back, taking her lips, his tongue slid silkily within the warmth of hers while his other hand pressed against her stomach, pushing her firmly against the hardness of his cock behind his denims.

Winter felt her desire build as Viper's hand unzipped her jacket. When it fell open, he pushed her top down until her bra was exposed. With a twist of his fingers, the closure came undone and her breasts were exposed to the chilly night.

"Viper…"

"Shh… no one can see."

Winter tried to turn her head, but Viper claimed her mouth again as his fingers twisted an already hard nipple. A soft gasp escaped her and Viper used the opportunity to deepen the kiss. Winter's hips began to grind back on his still covered cock.

Viper's hand left her breast to glide over her smooth stomach, unsnapping her jeans and sliding underneath to find her already wet for him. As he found her clit, teasing the small button in torturous swipes with his work roughened thumb, she was barely able to prevent herself from moaning out loud, not wanting to draw attention to them in the shadows.

Her legs tried to close to hold his fingers exactly where she wanted them, but Viper's foot tangled with hers, preventing her from moving. Winter was about to come when Viper removed his hand and returned to her breast, tracing her nipple with his wet fingers.

Winter was so lost in desire that it took several seconds

to realize the hands sliding and pressing against her pussy couldn't have been Viper's, with one hand in her hair and the other on her breast. Her loosened jeans slid further down her hips with the aid of a hand helping their descent.

Stiffening, Winter tried again to tear her mouth away from Viper as the hand explored her silken warmth. Shuddering in need with Viper's hand squeezing the flesh of her breast from the chest up to the tip of her nipple, Winter felt as if her nipples were on fire. When he pinched her nipples, the hand that had been caressing her pussy slid a finger deep inside, caressing her with long strokes. As her hips shifted, he added another finger.

Winter's body was a flame of passion burning out of control, desperately needing something, but the two men had built her so high, she began to whimper in need. The hand left her aching clit and seconds later, Winter felt a wet heat licking gently against her clit. Viper released her mouth to move to her neck, biting and sucking on the soft flesh.

"Please, I need to …" Winter stopped herself, unable to go on. She should have called a halt immediately, as soon as she felt someone else touch her body, but desire had stopped her.

"You want to come?" Viper's soft voice teased her ear. Winter frantically nodded her head. "I can't hear you." Viper sucked harder on her neck at the same time he pinched a nipple tightly.

"Yes." Even Winter could hear the need in her own voice.

As soon as she answered, the tongue on her clit pressed down, letting her feel the cold metal ball right where she needed it most. Winter knew without a doubt who was between her legs now and it only stroked her need higher. He used the metal ball against her clit like a master, knowing just how to slide it against the inside slit of her pussy before pressing it directly on the tiny bud her clit protected.

When she came, Winter felt Viper's hand cover her mouth to prevent everyone from hearing her screams. Only when she stopped shaking did Winter feel Knox remove his mouth from her with a final flourish that almost sent her over again.

Viper's hand smacked her ass hard to bring her back to reality.

"Don't you dare come again, you are saving the rest for me. But that's going to have to wait until we get back to the house; my balls are freezing off out here."

Viper gently turned her around and fixed her bra back in place before clasping it closed. He then re-buttoned her shirt and zipped her jacket back up. It took him less than two minutes when she would have fumbled in the dark trying to put herself back together.

Winter felt Knox move away as Viper redressed her.

Once he was done, he led her back to his bike, motioning for everyone to finish their business. Cash took a bucket of water and made sure the fire was out before he mounted his bike parked next to Viper's.

Winter held on to Viper as they headed back to the club. Her conscious was screaming at her for letting things get so out of control that she had let another man put his mouth on her.

Regret and fear stormed her senses during the ride, the wind only making the turbulence in her mind worse. When they pulled into the lot, she wanted to run to her car to escape back to her home, and reattach herself to the life and morals she could feel slipping out of her grasp.

She took off her helmet before climbing off the bike and stood silently, staring at her car as she tried to calm her racing mind and come to a clearheaded decision.

The other members left talking and laughing. When Beth would have approached with a flushed, ecstatic face, Razer pulled her past them. Seeing Winter's face, he instantly recognized that she was upset.

Viper watched the emotions chase over Winter's face.

It was an easy situation to read. She was regretting what had taken place. Her instinct was to run, that was what Winter always tried; she hated confrontations. Her life was like a rulebook. Whenever something didn't go as expected, she didn't want to confront it. Instead, she would try to go around it. That method didn't work for him anymore.

When she thought he wasn't attracted to her, she made excuse after excuse. All she had to do was ask, but she hadn't. Even now, she wanted to know where they stood, but she would rather run than risk an answer she didn't want to hear. She could face hoards of teens, face down school boards to get funding and stand up to furious parents over their spoiled kids, yet she had no confidence in herself as a woman.

The Last Riders were a part of his life, one that he had no intention of leaving. He wanted to share it with the woman he loved. Winter was that woman. If she would simply let her guard down long enough to see that he was willing to give her anything she wanted, she would stop letting her fears control her.

Viper had fallen hard for Winter during those two years he had been searching for Gavin's killer, however he had managed to keep from making love to her because he knew she wouldn't be able to accept his lifestyle. When she had found out who he really was, he hadn't been surprised she had thrown him out of her life. He had walked away. It was only seeing Beth with Razer when he realized that if Beth could accept The Last Riders, then maybe Winter could, too. The difference was Beth loved Razer enough to put herself out there, to take a chance that yes, she could be hurt, but the rewards would be worth it. Beth had set a high standard, one that he needed Winter to live up to.

"Let's go in the clubhouse," Viper coaxed with a soft voice.

She took a step forward, but it wasn't towards him, it was to her car.

"Do you know what it was like when I found out you had been hurt? I thought I would give you enough time to get over being mad and then try to convince you to give me a chance. This time I thought I would show you what my life was, and let you decide what you wanted. I was a motherfucker and I know that.

"What I didn't know was that, during that two years, I wasn't showing you the real me, you were giving me a part of you and I fell for that woman. I denied it to myself until you were hurt. I went to that hospital and I couldn't even see you. I had no rights toward you at all. You were unconscious, and they wouldn't tell me shit. I stayed at the hospital, and even when you woke, you refused to see me. I wanted to hold you and let you know I would take care of you, but you never gave me a chance.

"I watched the day the ambulance came to take you to the rehabilitation center, unable to even say good-bye to you. I accepted all of that because I deserved it. However, I knew what I was going to do when I found out you were coming home.

"You know the real me now, I haven't hidden one thing from you. Now you need to decide if you are going to stay and see where this goes, or are you going to try to run every time you let your guard down?"

"I don't want anyone else to touch me."

"Then they won't." Viper shrugged. "That's up to you."

Winter swallowed hard. "You don't care if I fuck someone else?"

Viper hesitated, knowing if he answered wrong that he would lose her forever, but he was going to give her the truth.

"If it's another member and I am there with you, then no, I don't. I've seen you staring at Knox and whether you want to admit it to yourself or not, you were curious about him. Was your curiosity satisfied?"

Winter felt tears come to her eyes. He was right. She

had been curious, not enough to ever act on it, just enough to wonder what it was that had all the women seeking him out. Viper wanted her, but not enough to really consider her his. She took another step towards her car.

Viper's hands clenched. He wanted to grab her and take her to his room and lock the door, but the decision was hers.

"Winter, you're missing my fucking point. I don't fucking care if you want to fuck someone else, but that doesn't mean that you have to, either. I'm saying it's your choice. I am still going to be with you whether you participate or not." Viper took a step toward her. "Winter, you could have stopped Knox at any time. Did you enjoy what happened?"

"Yes," she admitted reluctantly.

"Then don't get mad at yourself or me because you did. You were curious, now you're not. You curious about anyone else?"

"No," she said between clenched teeth.

"Cool. Are you ready to go in yet?"

Winter inhaled a deep breath and prayed for patience. She was determined to get a few things settled.

"Are you going to fuck around?" she demanded.

"No." Viper didn't even hesitate in his answer. "I won't be voting in anymore women in that way, either. Even with me and Razer taking our votes out, that still leaves the six they need to become members. If I think they are worth being members, then I am willing to give my marker."

He was giving her more than he had any other woman. If she walked now, it was her choice; he couldn't budge any further. He knew himself, what he needed, and was honest enough with himself to admit it. Winter had to do the same.

When Winter moved away from her car and finally towards him, Viper placed his arm around her, pulling her close.

"Does this mean I'm your old lady?"

Viper laughed. "Yeah, I guess it does. But there are other names I could call you that I like better." He picked her up and Winter's legs wrapped around his waist as he carried her up the flight of stairs to the house where the other members were bedding down for the night. Viper snagged her cane before going up to their room. Several of the bedroom doors were open and Winter buried her head in Viper's shoulder as they walked by.

"Sure you don't want to pick a room to watch?"

Winter didn't raise her head.

"No," she mumbled.

"Didn't think so. Want me to leave ours open?" he teased. Her scandalized answer had him wincing. "I don't know why you're screaming, your mouth was right by my ear."

"I do not want anyone watching us." She gave him a hard stare as he took off his clothes.

Her mouth watered every single time she saw his body. The women in the house were not going to be happy with her at all. His hard body with the tattoo's made her stomach clench every single time. The sleeve and the one on his chest and abdomen only accented the muscles underneath.

"You sure?" He stalked forward and Winter couldn't help taking a step backward. Viper with that predatory look was a little frightening.

He unsnapped her jeans and slid his hand inside, finding her wet. "I think you have a little wicked in you, woman." Pulling his hand out, he maneuvered her until she was sitting on the bed. Pulling off her boots then her jeans and panties in one tug, Winter leaned back on her elbows, thrown off balance by his intensity.

He opened the drawer of the nightstand and took out a condom. After tearing it open and rolling it on, he turned back to her.

Winters eyes widened as he picked her up, placing her

in the middle of the bed before he maneuvered himself between her thighs.

His cock found her slit and he drove it inside her with one hard thrust. Winter grabbed his shoulders as his dick began pounding inside her with a series of hard thrusts, making her gasp.

Jerking her top up and pulling her bra down, his lips latched onto her nipple, sucking and biting the tip until it became sensitive as her hips began thrusting back at him.

"I don't need another woman's pussy when I have your tight, needy one just waiting for me to fuck it."

Winter moaned. "You need to come; I can't last any longer."

"Didn't Knox take the edge off? I almost came just watching him go down on you. The tongue ring do it for you? The women talk about how good he is with it. He has several on his cock, too." Winter's hips slammed hard against him. This time it was Viper who moaned. "Woman, I don't think you have a little wicked in you, I think you have a lot."

"Quit talking."

"Why?"

"Because you're going to make me come."

"And that's a bad thing?"

"It is because I think it's going to kill me," she panted.

Viper laughed, his hips thrusting even harder.

"Which is getting to you more, the thought of Knox's cock or my cock in your pussy?"

"Both."

"I can solve your problem."

"You can?" Winter was a whimpering mess, her hands falling away from his shoulders and grabbing his taut buttocks, pulling his hips tighter against her. Viper adjusted his strokes to shorter, harder ones while his hand went between their slick bodies to play with her clit.

Winter screamed as she came, tearing at his ass unconsciously with her nails. Viper reached, snagging her hands in one of his and placing them over her head as his cock jerked his release into her heated sheathe.

Winter lay exhausted on the bed, unable to move. She felt the bed move as Viper went to the restroom. When he came back, he raised her limp body up to remove her bra before settling her on his chest.

"Can you set the alarm? I want to go to church in the morning," Winter asked, yawning.

"What time?"

"I want to get up about 8:30."

"I'll wake you," he promised.

"Thanks."

"Beth and Evie drive in together."

"Sounds good." Winter was barely awake with Viper massaging her lower back. As screwed up as her professional life was, this time together was worth it. Winter dozed off with that thought in her mind.

Viper felt the moment she drifted off with his hand sliding through her soft hair. His lips grazed her shoulder. After all the worry over her the last few months, this one moment was worth all of it. Leaning his head back against the pillow, he finally let his own body find sleep.

CHAPTER SEVENTEEN

Winter dressed for church while humming to herself. Viper grinned as he watched her, appreciating the blue dress showing her ass to perfection. Unable to resist, he came up behind her, running his hand along the smooth material circling her waist to pull her back against him.

"You're going to wrinkle my dress," Winter protested, smiling.

"Then you shouldn't make me want to take it off." His mouth teased her neck.

"Stop. I have to finish getting ready or Evie and Beth will leave without me," she said while brushing her hair. Winter fluffed her bangs before putting in her earrings.

Viper put his hands in the air stepping back. "Wouldn't want you to miss church. You need to go and get all the help you can, being wicked and all."

"Stop saying that." Winter blushed.

Viper pulled on his boots, sliding his bike keys into his pocket. "Nope, I like a little wicked, pretty girl."

Winter shook her head at his teasing. She turned to pick up her jacket, pulling it on to find him waiting by the door.

"What are you going to do with yourself today?" she

asked curiously.

"Go for a run with a few of the brothers."

"That sounds like fun," Winter said absently, searching through her purse for her lipstick.

When she finally started down the stairs, Evie and Beth were waiting for. Both women smiled as Viper buried his hand in her hair, tilting her head back for his kiss.

"I had to remind the good girl that the bad girl is going to get it when she gets back." Blushing furiously, Winter tore herself out of his arms. Viper's laughter followed them out the door.

* * *

"Beautiful sermon, Pastor Dean." Winter smiled at the Pastor as she exited the church.

"Thank you. It's good to have you back, Winter." He returned her smile, including Evie and Beth.

"Feels good being back, Pastor," Winter confessed. Beth and Evie stood behind her, waiting their turn to greet the pastor. As she moved away, she accidentally bumped into another parishioner leaving.

"Excuse me." Winter immediately recognized Randall Woods, the principal of the alternative school.

"Ms. Simmons." Winter turned red at the insulting tone in his voice that he made no effort to hide.

"Mr. Woods, it's nice to see you again." Winter forced herself to be polite.

"I am surprised you had the nerve to show up in church." His eyes went to Evie and Beth behind her. They, along with the pastor, were listening to her conversation with Randall.

Winter's shoulders stiffened. "What do you mean by that?"

"Everyone in town is well aware of where you have been staying, hardly the place a good Christian woman should be." His close-set eyes and tall muscular frame gave him a bullying stance as he towered over her. Now Winter understood the high rate of dropouts at the alternative school. The young adults already having issues with authority would not react well to his attitude.

"I wasn't aware it was any of your business, but since you have decided to make it yours, then yes, I have been staying with friends during my recuperation."

"You look fine to me." The look he passed over Winter's body sent blood rushing to her head in rage. It was plainly insulting and totally inappropriate standing in the doorway of a church. Evie took a step forward, but a hand on her arm held her back.

"Randall." Pastor Dean's calm voice drew everyone's eyes to him.

Randall Woods arrogantly turned to the Pastor and immediately lost the insulting look on his face because of the look in Pastor Dean's eyes.

"This is a house of worship and no one entering these doors will be treated with anything other than respect. You owe Winter an apology then I suggest you go home and read that bible in your hand and learn the real meaning of being a Christian."

"I apologize if my comments made you uncomfortable, Ms. Simmons." With his convoluted apology, he glanced back at the Pastor and murmured his goodbyes before hastily retreating.

"I am sorry, Winter," Pastor Dean said.

"You have nothing to apologize for. It's not your fault he's a jerk." Winter tried to ease the tension, aware of the curious eyes on her.

"I must not be doing something right if one of my parishioners can act that way right after one of my sermons. Goodwill towards man should last a little longer than it takes to get out of the church door," he said ironically.

"I agree, Pastor, that's why I'm going to shrug it off and go across the street to eat a huge stack of pancakes." Everyone laughed and the tension evaporated.

The women walked across the street and found a table

at the busy diner. Since Beth and Evie avoided rehashing the embarrassing event, Winter slowly relaxed, sitting back in her chair, smiling and laughing as they discussed Beth's wedding plans.

"Next weekend, I have to leave early Friday to meet Lily and her friend before going to Lexington. I have a meeting with the counselor who has been working with Lily since the bikers grabbed her," Beth said.

"How is she doing?" Winter asked, concerned.

"Really well, this counselor is good for her." That was all she would say before changing the subject to what to cook for dinner. It was her turn, and with Rider still serving his punishment, she wanted ideas for something simple to cook.

"Why don't you let me handle it tonight? You look tired after working all week," Winter offered. Beth looked tempted to accept.

"I shouldn't…" Beth said uncertainly.

Winter airily waved her hand in the air. "Let me handle it. I know just what to fix."

"If you're sure?"

"I'm positive," Winter said with a grin.

"Since you're in the mood to grant favors, could I ask for another one?" Beth asked, watching as Winter swiped one of her pancakes.

"Yes." Winter smiled, pouring the syrup over the stolen pancake.

"I always do Ton's shopping on Fridays. If I get everything, could you take them to his house on Friday?"

"I can do that." Winter finished eating the huge breakfast she had ordered. Afterwards, they went back to their car in the church parking lot. Beth and Winter discussed the children in their Sunday school classes as Evie drove home.

The house was quiet as they walked through the door. The men's bikes weren't out front, so Winter assumed they were still out on their run. As Evie and Beth went to their rooms, joking they needed a nap after their huge brunch, Winter went to Viper's room and quickly changed clothes before going back downstairs. She worked out for a solid hour before going upstairs to shower and change.

Then, deciding to get started on an early dinner, thinking the men would come in hungry, Winter went to the kitchen. Looking through the supplies and freezer, she chose to make a large meatloaf because it would feed a huge number of the members.

Going to the boxes that she had brought back from her house, she also decided on another course for those who didn't want the meatloaf. She went to the freezer again, pulling out a couple of packs of hotdogs, then got busy.

An hour later, she was putting the potatoes on to boil when she heard the front door open and loud voices as the members returned. The bottled water that she had picked up almost slipped from her hand when Train and Rider came through the kitchen doorway with the others. Several of the men had obviously been in a fight.

"What happened?" Winter asked Rider who was getting water out of the refrigerator.

"Nothing, we had a little altercation that has now been settled." He propped his hip against the counter as everyone else grabbed a drink.

"Where are the members from Ohio?" Winter questioned.

"On their way back to Ohio," Rider answered.

"What in the hell is that smell?" Train asked.

"I'm cooking dinner. I gave Beth the night off." Winter gave Rider a quick grin, watching the potatoes boil. "You can have the night off, too. Dinner's almost ready."

Even Rider was starting to look a little green. "What did you kill?" Neither man was obviously worried about hurting her feelings.

"Meatloaf."

"That doesn't smell like any meatloaf I have ever eaten." Rider was making gagging sounds.

"Oh, that's not the meatloaf. I made sauerkraut to go with the hotdogs. I wanted everyone to have a choice of entre."

The men stood staring at her silently.

The women, hearing the men come in downstairs, emerged from their rooms to eat dinner and reeled back from the odor.

"Whoa!" Dawn exclaimed.

Bliss turned to look at Evie.

"I thought tonight was Beth's turn. She always makes her spaghetti," she said plaintively.

"I thought she looked tired so I volunteered," Winter broke in, pasting a hurt expression on her face.

Giving everyone a glare, Evie put her arm around Winter's shoulders. "It smells delicious, doesn't it, guys?"

Silence greeted her statement.

"It smells like vomit," Knox said from the doorway.

"No, it doesn't, Winter." Evie again tried to soothe Winter's feelings while flipping off Knox behind her back.

"Let's get it all together, girls. I'm sure the men are starved after being out all day. You guys get cleaned up; dinner should be ready in an hour." Evie looked questionably at Winter.

"I am sure it will be done by then," Winter agreed.

"Start without me," Rider suggested before going out the doorway.

Winter looked around and didn't see Viper. "Where's Viper?" she asked a departing Train.

He hesitated briefly before answering, "Razer, Shade, Cash and Viper had to finish up a few minor details. They will probably be back after dinner." Winter's lips tightened when she could have sworn she heard him call them lucky bastards as he went out the door. The other men cleared out of the kitchen, leaving only the women behind.

"All right, let's get dinner done." Evie motivated the women and within the hour dinner was finished.

She had tactfully put the bubbling sauerkraut into a

bowl with a lid, explaining if anyone wanted it for a topping it was readily accessible. Jewell lit a candle and within minutes the sickening smell was evaporating. The steaming meatloaf was pulled out of the oven and cut into slices by Winter before quickly mashing the potatoes. She was just putting a dollop of butter on top when the members returned freshly showered.

Hesitantly, everyone grabbed a plate and began serving themselves while Winter sat at the table and began eating her dinner.

At first, the sounds of silence didn't penetrate her thoughts as she was beginning to worry about Viper. She also noticed Beth was constantly looking towards the doorway for Razer to appear.

"This is one of the best freaking things I have ever eaten," Jewell said as she took another bite of the meatloaf. The others' murmurs of approval made Winter flush in embarrassment. Even Rider's grouchy expression had changed to one of pleasure.

The remainder of dinner passed without the rest of the men's appearance. Bliss and Rider did clean up, Winter barely managed to stop him before he threw the sauerkraut away.

"I plan on having that for lunch tomorrow. I'll put it in the refrigerator." Winter placed the container in the back of the refrigerator.

"Suit yourself," he said, turning around to finish the dishes.

Winter went upstairs to work on Viper's paperwork. As the evening wore on, her anxiety began to rise. It was just beginning to get dark when the bedroom door opened and Viper walked in.

With bruised knuckles and a bruise on his cheekbone, he had obviously participated in the fight, however he didn't look too busted up. Relief flooded through her system as he began to get undressed.

She turned in her chair to face him with her arms

folded across her chest.

"What is that stern look for?" Viper grinned at her, bare-chested.

"Have you been fighting?" Winter winced at her tone of voice. Well, at least she hadn't lost her principal voice.

"Yes, ma'am. What ya gonna do about it? Put me in detention?" he mocked her.

Ignoring the smartass remark, she plunged ahead, "Who have you been fighting with?"

Unzipping his jeans after taking off his boots, he stared back at her before answering, "Sorry, that's club business." Unashamedly walking towards her, he brushed her soft check with his thumb.

"I need a shower; want to join me?" Winter gave him an angry glare in response before becoming caught in his intent gaze.

"I already had one."

Viper's hand came out to curve around her neck, pulling her up out of the chair and not stopping until she was plastered against his naked body. His lips buried themselves in the cleavage her shirt left exposed as his other hand reached around to grab her ass and pull her hips closer to his, rubbing his cock against her soft stomach.

"You know the best thing about fighting?" he whispered against her breast.

"No, what?"

"The adrenaline rush makes you want to fuck."

Winter trembled, feeling the coiled tension in his body. "It does?"

"Yes, it does. So, it doesn't matter if you had a shower, you're about to get wet again," he warned her.

His words were already coming true. Winter felt her belly clench in desire as he jerked her top down to expose her breasts further. Taking a nipple in his mouth, Winter lost what little inhibitions she had left and responded to Viper with a passion that stunned her.

When she leaned forward, taking one of his nipples in her mouth, biting the nub gently with her teeth, she felt his cock jerk against her belly. Viper stood motionless as her lips left his nipple, exploring his chest, before moving downwards. Winter got on her knees as her lips traced the tattoo on his flat abdomen. Desire was urging her on as she felt his hand move from her neck to her hair, guiding her mouth to where he wanted it to go.

Winter took the tip of his cock into her mouth and heard his hiss of pleasure. She explored the head with her tongue before sucking him into the warmth of her mouth, setting a rhythm that had both of his hands in her hair, grasping her closer to his thrusting hips.

"Take more," Viper groaned. Winter's hands found his balls, exploring them before circling the base of his cock with her hand. Exerting the slightest pressure, she began to move faster to give him the sensations he needed. Viper tensed, ready to withdraw, but her hand tightened, preventing him from doing anything except thrust deeper into her greedy mouth.

"Pretty girl, you're killing me," he groaned.

Withdrawing, Viper lifted her into his arms. Carrying her to the shower, he started the warm water before stepping inside. They washed each other, exploring their bodies, gradually building their desire before Viper sat down in Winter's bath chair and pulled her onto his lap. They were both wrinkled when they managed to get out of the shower.

"Are you hungry? I could go downstairs and fix you a plate," Winter offered.

"We ate before we came home. Rider called us and warned us about your cooking," he teased.

Winter laughed. "That jerk ate two plates."

Viper gently shoved her down on the bed and Winter looked up at him in surprise.

He gave her a mocking smile as he took an ankle in each of his hands, pulling her towards him. "What did I tell you about adrenaline?"

CHAPTER EIGHTEEN

The next morning, Winter glanced at the worksheet before going next door to the factory. She was going to get her punishment over with so that no one could say she was shirking it because of Viper.

When she entered the factory, she was stunned at the size of the operation as the members were all busily at work. Jewell and Bliss seemed to be filling orders while the other women were in an assembly line packaging the orders and the men were all doing various jobs with the machines. Seeing Train standing with a clipboard in his hand, she asked him where she could find the seeds that needed to be organized.

Nodding his head, he walked through the factory with Winter on his heels, curiously studying the items being packaged. She couldn't help questioning one of the items.

"Customers order bottled water?"

Train paused to show her the water. "It's not just any water. It has vitamins and nutrients. Our customers are in disaster areas or they are disaster preppers who can survive on the water when food is in limited supply," he explained.

Winter looked around. It was amazing to her how they had built a company based on items that, when a disaster struck, became more valuable than gold.

Train showed her several of the gadgets that they made while he walked her to a door in the back of the factory. As they entered the room, he flipped on the lights. The room contained three refrigerators and two deep freezers that had inventory lists posted on the front.

"There they are." He nodded toward the refrigerators.

"Where?" Winter asked confused.

Train walked forward, opening one of the refrigerators. Inside were hundreds of plastic baggies with little seeds inside.

Winter's mouth dropped open. "When we fill the orders, they can often fall out of place. They are filed based on numerical order."

"What order? It's a mess." Winter was amazed they could find anything the way the hundreds of small baggies were haphazardly placed inside.

"That's why they need to be straightened out. By the way, they need to stay cool, so don't leave the door open long, the fridges are set at a certain temperature. Take a few out at a time to get them organized." With a goading smile, he left her alone in the room.

Winter opened the door and studied the mess inside. Closing it, she went to the other two refrigerators to find more of the same. She couldn't understand how anyone could find anything inside; they were long since out of numerical order. Rolling her sleeves up, she began work on the first refrigerator. Twenty minutes later, she was leaving the factory with a determined expression. Rider was outside working on his bike when she asked him to get her keys and purse from the house.

Returning with her things, he handed them to her.

"Escaping your punishment?" he joked.

Winter merely gave him an annoyed stare that cut off his laughter. Getting into her car, she was proud of her herself for not hitting him with her purse.

The Dollar Bin was her first stop. Taking a cart as she

entered the store, it didn't take long to find the items she needed. The store was relatively slow for the morning and she was going through the door after paying for her purchases when she passed Carmen with her parents.

"Good morning, Ms. Simmons," Carmen's parents greeted her. Carmen refused to say anything, not meeting her eyes and giving her the cold shoulder treatment.

"Good morning. I didn't know you were back in town," Winter remarked to Carmen's parents.

"Not for long. We came to town to sell the lot our house was on," Mrs. Jones replied sadly. "I'm sorry we didn't come by the hospital to see you. We are so sorry that our daughter's misjudgment caused Jake to take his anger out on you."

"Don't—" Winter started to say when Carmen interrupted her.

"Jake didn't do anything to her. I keep telling you, but no one will listen," Carmen angrily glared at Winter. "I don't know who attacked you, but it wasn't Jake."

Confused, Winter questioned Carmen, "But he's already been sentenced. I read it in the newspaper that he confessed." Winter had been dreading being called as a witness, so she had been relieved to know she wouldn't have to testify.

"He was scared after he burned down our house. He was angry and made a mistake, but he didn't touch you. The prosecutor offered him a plea deal and he knew no one in this town was going to believe him, so he took it. But I believe him," she said angrily. "He wasn't the one who hurt you."

Winter could tell she was still just as infatuated with him as she had been during the summer.

"I don't remember anything from that night, but I will ask the sheriff if there is any possibility there could have been a mistake." Winter saw the hope in the girl's face and sought to caution her. "Carmen, he was on school property earlier that week, and I know he was pretty angry with me for telling your parents that he was mistreating you."

"He didn't do it," Carmen repeated stubbornly.

As Winter and Carmen's parents said goodbye, Winter hoped they would be able to find a new start away from Treepoint.

* * *

The members all stared at her as she walked back into the factory, carrying her bags. Returning to the back room, Winter organized the refrigerators for the rest of the day. She didn't even stop for lunch, wanting to get the job done. She was so occupied in sorting the seeds that she didn't notice the door opening.

Warm arms circled her waist, tugging her back into a warm body.

"Having fun?"

Winter shook her head. "Your system sucked, but it's finished."

Viper released her to open the refrigerator to find several baskets with seeds. Instead of hundreds of baggies. She had organized them into larger bags and by numerical order. Viper whistled in admiration as he closed the door and opened the other one, which was also organized. Looking at her with a raised brow, he opened the last one to find it, too, organized.

Winter gave him a gloating smile.

"I'm impressed." Viper meant the compliment.

"You should be," she continued to gloat.

Viper smiled at her exuberance. "You do know it won't last?"

Winter lost her smile. "Why not?"

Viper shrugged. "You'll see."

"It's a good system."

"I agree, but it still won't last. That's why it's one of the punishments. It's a constant job that needs to be kept in check."

Winter could understand that. "At least it won't be my

job." She wound her arms around his neck. "I don't plan on needing any more punishment. I learned my lesson."

"I hope not." His hand rubbed her ass. "I have several more interesting punishments in mind for you than organizing a refrigerator."

Pulling out of his arms, she went to the door and held it open. "Not today you don't, I'm starving."

They went to the house and ate dinner, relaxing on the couch in his bedroom, watching television and talking. Viper laughed at her complaints about the different varieties of green beans and ignored her suggestions of taking it down to one variety. That way, if she earned that particular punishment again, the less to organize, the better.

Tired, Winter stretched out beside him. Noticing her movements, Viper took her hand and pulled her to her feet. "Bedtime for you."

Winter leaned against him, unable to prevent herself from wincing. Viper leaned down and lifted her into his arms then carried her to the bathroom where he turned the shower on until the room filled with steam. Helping her remove her clothes, they silently took a shower. After drying off, Viper helped her to bed and reached for the ibuprofen on the nightstand. Handing her the bottle, he went to the small refrigerator to retrieve a bottle of water. Taking the pills, she laid back down and then was pulled to his chest.

"Take it easy tomorrow; you did too much today," Viper advised.

Winter nodded her head in his shoulder. "I'll be fine."

"Yes, you will, pretty girl," Viper promised.

* * *

The next day, Winter took Viper's advice. Taking it easy, she caught up on his reports and then decided to read a book until she became hungry. When she went downstairs, she found Rider and Train cooking lunch. It didn't involve much cooking other than placing the frozen pizza in the oven. Deciding to forgo the pizza, she made herself a sandwich. Taking a bottle of water, she started to leave the room.

"If you lay the pizza directly on the wire rack, it will cook the crust better with it being frozen." The men thanked her for her suggestion.

Winter hummed as she went back upstairs to finish her book. Viper brought dinner up to her later that night. Afterwards, they had a quiet night together before going to bed.

Viper was still sleeping when Winter got out of bed early the next morning. Dressing in her workout clothes, she went down to the weight room to do her exercises. She missed having Donna there when she worked out, but they had agreed she no longer needed her every day; instead, she now only came by once a week.

When she finished, she went upstairs and took a seat at the kitchen table. As she slowly drinking a cup of coffee as she heard a few sounds upstairs, aware that the others would be getting up to get ready for work.

As she continued to sit, relaxing, the kitchen door opened and Shade walked in, looking tired and irritable. She watched as he poured himself a cup of coffee. He still didn't speak to her, but she wasn't upset by it. Winter had learned he wasn't much of a talker. After he took a few sips of his coffee, he moved towards the stove. Opening the oven door, he stared at it several minutes before closing it.

Shade went to the kitchen closet. She noticed he was gathering cleaning supplies and then filling a bucket with soapy water. He then went to the refrigerator, opened the door, and within seconds, he was slamming it shut. Turning green, he hastily moved away to lean on the counter.

Winter took another sip of her coffee. "The punishments are a bitch, aren't they? I thought mine was bad, but at least I don't have to clean that oven or the fridge," she remarked conversationally.

Shade looked back and forth between the offending appliances. Winter knew he was trying to figure out which one to start with.

"I would start with the oven. Give your stomach time to settle, it's a little early to clean something that smells so bad." Winter stood up to freshen her coffee and watched as he stood, debating in front of the oven.

"Of course, I could help you with your problem." He turned to face her, his eyes narrowing in on her innocent expression.

"I could clean the oven, fridge and pantry for you." His eyes went to the pantry door, but he made no move to see what condition it was in. Everyone knew it was a close second to the seeds in punishments.

"What do you want?" he asked grimly.

"It's going to take me at least a couple of hours to scrub that oven down. In case you didn't know, that's cheese on the bottom. The fridge is even worse, it smells like Armageddon, and the pantry has an ant infestation," she said, taking another sip of coffee.

"What's your price?" he repeated through clenched teeth.

Winter faced him squarely, looking him straight in the eyes as she told him exactly what she wanted. "I want your vote. Look at it this way, it's going to take several hours of work to clean this mess up. If we had sex, it would take ten minutes. You're getting a better deal. Besides, we both know that you're not going to vote me in with sex anyway."

Shade stared at her before shrugging. "It's all yours."

Winter frowned that he had given in too easily, but she wasn't going to question her luck. She started to go into the pantry to begin as Shade reached into the cabinet.

"I'll have to tell Viper that he must be getting old if you think sex lasts ten minutes."

Her poor choice of words was going to piss off Viper

and the bastard knew it from his smug grin.

He poured himself a cup of coffee as he started to sit at the table. Winter went to the refrigerator and opened the door. He was out the door before she had finished the movement.

Reaching inside, she took out the leftover sauerkraut, placing it in the trash bag before carrying it outside the backdoor to the trashcan. When she came in, she lit a candle and opened a box of baking soda. She was busy cleaning the fridge when the members started coming in for breakfast.

She was almost finished when Viper trailed in. He watched closely as she closed the door to the refrigerator. "Why are you doing Shade's punishment?"

"I decided to give him a helping hand." Viper fixed himself a bowl of cereal.

Winter noticed him glancing at her in speculation a couple of times, but she ignored it and kept cleaning.

That night in bed she was almost asleep when Viper brought up Shade.

"He told me he gave you his vote."

"Yes." She curled closer to his side.

"I didn't know we had an ant infestation."

"We don't," Winter confessed.

"You're a dangerous woman, Winter Simmons."

* * *

Winter knocked on Ton's door, which opened several minutes later to a bleary eyed Ton with a sour expression on his face.

"I brought your groceries." Winter gave him a bright smile.

"Beth never comes until after ten," Ton grouched.

"I'm an early riser."

"I bet Viper loves that," Ton said snidely. Winter blushed at his remark. Viper was not an early riser. He worked hard, but he did like sleeping in the mornings. Unless he had a meeting, he never got out of bed before nine.

"The groceries are in the car," Winter told Ton. Beth had warned her he would take it as an insult if she packed the groceries inside herself.

She hastily moved out of the way of the screen door before Ton stomped to her car, lifting out the box of groceries. She followed him inside uncertainly while Ton put the groceries on his table. She wondered why Viper hadn't just brought them himself.

"Do you need anything else while I'm here?" Winter offered.

"No. Since I'm up, do you want a cup of coffee?"

"I would love one." While the coffee was brewing, Ton moved around the kitchen, putting up his groceries. When the coffee was finished, Ton poured each of them a cup.

They carried their cups to the living room and sat on the couch. Winter loved his cabin, it was rustic and homey.

"Beth told you she was going out of town today?"

"She mentioned it. Told her she didn't need to worry about the groceries," Ton answered her question.

"Why didn't Viper just bring them by?"

Ton looked at her with surprise. "I haven't seen Viper since the day at the diner. He's pissed at me, and when Viper gets mad, it takes him a while to get over it."

"I didn't know," Winter said, regretting her question.

"He's right. I let my anger get the better of me and I put the women in danger because I couldn't control my temper," Ton admitted.

Winter felt sorry for the man. It couldn't be easy for a man who had lived an active life in the military to suddenly find himself with nothing except time on his hands. Losing a son and declining in health could only exacerbate the problem. The man needed something to keep him occupied, but Winter didn't know what to suggest. She would have to give it some thought.

"Perhaps I could talk to him?" she suggested.

"It won't help. He'll gradually come around." Ton

shrugged.

Winter guessed it wasn't the first time the father and son had butted heads and it wouldn't be the last. Not only did they share the same genes, but obviously the same temper.

Winter rose to go. She had made an appointment and didn't want to be late.

"Beth won't be back until Monday. If you need anything, just call." Winter saw a paper and pencil by the phone and wrote her number down.

"I have been taking care of myself for a long time," Ton grouched.

"I am sure you have." Winter smiled. "But I am at a loose end right now, so it would give me something to do."

Ton's face turned red. "Those stuck up townspeople take your job?"

"They're going to try," Winter responded.

Ton nodded. "Don't let them push you around. Stand up for yourself."

"I plan to," Winter said with determination.

Winter left Ton inside. She was about to get in her car when she noticed the garage door was partially ajar. Ton had forgotten to turn out the light after storing some of the supplies that Beth had sent. She walked over to turn off the lights for him.

Opening the door wider to find the light switch, she curiously glanced around the garage. A large blue tarp that was covering a huge mound had slipped to the side, revealing a motorcycle wheel. It had obviously laid there for a while, since dust and spider webs covered it.

Winter quietly walked over to the tarp and lifted a corner to reveal what was left of a motorcycle, or at least, that was what she thought it was. It looked like it had been in a crash; the frame was bent and it was torn to pieces. Winter swallowed, imagining anyone on this bike when the damage occurred surely hadn't been able to walk away alive. It was that bad.

"I thought you were leaving."

"I saw that you had left on the light," she answered.

She didn't take her eyes off the bike. "What happened?" Ton didn't answer so Winter turned to face him. "Whose bike is it, Ton?"

"Viper's."

"He crashed his bike? When?" Winter swallowed tightly.

"He didn't crash it. He did that himself."

"But why?" Winter asked, shocked.

"Don't know. You'll have to ask him. He just brought it here and told me to leave it alone. I offered to help him rebuild it, but he said no. He loved that bike; him and Gavin picked it out together when they got out of the service." Winter saw another bike covered in the corner.

"That one Gavin's?" Winter pointed to the bike.

"Yes."

Winter brought her attention back to the mess in front of her.

"When?" Winter asked again.

"The best I can figure is the day after your attack," Ton sighed.

Winter turned white. Turning on her heel, she didn't say another word.

Getting in her car, she pulled out and drove into town. Impulsively, she drove to her home.

Going inside, the quiet struck her. At the clubhouse, there was always someone moving around, music playing, talking or fucking.

Winter walked from room to room. Going back to the living room, she took out her phone and called to reschedule her appointment, not even paying attention to when it was rescheduled.

Winter buried her face in her hands. The image of Viper's bike wouldn't leave. All the implications flowing through her mind.

Her phone rang next to her, but she didn't answer. Twice more within the hour the phone rang. Finally, coming to a decision, she picked up her phone. It had been Beth who had called, and when she couldn't reach Winter, she had become concerned and called Viper. The last two calls had been from him.

She couldn't talk to him yet. Winter sent a text, saying what she couldn't bring herself to say face-to-face.

"We're over."

CHAPTER NINETEEN

Winter hadn't moved since she had sent the text. The chair faced the window so she could see the sun going down. The party would be getting started and Viper would be there alone, angry at her text. She knew without a doubt in her mind how he would react. The only question in her mind was which woman he would pick first.

She wasn't aware of when she started to cry, hadn't even noticed the wetness on her cheeks. Winter was too focused on the pain coming from her chest, afraid she wouldn't be able to catch her next breath. The hiccupping cry that left her throat was her first realization that she had been sitting there for a length of time quietly sobbing. Her hands smoothed away the tears from her cheeks.

She was about to get up to go to her bedroom when inside the quietness of the house she heard the loud motors coming down the street. It sounded loud in the quietness of the neighborhood, filled mainly with elderly homeowners.

Winter sat still, unsure what to do. She hadn't turned on the lights when it had become dark, preferring to sit in the darkness. Now the whole room was being flooded with lights from the outside. A knock on the door had her rising, reluctantly accepting the inevitable. She was going to have to face Viper.

Opening the door, she took a step back as he walked angrily into the room.

"Why are all the lights off?" He came to a sudden stop. Without waiting for her reply, he found the switch and flipped the lights on. The light showed the devastation on her face the crying had caused. Viper stared at her quietly, taking in her puffy, pain bruised eyes.

"What's going on, Winter? Why did you send me that text?" Viper asked gently.

Winter turned her back, moving towards the living room, further away from his intimidating presence.

Viper followed her, concerned.

"I think it should be self-explanatory. We're over. I am moving back into my home, something I should have done long ago."

"You could have moved back anytime, Winter. Why now? You were fine when you left the clubhouse this morning. What changed between then and now?"

"I went to Ton's this morning."

"I know, you told me this morning that you were going. Did he say something to you?" he asked angrily

"No, but you shouldn't stay mad at him, Viper."

"My father is my business," Viper said in a hard voice.

"There it is," Winter said softly.

"What in the fuck are you talking about?"

"I saw your bike there, Viper. You trashed it the day you found out about my attack, didn't you?"

Viper stiffened, sensing a trap.

"If you didn't feel guilty, then why did you trash your bike? All this time, during the last few months, you have just been soothing your conscious, Viper. You told yourself and me that you didn't feel guilty, but I think inside you did and that's why you were determined to take care of me when I came out of the hospital."

"You came up with this just from seeing my fucking

bike?"

"Not only that, Viper. Let's be honest, why would you quit having sex with the other women? It had to be your guilty conscious." She turned, giving him her back while she tried to get control of herself. Her hands clenched, her nails biting into the flesh of her palms as she turned back to face him.

"Why would you pick me over them? Look at me. I'm not even pretty." Drawing back her bangs, she pointed to the ragged scar on her forehead. "I don't have a gorgeous body. Mine has scars from the surgery on my back." Winter's legs were trembling as she sank down onto the sofa, burying her face in her hands.

"You'll get tired of me one day when a new prospect or hanger-on walks in the clubhouse door and you'll leave me again. That's what you always did, Loker. You left me for other women before and you'll do it again."

"Winter, look at me," Viper said gently.

Winter reluctantly looked up. He was staring back at her with tears in his eyes. "Pretty girl, this time it's not me leaving, it's you."

"I'm still in love with you, Loker," she heart-wrenchingly confessed as tears slid from the corner of her eyes.

"I know, Winter. I've known all along you never stopped loving me. I knew when you stayed at the clubhouse, when you started helping me with my work, and when you decided to become a member of The Last Riders." The only one Winter had managed to fool was herself, she thought in self-contempt.

"It was the only thing I had to hold onto to make the nightmare of almost losing you bearable. I believed that once you found out who I was, you wouldn't be able to accept that, and I wanted you to have the choice. The accident did change my feelings, I agree with you there, but not the way you think, Winter." Viper saw the resignation in her eyes. "My feelings changed because I was no longer going to give you a choice in the matter. I pretended I was, even to myself. Right up to the point you sent me that text. You're mine, regardless of whether you want to be or not. If you even think of looking at another man, I will kill the motherfucker. If you try to leave me again, I will lock you in my room. And if you ever, and I mean ever, tell me you're not pretty again, I will beat your ass until you can't sit for a week. Do you understand me?"

Winter didn't know a man could yell and cry at the same time. For the first time, Winter ran into his open arms.

Viper's arm's closed tightly around her, burying his face in her neck "I was so fucking stupid. I almost lost you. If that punk ever gets out of prison, I'm going to kill him."

"You kind of have a violent streak, do you know that?" Winter informed him. "I saw Carmen the other day and she doesn't think Jake was the one who hurt me. She said he only confessed because of the plea he was offered."

"He took a plea deal because he was guilty as hell. Cash is the one who tracked him into the mountains," he said unsympathetically.

"She seemed pretty convinced, Viper."

"I'll talk to Cash."

She nodded her head against his chest.

"Can we go home now? Your neighbors will probably start calling the sheriff's office and there is no reason to ruin his Friday night."

Winter lifted her head. "Is that all you guys look forward to is Friday?" she teased.

"With you in my bed, it's Friday all week."

Blushing at his compliment, she stepped away from him to get her purse and phone. They went to the door and Viper flipped off the lights, making sure the door was locked before they went to his bike. Winter kept her head lowered, embarrassed that the whole club was on her doorstep.

Winter climbed on the huge bike behind Viper and

two-by-two they pulled out with Viper in the lead and Razer bringing up the rear.

She tightened her arms around his waist and leaned her head on his back as they flew through the night.

* * *

Winter folded the clothes and put the laundry basket on the table in the laundry room for the members to come and get their clothes. She was humming as she put the clothes in the dryer.

"There is someone here to see you."

Winter turned in surprise to see Viper standing in the doorway.

Winter was surprised. No one had visited her since her return. "Who is it?"

"Don't know. She said you had an appointment with her this morning and you missed it." He looked at her quizzically.

"Damn, it must be my lawyer from the teacher's union. I had an appointment with her last week and canceled it. I forgot we had rescheduled it for today." Angry with herself for forgetting such an important appointment, she hurried upstairs, leaving Viper to his workout.

The lawyer was waiting for her in the front room. The woman was immaculate in a dress suit, just the way she used to dress for school. Winter didn't miss that aspect of her job.

The woman extended her hand. "Ms. Simmons?" She was tall, and curvy, making Winter feel small beside her.

"Yes. Ms. Richards? I want to apologize for missing our meeting this morning."

The woman smiled. "I should have called yesterday and confirmed the appointment. Let's both admit we're to blame and move on from there. Is there someplace we can sit and talk?"

Winter bit her lip. She didn't want to take her upstairs to her and Viper's room, which left only one place.

"Would the couch by the window be okay?" Winter

pointed to a couch with a side table. It was at the end of the room so that if any of the members came in, they wouldn't be able to hear their discussion.

"That would be fine."

Winter was nervous. None of the members were working since Friday was their off day. With any luck, their meeting would be quick. Both women sat on the couch and Winter watched as Ms. Richards placed her briefcase between them.

"I requested your work record from the superintendent's office and I was happy to see that during your employment you were an exemplary employee. That is going to help our case. I understand that they wanted you to resign and you refused."

Winter explained about her attack and the following months of her recuperation. She didn't hold back any information, well aware of how dirty some of these cases could become.

"Are you fully recovered?" Ms. Richards kept her face impassive throughout her explanation.

"Not fully. I still have several issues with my leg and back, but nothing that would prevent me from doing my job."

"So, there aren't any physical issues that would hinder you from moving back into your home?" she asked.

"No." Winter refused to look away. "This is my home now. It will not affect how I do my job. I haven't committed a crime. The school board might not approve of my living arrangements, but I do know that I haven't been convicted of any crime."

The lawyer nodded her head as she studied the paperwork. "I think we may be able to get your job back. Worst-case scenario is they let you go with a damaging reference. I am going to try to set a date for a meeting with the school board as soon as possible, but they are going to try and delay it. I really don't see you returning to school this year."

"I expected that," Winter acknowledged.

"I'll call and make another appointment to go over a few other things after I hear back from the school's attorney."

"I promise not to forget it this time," Winter stated.

Ms. Richards was putting the papers back in her briefcase when Knox came down the stairs with Natasha and Jewell at his side, the women laughing at something he said. The women were wearing t-shirts and panties and Knox had on just a pair of jeans. Winter wanted to sink through the floor.

Knox and Natasha sat at the bar as Jewell got them each a beer.

Ms. Richards rose to her feet with her briefcase. "It was nice meeting you, Ms. Simmons."

"Please call me Winter." The lawyer nodded, but didn't extend the same courtesy.

A shrill laugh sounded loud in the room, drawing their attention to see Knox rubbing his cold beer bottle against Natasha's breast. Winter was just thankful that he hadn't bared it first.

"Let me show you to the door." Winter hurried her to the door, trying to block her view of the three at the bar, but with her so much taller than Winter, it was useless. She didn't need to bother; the woman didn't glance in that direction again, no longer able to hide her contempt of the situation.

Winter braced her shoulders following her to the door. It was no one's business how she lived her private life. She didn't worry about what skeletons were in everyone else's closets.

Winter knew it was a lost cause. If she lived in a larger city where she could remain fairly autonomous, the outcome might be different, but Treepoint residents judged with their own set of values.

Knox and the women finally noticed the stranger in the room, and he removed his hand from Natasha's ass, letting the t-shirt cover her flesh. He gave the woman a smile, but it was not returned. Ms. Richards turned her head away, flat out snubbing the man. Winter almost laughed at his expression.

"I will be talking to you soon." Winter closed the door behind the lawyer, both hopeful and resigned as to what would happen.

CHAPTER TWENTY

Winter slid her feet into the sandals she had purchased to match her outfit. She was dressed in a simple blue dress that paired with the flashy sandals which gave her a casual appearance. Brushing her hair, she decided to leave it loose since it had grown over the last two months and she was now able to pull it back.

The noises coming from downstairs were getting more vocal; Beth's bachelorette party had been looked forward to for the last week, building the women's enthusiasm to a fever pitch.

Several of the women had gone to town for a new outfit, herself included. The apparel varied, from simple to the biker bitch. She had chosen simple, knowing Lily would be there and she would be nervous about sticking out among the women.

"Let's go!" Natasha's yell from downstairs had doors from the upstairs banging open as the women rushed to answer her summons. Winter grabbed her purse, making sure her license was inside. She planned to be the designated driver, although she didn't have high hopes of keeping the rowdy women's drinking under control.

The women were all waiting at the bottom of the stairs

while the men slung back beers at the bar, unhappily watching the women all decked out to party without them.

Razer on the other hand, had his arm around Beth's shoulders, who was wearing a pink 'Bride to be' t-shirt and a modest blue jean skirt. She was a knockout in her outfit and the happiness shining from her eyes caught Winter in the throat.

"What are you thinking about?" Viper asked, coming to her side.

"They are perfect together." Winter nodded toward the engaged couple.

Viper smiled at her, pulling her to his side. "You look pretty tonight."

"You're not disappointed?"

Viper frowned at her answer. "Why would I be disappointed in the way you're dressed?"

""I am not dressed like the others." She stared enviously at Evie's high-heeled biker bitch boots. She couldn't even wear high heels because of her back.

"Winter, you look beautiful. I don't care what you're wearing, but if you want to borrow those boots for later, I'm all for it. There won't be much walking involved, though." She laughed at his reply.

She had learned over the last two months that he had a fetish for high heels. She couldn't walk in them for more than a few minutes, the few minutes she tried, before Viper would drag her into his arms and show her his appreciation.

"Let's go or Bliss is going to miss the party." Evie nudged everyone out the door. As Winter took a step forward, Viper swept her up into his arms.

"There is no way you're going down those steps in the dark." Winter circled his neck with her arms and let him carry her to the vehicle. They had decided to take Beth's SUV because it would hold almost everyone. Evie would drive her car with the rest, but if she planned to drink, Mick would drive them home and the men would pick up the car tomorrow.

The women broke into a chorus of raunchy songs on the way to Rosie's. Winter couldn't help laughing at their antics, enjoying camaraderie among the friends. Lily was already at the bar, waiting for them to arrive.

Beth had dropped her off there before going to the clubhouse to get dressed. Winter had been surprised, but Beth had explained that Lily had wanted to decorate the tables. Mick had promised to keep the doors locked until they returned; so she had felt safe leaving her with the burly bartender. Lily had gone to church with Mick for years and was not frightened or intimidated by his huge frame.

The women arrived at the bar and at their knock, Mick unlocked the doors and the group of women entered, ready to party.

Lily had done a good job decorating. There were balloons everywhere and bride to be banners. Winter couldn't help smiling as Lily anxiously waited for her sister's reaction. Beth caught her close for a hug, pulling her into the large group at the table. Lily had pushed several tables together so they could all sit together.

Mick brought a huge tray of drinks and Winter watched as everyone grabbed a glass.

"What did you fix for us this time?" Evie asked. Mick liked to pride himself on the drinks he made. He could serve beer and whiskey all day, but he liked to surprise the women with the girly girl drinks they liked occasionally.

"Pixie-Stix martinis."

"Whoop, Whoop!" The women yelled.

"Damn, Mick, you outdid yourself this time," Evie complimented him after taking a drink. Winter could have sworn the hard ass bartender blushed bright red. He set a drink in front of Lily and Winter with a wink. "Fixed you two girls some Designated-Tinis."

The whole table laughed, including Lily. Mick turned on the sound system and several of the women began to dance together on the dance floor. There was a metal pole in the middle and several took turns dancing around it erotically. Winter's eyes narrowed, remembering the pole in the basement of the clubhouse, which had seemed out of place. The women were just too good for not having much practice.

Bliss smilingly took her turn, wrapping a leg around the pole, giving a performance that had the women members yelling their encouragement, while Winter, Beth and Lily sat with their mouths open.

Viper was fucking never going into the basement again! Winter thought, watching Bliss finish sliding down the pole with one leg from the top to the bottom. Everyone clapped, with Ember moving forward to take her turn. Winter moved her chair so that she didn't have a view of them exhibiting a skill she had been unaware they possessed.

"How's school going?" Winter asked Lily whose eyes were glued to the pole dancing.

"Good," Lily answered.

"How was spring break?" That pulled her attention away from the pole dancing.

They talked about going to the racetrack, moaning about how much money they lost before going on to tell her about Beth's wedding dress. Beth had her second fitting, enabling her to pick it up while in Lexington.

"Did you try on your bridesmaid dress?" Beth questioned Winter.

"Yes." The women had purchased their dresses from a local shop in town. "They're gorgeous, you made a great choice."

Beth smiled happily. "I can't wait to see everyone in their dress."

"You're not getting nervous?" Winter questioned the calm bride to be. Beth certainly couldn't be called a bridezilla.

"Not at all," Beth answered. "I want everything to go according to plan, but if it doesn't, we'll adjust. I'm counting on you to keep everyone on schedule."

"That, I can do," Winter promised.

Evie and Natasha came up behind Beth, tugging her away from the table to the dance floor. It didn't take long for her to relax, dancing from woman to woman. It was easy to see Beth had developed a close relationship with them.

Lily watched the interaction of her sister with her friends with a face filled with happiness. It was obvious Lily wasn't jealous of the other women; she was happy her sister was fitting into her new life.

"Want to join them?" Winter asked.

"Yes." This was the Lily that Winter loved. The mischievous, spunky woman that, when she let her guard down, was stunning to witness. Winter couldn't believe that while they were dancing, Stori and Dawn started taunting Lily to pole dance. At first, Lily ignored them, making comical remarks about their own dancing.

"Bet you can't get that skinny leg to hold you up on the pole," Jewell taunted her, staggering forward after she had twirled around the pole several times in succession.

A look came into Lily's eyes that Winter had seen a couple of times during her high school days. Lily didn't like anyone to bet her she wouldn't do something.

She danced toward the pole, grasping it with one hand, winding one long, shapely leg around the shiny metal before gracefully lifting herself up, performing a series of maneuvers that showed the women how to really pole dance. Every single one of them stopped dancing to watch. Beth cheered her on as she finished in a maneuver that had her sliding down the pole in a circling ball, stopping herself from hitting the floor hard with just an inch to spare.

Silence filled the room as she rose to her feet, her face red from her exertions. Then the clapping began.

Winter had to ask Beth, "Did you know she could do that?"

Beth shook her head, going to her sister.

"Where did you learn that?" Beth asked.

"The gym that I go to has classes. That was the only exercise class that fit into my schedule," Lily told Beth who was begging her to teach her some of her moves. Winter went to the bar for bottled water.

She had gone for her second bottled water later when she noticed the time. Finding Bliss, they went to Beth who was sitting at the table with Lily and Evie.

"I'm going to take Bliss back to the clubhouse. Can I borrow your keys?" Winter asked holding out her hand.

Beth dug inside her purse to find the keys before handing them to Winter.

"I'm ready to go, too. Do you mind giving me a ride?" Lily stood up from the table, giving her sister a smile. Winter was well aware of why Lily was ready to leave. Several of the women were becoming intoxicated. Beth didn't try to talk Lily out of going, having given her the option earlier in the evening.

"I wish you didn't have to leave, Bliss. I'm sure Crazy Bitch and Sex Piston will behave." Beth tried to excuse her friends' anger at Bliss. Winter herself didn't know why the biker women wanted Bliss so bad. Everyone refused to tell her. When she had brought the subject up to Beth, the hurt look in her eyes had her quickly dropping the subject.

"I don't mind. I get to go back to the clubhouse with no other women around but me." Giving a hug to Beth, they turned to leave the bar. Everyone missed the worried look Lily gave her sister before she turned to follow them out the door.

Winter decided to drop Bliss off first, as her incessant talk about the men was making both Winter and Lily uncomfortable. By the time they were at the clubhouse, she wanted to shove a rag in her mouth to shut her up.

After they watched Bliss enter the house, Winter reversed the car, pulling back out onto the road. The silence was deafening.

"The club members are pretty tight, aren't they?" Lily

questioned.

"Yes," Winter said cautiously.

"Bliss has had several relationships with the men, hasn't she?" This time her question was more probing.

"I try not to involve myself in that aspect of the club," Winter evaded a direct answer.

"I think she had one with Razer. Beth won't tell me, but they broke up for a while and the way her biker friends react, I think it was Bliss," Lily said, trying to draw an answer out of her. Winter was surprised Lily was asking her about the break up between Beth and Razer.

"I don't know. Truthfully, Lily, that was before I had moved into the clubhouse."

Lily went silent, staring out the window. They had passed the club and were beginning to go down the mountain road when blue lights flashed in her rearview mirror.

"Damn," Winter said, pulling over to the barely existent shoulder of the road. Coming to a stop, she pushed a button, sliding her window down as the deputy approached.

"Driver's license and registration," the deputy requested.

Winter pulled out her driver's license from her wallet, giving Lily a reassuring smile. She held out the license to the deputy standing on the dark road.

"I have to look for the registration; this is my friend's vehicle." Winter moved to reach inside the glove box.

"Keep your hands where I can see them." The deputy moved his flashlight until it shown onto her license in his hand. Winter stared up into the deputy's face, his unpleasant voice ringing a bell in her memory.

"I've met you before when I lived in town. You were the deputy who came to my house with the sheriff." Winter didn't miss the ugly expression that passed over the deputy's face.

"I remember you, too. You're the slut who likes to get

her kicks playing hard-to-get," he said snidely.

Winter couldn't believe the deputy was talking to her in such a hateful manner. Lily's indrawn breath showed her own surprise.

"Get out of the car, both of you." The deputy took a step back from Winter's door, motioning for them to get out of the SUV with the flashlight in his hand. Winter tried not to become frightened. He was an officer of the law, but the threatening vibes emanating from him were sending chills across her neck in warning.

Lily climbed out, walking around the front of the SUV. Coming to stand next to Winter. She took Lily's hand in hers, trying, without words, to reassure the young girl. The fear was obvious in her eyes as the deputy moved closer to Winter.

"You been drinking tonight?" he questioned obnoxiously.

"I haven't been drinking," Winter answered him truthfully. He stared arrogantly down at her before his eyes slid towards Lily. His change in appearance was sickening; he made no attempt to keep his lustful expression from showing.

"You had any drinks tonight?"

Lily simply shook her head no.

"If that's all, we'd like to go, Deputy." Winter desperately tried to end the encounter.

"You'll go when I tell you to go." The deputy turned back to face her. As he did, the hand holding her license brushed up against her, knocking it out of his hand. When it landed at her feet, she automatically bent down into a squat to pick it up. As she did, her eyes glanced at his boots. They were very distinctive with a buckle and star on the side. Winter had seen them before.

Trembling now in terror, she stood up, trying to keep her terror from showing, however she was unsuccessful.

His eyes bore into hers and she knew he had figured out that Winter was aware of he was. Before she could react, he backhanded her, throwing her into the side of Beth's vehicle. Lily screamed, moving toward Winter until the deputy grabbed a handful of Lily's hair, stopping her.

"Now, there isn't any need for you to be scared. I'll take care of you right after I finish with this cunt." Winter's hand grabbed the door to right herself, slowly moving away from the deputy.

"You remembered me, didn't you? I was hoping you would." He shrugged. "A man likes to know he's made an impression," he said, dragging Lily by her hair as he stepped in front of Winter, preventing her retreat.

"Why?" Winter asked. If he was going to kill her, she would at least like to know why he'd tried to kill her at the high school.

"You almost got me fired. If my dad hadn't used his connections, I would have been. Of course, the old bastard warned me he would disown me if I got in trouble again," he said, slamming the butt of his flashlight into Winter's stomach as the air rushed out of her. She fell to her knees, gasping for breath as he slung Lily hard into the SUV door.

"Get in there and turn off the lights and motor," he yelled. "Now!"

Winter watched as Lily's fingers tried to open the door, but they were shaking so badly that they couldn't grasp the handle. When Winter managed to get to her feet, Deputy Moore, seeing her move, released Lily's hair long enough to grab Winter's arm. Winter tried to break free, struggling against his hold.

"Lily, run!" Winter screamed. Lily hesitated. Winter could tell she didn't want to leave her behind.

"Go get help. Run!"

"I'll kill her if you move." Deputy Moore tried to drag Winter closer to Lily so that he could grab her, but Winter struggled desperately against his hold, trying to give Lily time to get away. Frustrated, the deputy quit trying to reach Lily, pulling out his gun instead.

Lily started running on the road, however the sound of a gunshot had her veering off into the wooded hillside. As Deputy Moore fired another shot at her, he tried to adjust to a better position to shoot at Lily, but Winter kept striking him, using her nails to dig into the flesh of his arm.

"You stupid bitch, I'm going to put a bullet through your head if you don't stop!" he screamed at her.

Lights suddenly hit them from an oncoming car, highlighting their struggling figures in the darkness of the night. The car slowed before pulling to the side of the road. The doors opened and women began climbing out of the car.

"If you say one word to them, I will kill you and then kill them," Deputy Moore warned her. Winter stopped struggling. The pain in her back was excruciating and her legs were trying to give way, making her hang limp in his brutal grip.

"What the fuck is going on here?"

Winter looked at the women, recognizing them from the night at the Pink Slipper. Winter realized the woman demanding an explanation from the deputy was Crazy Bitch and that Sex Piston was the one crossing the road, coming towards Winter and the deputy.

"Get back in your car. This is none of your business. I pulled her over for driving under the influence and she is resisting arrest." His harsh voice didn't stop the women moving forward.

"Why do you have Beth's ride?" Sex Piston asked Winter.

Winter knew she had a choice. She could tell Deputy Moore wasn't going to let any of them go. They would be able to identify him when she turned up missing. He only had one option, but Winter didn't.

"Get help, help from Beth. Tell her to get Razer. Run!" Winter screamed at the biker women as she resumed her struggles to get away from the deranged deputy.

"Stop it!" He lifted his gun towards Winter, but before

he could fire it he found himself under attack from Sex Piston and Crazy Bitch.

Trying to protect himself from the two women, he was forced to release Winter, who lost her balance and was knocked to the ground from the struggling trio. Winter watched as Crazy Bitch tore the gun from his grasp while Sex Piston was trying to rip out his hair. Out of the corner of her eyes, she saw all except one of the remaining biker women running towards them, the one left behind reached back inside the bright green car and brought out a baseball bat. Running towards them, Killyama came up behind the struggling deputy.

"Get out of the fucking way." The bitches moved aside, leaving him to Killyama.

Winter had no sympathy for the man as she watched her bring the bat across his back, knocking him into the SUV. Giving him another hard whack between his shoulder blades had him falling to the ground beside Winter.

One of the women knelt down beside Winter. "Are you okay?"

"Yes. Get my phone out of the car and call Viper." T.A. got to her feet, going to the SUV and placing the call.

Killyama was finally satisfied that the deputy wasn't going to move now that she was standing over him with a bat and Crazy Bitch had pointed the gun at his head.

"What in the fuck was going down?" Sex Piston asked.

"He was trying to kill me. He attacked me once before, but he wasn't identified. He knew I recognized him and he was going to kill Lily and me." Winter's almost incoherent explanation had Lily's predicament flooding into her mind.

"Oh God, Lily," Winter moaned. "She took off running into the woods!" Winter screamed, trying to get T.A to help her to her feet. "We need to find her!" Winter screamed again. "She may be hurt, he shot at her twice."

""Calm the fuck down," Killyama said. "We're not going to run around these woods in the dark. Wait for the men." Deputy Moore started moving. "What did he do to you?" she asked with a mean glint in her eye.

Winter stared at the woman holding the bat. "He almost beat me to death, left me outside all night on the ground. He didn't finish the job, so he was going to kill Lily and me." Winter was shaking so badly, she had to hold on to T.A. to prevent herself from falling.

"You a friend of Beth's?" Crazy Bitch asked.

Winter nodded. "I'm one of her bridesmaids."

"We are, too," she said absently, staring down at the deputy who had managed to get to his knees. Shoving the gun into the waistband of her jeans, she held out her hand.

"I'm going to see that you all are arrested, assaulting a police officer..." Deputy Moore tried to put the fear of the law into the biker woman.

Killyama handed the bat to Crazy Bitch. "I'm going to show you assault, mother fucker..." Crazy Bitch brought down the bat, this time over his shoulder.

"I... am... going... to.... beat... the... shit..." each word was timed with a hit by the bat.

The sound of the bat striking flesh were then drowned out by motorcycles. The loud sounds could be heard even before they saw the lights turned the corner. Crazy Bitch stopped hitting the unconscious man to watch The Last Riders park their bikes close to Beth's vehicle.

Viper got off his bike, running directly to Winter.

"What happened?" Trying not to let her hysteria get the better of her, she attempted to remain calm enough to explain what had happened, however she lost it completely when she told him about Lily.

Viper took command. "Sex Piston, take Winter and Beth's vehicle back to Rosie's. Don't open your mouths about what happened. You never stopped. You came directly to Rosie's after you left your home. Understand me?"

"You going to finish this motherfucker or do you need me to stay and help?" Killyama asked sincerely.

230

"I think we can handle this piece of shit from here. Go on to the bar, get drunk and have some fun. Forget this happened." Viper's eyes bore into the biker bitches' faces. Getting the message, they climbed back in their car; the tires screeched as Crazy Bitch floored the gas pedal.

"Razer, call Beth, tell her what happened and not to tell anyone. You tell her we'll find Lily. Winter, get in the SUV and go with Sex Piston. You need to keep Beth calm." Sex Piston was behind the wheel before Viper finished talking. Winter shakily walked to the passenger door, getting inside with Viper's help.

"Find her, Viper," Winter begged.

"Bet on it, pretty girl," he said grimly. "You sure he's the one who almost killed you?"

Winter didn't hesitate. "Yes, I'm sure," she said, closing the door without a glance at the man surrounded by The Last Riders.

Sex Piston did a U-turn before driving off in the direction of the bar.

CHAPTER TWENTY-ONE

"Cash, Shade, Rider, find Lily." The men moved, each going to their bikes, pulling out what they needed before disappearing into the dark woods.

"Razer, Knox, Train, you're with me."

Viper walked over to the deputy who had wet himself when Killyama had started beating him. He squatted down next him.

"Call the sheriff; tell him those women attacked me," Deputy Moore cried, lying on the ground as he stared up into a face staring stonily back at him.

"That was my woman you almost beat to death. She laid in a back brace for weeks, having to have pads under her to take a piss. You left her on the fucking ground in fucking agony for hours. She had weeks of rehab just to move from the bed to her wheelchair."

The deputy was now sobbing for mercy, yet Viper showed him none.

"You've just lived your last day."

* * *

Cash, Shade and Rider moved silently across the hillside, looking for a sign of which direction Lily had gone to give them a clue where she had run. Expertly, Cash shone his flashlight back and forth across the ground. They were lucky because it took them less than fifteen minutes to find her first track.

Moving apart a few feet, they began a search grid, steadily working their way closer to her. Cash was familiar with the mountain, searching for areas it would be easier for her to run. It was Shade who found a ripped portion of her dress with blood on it. As he gripped it tightly in his hand, they moved forward, changing direction just slightly.

"We're fucked," Cash said, recognizing a marker.

"What?" Shade snarled.

"We're on Porter land."

"So?"

Cash shook his head, squatting down by a tree. "She rested here, someone found her and she left with them in that direction." He pointed at an area to their left.

"How the hell do you know all that?" Shade asked, staring at the ground.

"Because whomever took her was riding a mud puppy. The good news is, it left us a trail a blind man can follow." Now that they had easier signs to follow, it didn't take them long to come to the large house built into a clearing.

"Son of a bitch." They hunkered down as close to the house as they could get without being seen from the occupants within.

"Let's go," Rider said when they saw the four-wheeler they had been tracking parked in front of the house.

"Get down," Cash hissed.

"Why? Let's just knock on the fucking door," Rider tried to reason.

"You knock on their door, the coroner will be scraping what brains you have left off that front porch. Listen to me; the Porter's are the biggest weed growers in the county." Cash tried to explain the danger they were in. You just didn't walk onto a weed dealer's property in this area of the county.

Cash didn't take his eyes off the house. Coming to a

decision, he turned to Rider and realized Shade was gone.

"He's going for her, dammit." With no other option left, he ordered Rider to stay where he was. Coming out of the cover of the trees, he walked to the front door. He didn't make it close before the door was opened. Cash knew the son of a bitch who came out of the door holding a shotgun pointed at him.

"Get off my land."

"Greer, it's Cash Adams."

"I can see who you are, fuckwad. Get your ass off my property." Greer didn't raise his voice; the shotgun got his message across.

"My friend's fiancée's sister found herself in trouble tonight and took off into the woods. We're trying to find her."

"Haven't seen anyone tonight, other than you and that chicken shit you have hiding over by that tree," Greer said, cocking his shotgun.

"Rider, come out." When he didn't, Cash knew where Dustin was.

"Dustin, you better not hurt him or you're going to have deal with The Last Riders. You won't have anything except scorched earth left to grow that weed you're so proud of."

"Shut the fuck up, Cash," another voice from behind his back spoke, pressing a gun muzzle against the back of his head.

"I was wondering where you were, Tate. Will you tell your crazy assed brothers to back off? We just want Lily and we'll go." Cash tried to reason with the oldest brother.

"There isn't any woman here!" yelled Greer.

"He always was a dumb fuck," Cash sighed. "You better make them see reason, Tate. You don't want trouble with The Last Riders."

"You think you're going to scare me with a motorcycle gang?" Tate asked quietly.

"The woman is ours. She got lost and we're trying to

find her to give her back to her sister, Tate."

The gun muzzle pressed harder against his head. "Why should we give her back? Maybe this time we should steal one of your women, Cash. See how you like it."

"Stop it, Tate. Put down that shotgun, Greer. Dustin bring out his friend." In the doorway, Cash could see a woman come outside. The shining spotlight only allowed him to see her silhouette as she leaned against the front porch post.

"Put down your guns and leave them alone." All three men slowly lowered their weapons, reluctantly following the woman's firm orders.

"Rachel, get back in the house," Greer told her.

"No need. While you three dumbasses were out here arguing, their buddy was climbing in the bedroom window."

Tate shoved Cash's shoulder as he walked past him to the porch. Dustin came out with Rider in a stranglehold, throwing him forward before he went to stand on the porch.

"Rider!" Cash stopped Rider before he could attack Dustin. Rider stopped, but Cash knew he wasn't happy being called off.

Cash and Rider both walked to the front porch. As he moved closer, he saw Rachel. He hadn't seen her since she was a kid. Her long hair was plaited down her back, coming to an end at the curve of her ass. She stared back at him with direct grey eyes and a winsome smile.

"Well, if it isn't the famous Cash Adams," she said mockingly.

Cash took in the oversized flannel shirt and loose jeans.

"How are you, Rachel?"

"I was doing pretty good until I heard gunshots when I was checking my plants, went to see where the shot come from and found Lily sitting on the ground spaced out," she said with a worried frown.

"We will take her back to her sister," Cash said,

studying the changes in her body since the last time he had seen her in town, surrounded by her brothers.

"I want to talk to Beth before anyone takes her anywhere," Rachel told him firmly. Cash didn't argue, pulling his cell phone out to call Razer. Rachel was trying to protect Lily. He admired the way she was able to control her crazy ass brothers while letting Cash know he wasn't taking Lily anywhere without Beth's okay.

"Razer, there's someone that Beth needs to talk to…"

* * *

Shade leaned against the wall, evaluating the situation before making a move towards Lily. Rachel had left, leaving them alone after a quick word. He was lucky that he had met her before, when he had made a couple of purchases for the brothers.

Lily was sitting in the corner of the bedroom on the floor with her face in her knees, arms wrapped around herself, rocking back and forth. The red rubber band the counselor had given her was on her delicate wrist. Penni had told him the counselor had told Lily to snap it against herself when she became too frightened to deal with a situation. Penni had also told him that, at first, she would see Lily snapping it constantly, but it had begun tapering off to only a few times a day.

"Lily?" Shade tried to soften his harsh voice. He had seen her this way a couple of times. Beth had told Razer that only time would draw her out of her self-induced trance. It was her safety mechanism.

Shade slowly walked toward Lily before hunching down in front of her rocking form.

"Lily." This time his voice was more forceful, commanding her attention. The rocking stopped. Coming to a decision, Shade reached out, lifting her into his arms. It wasn't the smartest decision as he found himself with a wildcat in his arms.

The unexpected fury of the woman had him forcing her against the wall to gain control of the nails going for his eyes. Pinning her there with his body, he didn't try to grab her hands, merely blocking her moves.

"Lily, stop it now!" he said in a firm voice. "Aren't you worried about Winter? She's worried about you. She was crying she was so worried, Lily. Beth is probably scared out of her fucking mind." Shade kept her pinned against the wall as he kept repeating Beth's and Winter's names. Finally, he saw a light of reality break through her blank expression.

"Shade?" her voice whimpered.

"Yes, baby."

Lily sucked in deep breaths as if her chest was going to explode. Her hand wiped at the tears on her face. "Is Winter safe?"

"Yes, Beth's friends stopped and helped. Winter is waiting with Beth. They are both waiting to hear from us. You okay?" Shade asked, worried about the blood he had found on her clothes. His eyes searched her body, finding a scratch with drying blood on the underside of her forearm.

Lily nodded her head, still trying to catch her breath. "Lily, breathe slowly," Shade ordered her in a hard voice.

Lily jumped, but her breaths gradually slowed. He took a step back, giving her some room.

"Can we go now?" Lily asked, her soft voice gaining strength. She sidled passed Shade, making sure her body didn't come into contact with his.

"Yes." Shade backed away more, giving her enough room to slide by him.

He opened the bedroom door, letting Lily go ahead of him, following her outside.

Lily walked out the door, coming to a sudden stop when she found the yard filled with The Last Riders.

Winter watched from the back of Viper's bike as Beth jumped off Razer's bike, running to her sister, nearly knocking her down. Shade's hand on Lily's back held her steady and Winter smiled. After the sisters talked for a few minutes, they moved toward Razer's bike.

Shade got on his own bike, which had been brought up the old mountain road by Knox, and started the motor. Knox was now riding with Rider. Viper fired his engine, too, waiting.

Shade rode his bike up next to Lily. "Lily."

"Winter could tell by her face she didn't want to ride on that bike, she wanted the safety of her sister's arms. She wasn't ready to lose her comforting strength after the nightmare of the night. Winter heard Beth ask Razer to call Mick to bring her car.

"Get on, Lily. I'm taking you home." Shade's firm voice had Lily moving reluctantly towards him. She climbed on behind him, holding his sides with her legs, trembling hands taking his helmet. As soon as it was on, Shade throttled his engine.

"Let's go home, pretty girl." Viper pulled out in the lead with the other's following down the winding road. Winter wasn't afraid of riding in the dark anymore. With The Last Riders, she didn't have anything left to fear.

CHAPTER TWENTY-TWO

Winter nervously smoothed down her skirt. Viper grasped her hand, giving it a squeeze.

"Don't look so nervous," Viper said smoothly.

He wasn't helping; Viper was part of the problem. He was dressed in one of his suits, looking like the cold-hearted bastard he had been before her assault.

"That's easy for you to say, they're too scared of you to say anything nasty to you."

"If they know what's good for them, they won't say anything nasty about you, either," Viper said in a threatening voice.

Ms. Richards came out of the closed doors of the School Board's meeting.

"They are going to call us back in a few minutes. They're going to open the meeting to the public. I wish you would have taken my advice and waited for your hearing."

Her lawyer didn't sound very happy with her decision. Winter could understand her apprehension as she looked around the hallway at the public ready to fill the meeting room.

That morning, as she was leaving, she had found everyone waiting for her in the kitchen, including Viper who had disappeared while she was in the shower.

All the women, dressed in their regular clothes, brought Winter to a standstill. They had informed her that they were going with her to the meeting. Of course, afterward they planned on dragging her to the local tattoo shop for her long overdue tat.

Viper had told her, the day after the deputy's attack, that all eight original members had given her their vote for trying to save Lily's life. Winter had managed to avoid the tattoo until now. The women were determined that it was time that she made it official. She was a Last Rider. Winter gave in with a smile, knowing they were right.

Ms. Richards, on the other hand, was not as moved as she was by their show of support, asking snidely if she wanted her job. Winter had remained quiet, sucking up the haughty woman's comment. When Viper would have let the woman have it, Winter merely shook her head pleadingly, simply wanting to get the ordeal over.

The doors to the school board meeting opened, giving the public entrance to the rest of the meeting. As they were about to go through the door, the outside door opened and the biker bitches came through. Winter's face paled at their appearance. They were wearing their tight blue jeans and leather jackets with biker boot heels. Winter seriously wanted to melt into a puddle. Beth, seeing them come through the doorway, hurried forward hoping to prevent them from coming into the meeting.

"Sex Piston, did you need something?" Beth asked quickly, hoping to get them out of the building before they were seen.

"Nope, when you texted me this morning saying you couldn't keep your hair appointment and why, we decided to come, too. If it was important enough for The Last Riders women to be here, then we needed to be here. The bitch needs all the support she can get." Sex Piston nodded her head at Winter.

"It's all right; the room is already almost full. I don't want you to go through the bother. Why don't we meet in the diner in an hour?" Winter came forward, also trying to divert them.

"Girl, there's nothing more important than standing up for another bitch," Crazy Bitch butted in, her breasts barely squeezed into her tight t-shirt.

T.A., Killyama and another one that they introduced as Fat Louise ignored her, moving on towards the meeting room. Ms. Richards, striding out of the meeting room, came to a full stop when she saw who Winter was talking to.

"What are you doing here?" she asked sternly.

Winter didn't understand her question until she realized she was talking to Sex Piston.

"Giving our bitch moral support. Why you here, Diamond?" Sex Piston answered.

"I have told you not to call me that," she hissed.

"It's your fucking name, bitch," Sex Piston hissed back.

Her haughty lawyer lost her cool. "Don't talk like trash."

"I'm gonna tell mom you called me trash," Sex Piston told her.

"You do, and if she calls me, I'll smack you silly," Ms. Richards warned.

Winter's mouth dropped open when it dawned on her that they were sisters and Sex Piston was obviously the younger of the two. The resemblance was there. Both had the same shade of red hair and hazel eyes. Sex Piston was thinner than her sister, who wasn't really heavier, just curvier.

Ms. Richards inhaled sharply before she gathered her professional persona around her like a cloak.

"If you lose this case, it won't be my fault. You cannot flaunt your lifestyle and expect to keep a job in this community," she told Winter. "I can't perform miracles. If you really want to support her, go home, Sex Piston, and take your whore friends with you." She started to leave, but turned back to Sex Piston for her final insult.

"If mom calls me, I'll tell her to fuck off, so it's up to you if you want to start another fight between us." She concluded the conversation without a word of goodbye to her sister.

Sex Piston stood there and Winter could see that her sister's words had hurt.

Winter stepped forward and wrapped an arm around her shoulder.

"Let's go in, Sex Piston." She owed these women her life. She wasn't going to insult them by asking them to leave.

Once everyone was seated, the meeting was called to order. It started with discussions of the budget.

At the conclusion of the budget portion, Ben Stiles read the next item on the docket, which was to terminate Winter's employment. Ms. Richards stood to her feet. When they gave her permission to speak, she gave clear and concise reasons why Winter should not be fired, stating her professional record and the contributions she made to the school system as a whole. Not just the high school, she often volunteered performing duties beyond her job description. Several of her students had shown up also to support her, giving their testimonials of what she had been able to accomplish for their future. Then her fellow colleagues were asked to speak.

"They hire her back, I'm going to go back and get my diploma," Crazy Bitch whispered loudly to Sex Piston.

"You're too old," Sex Piston told her, not trying to whisper.

"I'm not too old; I'm just twenty-five."

"That's too old. Those snooty bitches," Sex Piston nodded toward the high school teachers that came to support Winter, "would be afraid you'd fuck the boys and turn the girls into bitches."

"Don't want no young dick," Crazy Bitch refuted, not denying the possibly about recruiting the girls.

"You'd fuck young stud dick," Killyama broke into the conversation.

"Don't fuck young dick. Wouldn't fuck them stuck-up bastards behind that big desk, either," Crazy Bitch argued back.

Winter bit her knuckle as they talked, having long since regretted inviting the biker bitches to stay.

"Two of them are women," Sex Piston said popping her gum. Actually, there were three female board members, Winter counted.

"Which ones?" Both Crazy Bitch and Killyama scrutinized the school board members.

The board stopped further testimonials, calling for a vote while several members glared at the women.

Winter jumped to her feet. "Before you judge my future employment, I would like a chance to speak."

"Go ahead." Ben Stiles motioned her towards the podium.

"First, I would like to thank the School Board for taking time in their busy schedule to give me a fair opportunity to explain." Winter described her attack and her recovery at The Last Riders. "I will not deny I am in a committed relationship with Mr. James, who is the president of The Last Riders, but in all fairness, the board must admit it is not in my contract that I couldn't live out of wedlock with a male. Furthermore, I feel that it is hypocritical to hold it against me for living with Loker James when two members of the school board share a similar situation.

"Loker James has also become an important member of our community and will, in the near future, be one of Treepoint's largest employers. Next week, they will start hiring for over fifty positions that will also pay a very generous salary with full benefits."

The school board perked up immediately, new business

meant collecting more in taxes.

"If I cannot find employment in Treepoint, we have decided to move to Ohio, where Mr. James has an existing factory and I will be able to find a job in the field of education, which I love. Mr. James has no ties to this town. It was his brother who was murdered by one of the very members who used to sit on this board. Both of us would like to see his brother's dream of helping our financially-deprived community find opportunities and wouldn't want this board's decision to affect the community by denying them much needed employment."

"Ms. Simmons, your job has already been filled by your vice-principal, Jeff Morgan," Ben Stiles informed her with a frown.

If the townspeople found out they didn't get high paying jobs because of the school board firing Winter, it could backfire on them. There wasn't a person in the meeting room who didn't know that. In their economically depressed area, money came before morality.

"I don't want my job back at the high school. I want to be the principal at Riverview since Mr. Woods has long been overdue for retirement. The extremely high rate of dropouts exhibits that he is unable to understand his student's needs. I feel, in all truthfulness, that I can make a change for the better at the alternative school. My records will show that Treepoint High School had the lowest dropout rates in twenty years during my years as a principal."

The school board members stared back and forth among each other. Winter knew that Mr. Woods was heartily disliked. The only reason that he was still employed was because no one wanted the job. It was a punishment to be sent there. Mr. Woods had earned his job there when he had an affair with the gym teacher and had been caught in the equipment room.

"The School Board will return to a closed session and take a vote. We will notify Ms. Richards within the next forty-eight hours of our decision."

Winter sat back down in her chair.

"Is that three days?" Crazy Bitch asked.

"Yes," answered T.A.

"Which one do you think Bliss is?" Sex Piston asked, getting to her feet.

"I bet it's the sweet thing at the end of the row," Killyama's threatening voice lowered as they moved away.

Winter turned, glancing sideways. She suddenly had a feeling that their appearance at today's meeting wasn't as altruistic as they had pretended.

As the meeting closed, everyone filed into the hallway. Winter and Viper came to stand next to her lawyer. "Thank you, Ms. Richards, for your help."

"I will let you know as soon as they notify me," Ms. Richards said.

Evie, Bliss and Natasha interrupted. "Winter, we'll meet you at the diner. Bliss and Natasha want to get something to eat before we go to the tattoo shop."

Ms. Richards paused before leaving, reaching into her purse to pull out a card. "Which one is Bliss?"

"I am," Bliss said, stepping forward.

Ms. Richards handed her a card. "Call me if you ever need legal representation, I handle personal injury cases also."

"What was that about?" Viper questioned after the woman left.

"I have no idea," Winter lied, winding her arm through Bliss's as they walked toward the exit.

CHAPTER TWENTY-THREE

Winter lay on the bed, pretending to read a book as Viper zipped his black jeans on before sitting down on the chair to put on his boots. His hair was still damp from the shower they had taken together where she had tried to lure him into having sex before he began to get dressed. He had subtly thwarted her attempts, though.

She had wanted to make sure he wasn't horny before he went to Razer's bachelor party. Evie had let it drop that Knox had hired a stripper.

Her fingers tightened on the book as Viper put on a leather vest with no shirt, showing his tats. Winter swallowed hard, his sleeve never failing to draw a response from her body.

"When are you going to start getting ready?" Viper asked, sliding his keys into his pocket.

"Why should I get dressed to watch television alone?"

"Why would you be alone?"

"Because Beth is with Lily at her house and the rest of the women are going to Rosie's with the men."

"You don't want to go?" Viper asked, trying to keep his lips straight.

Winter looked at him in surprise. "You never said

anything, I assumed I wasn't going."

"You got our tat on you?"

"Yes." Her first and last tat, she was determined, but she hadn't liked the look on Viper's face when she had informed him of that decision.

Winter jumped off the bed, going through her clothes to find something to wear. "Jerk, you could have told me and I would have bought a new outfit," she said, unhappily staring at her choices available.

"There's an outfit for you in the closest in the brown dress bag."

Winter opened the closet door, searching until she located the bag at the back. Pulling the bag out of the closet, she unzipped the garment bag, pulling out a black leather skirt that she was sure would cover her without being too short. The top was black lace across the top, with no straps and leather fringes that would both conceal and hint at her waist and abdomen. Winter loved it, they were perfect. There were even thigh high boots that were flat on the bottom. It was her first biker bitch outfit.

"Thank you, Viper. I love it," she said, jumping into his arms and kissing him in thanks. He deepened the kiss until Winter thought he might change his mind about having sex before the party, but he released her.

"Thank, Beth; she's the one who bought it for your first party," Viper told her with a smile.

"Where did the ugly outfit come from that I wore?" Winter asked with a suspicious glare.

Viper went through the door. "I bought it. Conner would never have chosen the other women if he had seen you in that getup." He barely managed to shut the door before she threw one of her boots.

* * *

Razer pulled out a chair in front of Winter with his back to the stripper swinging her body against the pole. He hadn't let his eyes stray to the dance floor once. Winter herself wouldn't have believed it if she hadn't witnessed it, which she had finally deduced was why she was there. Razer had every intention of covering his ass. If Beth asked her, Winter would be able to tell her, in all honesty, that Razer hadn't strayed.

Lifting her beer, she looked at Viper. Of course she couldn't say the same; he was obviously enjoying the show.

"I'm getting ready to smash my beer bottle into that hard on your getting," Winter threatened. Viper laughed, turning his chair to face her. Mollified, Winter put her beer back on the table.

When Viper and Razer began talking about a new method of growing plants, Winter zoned out, not in the least interested. The stripper finished with a flourish, putting on a silky pink rope that she didn't bother tying. Several of the members followed her to the back of the bar.

Winter finished her beer, feeling the urgent need to use the bathroom, and excused herself to go to the restroom at the back of the bar. After using the toilet, Winter washed her hands, throwing away the towel as she left the restroom.

She tried to keep her eyes forward, but her curiosity got the better of her and she looked over towards where she had seen the stripper go. She slowly came to a stop in the shadows of the long hallway.

The stripper was giving a lap dance to Shade who was sprawled on one of the chairs. He was wearing blue jeans and had pulled off his t-shirt. He was leaner than Viper and the rest of the members with perfectly cut abs. Both arms, neck and chest were covered in a myriad of tattoos. His facial expression was fierce as he watched the woman shake her breasts an inch from his face. As she straddled his lap, she ground her pussy down onto a cock that Winter could see was huge, even covered in his jeans. The woman obviously knew him because, as she was grinding down on him, she was pleading.

"God, please, Shade, please." The woman's face was a

tortured mask.

"What you want, bitch?"

"Your cock. Please, Shade," she whimpered.

"Where you want it?"

"My pussy."

"Can't give it to you now. You come back to the clubhouse, I'll give it to you all night." The woman nodded frantically.

"Go give my brothers their dances. If you want to give them anything else, you can give them your mouth. Save your pussy for me." The woman shakily moved off Shade, moving towards Knox who was eagerly waiting his turn.

Winter stayed to the shadows until she was able to get to her table.

"Where the fuck have you been? I was going to come looking for you," Viper questioned her as soon as she sat back down.

"I had to use the restroom; the beer was making me sick. I stayed until I was sure I wasn't going to vomit."

"Eat some pretzels," Viper said, noticing her flushed cheeks.

Razer's speculative gaze wasn't making her feel any calmer. Winter was having second thoughts about talking to Beth. Perhaps a slight warning wouldn't hurt anyone and Lily would stand a fighting chance to…

"No, Winter. Leave it alone. You don't want a mad Shade to deal with. I certainly don't want to deal with him," Razer warned her, reading her thoughts.

"I don't know what you're talking about," Winter replied, using her fingernail to tear at the beer label.

"Leave it alone," he said with finality.

Winter finally nodded her assent.

Winter almost spit out her beer when the bar door opened and Lily walked inside, wearing jeans and a loose pale blue top that highlighted the darkness of her hair. Lily's eyes searched the bar before finding Razer at the table. Her face was full of tension and you could see fear in the back of her eyes as she approached their table.

"Fuck. What's she doing here?" Viper muttered under his breath.

"I don't know." Winter was also at a loss.

"May I join you?" Lily asked, trying to appear casual.

"Yes," Razer spoke for the table.

Lily greeted them, deliberately keeping her eyes on their faces.

"Razer, could I talk with you privately? I've tried to find several opportunities, but with Beth and you constantly together, it's been hard to find a moment."

"Go ahead and talk. Beth and I have no secrets from the club," Razer told her.

"Perhaps I could find another time," she said, beginning to rise from the table.

"Lily, sit your ass down and tell me what's on your mind," Razer said softly.

A soft scream of frustration could be heard from the back of the bar. Lily turned instinctively to see what was happening and faced a wall of biker's staring back.

"What happened?" Lily asked.

"One of the girls probably saw a rat," Winter said, glaring at the brothers.

"Oh," Lily said. Taking a deep breath, Lily spoke her mind. "Razer, you know I love my sister."

"I know that you two are very close." Razer's eyes were watching Lily's hands.

"We are. Our parents adopted me, but Beth and I are as close as if we shared the same parents. We tell each other everything," Lily confessed, not noticing that now Razer was becoming tenser. "When you and Beth broke up, she came to my dorm and shared with me how badly she was hurt."

Razer listened attentively, still watching Lily's hands. His jaw grew tighter and tighter.

"I am aware bachelor parties are meant to be fun, the man's last night of freedom, and I wouldn't want to take that fun away, it's just that…" Lily paused, her eyes going to Bliss dancing with Rider. They had toned down their erotic dancing when they had seen her enter the bar, but Bliss couldn't hide the sexy outfit she was wearing.

"I don't want to see her hurt that way again," Lily said miserably.

Razer suddenly leaned across the table, his hand covering the one flicking the rubber band repeatedly against the bright red flesh of her skin.

Winter swallowed hard.

"Lil' sis, you're breaking my heart, please stop." Lily's hand became still under his. He nodded towards Winter.

"You trust her?" Lily turned her head to observe Winter before turning back to Razer.

"Yes," answered Lily.

"Do you trust her enough that she would tell Beth if I'm stepping out on her?"

This time Lily didn't look at Winter, but her answer was the same.

"Yes."

"She's attached to my hip the rest of the night. When she leaves, I leave."

"Okay." Lily smiled at Razer in relief. *Geez, the girl is too beautiful,* Winter thought in worry.

"I am marrying Beth because I love her, which means I'm not going to do stupid shit to hurt her again. Beth has learned to trust me and I want you to also." He moved his hand, touching the rubber band. "You don't need this anymore to keep from being afraid, lil' sis." Razer leaned further across the table. "I swear on my life, I'll never let anyone hurt you again."

Lily gave him a heartwarming smile before getting up from the table and hugging Razer, who hugged her back before sitting her away from him by several inches.

"Now, let's get you out of here. You have another year before you can legally be in a bar," Razer joked. "Mick made an exception for Beth's bridal shower, but he might get pissed off if we start making a habit of it."

Lily laughed. "He can't get in trouble. I turned twenty-one my last birthday. I thought Beth told you. Everyone just thinks I'm a year younger because Mom and Dad were so concerned I was behind in school when they adopted me."

"Is that so?" Razer asked.

"I would have thought she would have told you. I guess she was waiting for me to tell you, now I have. Now Beth has no more secrets from you, does she?" Lily teased as Razer ushered her quickly out of the bar.

"I think she might have one or two," Razer replied grimly, already hearing the commotion from the back.

Startled screams from the women were heard as they tried to get out of the way.

"Are you sure everything's all right? Mick should really take care of that problem."

"I imagine that's what he's doing right now," Razer said, walking faster, looking back over his shoulder.

Razer escorted Lily to her car, watching until he no longer saw the taillights before going back towards the bar. The women had all escaped outside, staring back inside as the bar became engulfed in fighting.

"Fuck." Razer was sure he didn't want to go back inside.

"Looks like Beth isn't as unaware of Shade's interest in Lily as you thought she was." Winter mocked Razer's reluctance to reenter the bar.

"You told Lily you would protect her, you swore," she reminded him, amused at his predicament.

"Shade's going to fuck me up for my wedding night. Beth hasn't let me touch her the last month to build the suspense. When he gets done with me, I won't be able to do shit." Razer winced as a loud crash resounded from within.

"I'm sure Beth will show her appreciation," Winter consoled.

"She fucking better," he said before striding into the bar.

CHAPTER TWENTY-FOUR

Winter came out of the bathroom wearing a towel crossed at her breasts. Viper was sitting at his desk with his hand in a bowl of ice. Luckily for him, he kept extra ice trays in his mini fridge. What little ice was in the freezer downstairs had been quickly used for the other brothers' injuries.

"Feel any better?" Winter tried not to smile.

"No, my hand is stinging like hell. I don't know what you think is so fucking funny."

"I don't know, maybe because you let one man beat the crap out of the whole group of you."

"He's a mean motherfucker and he knew we don't want to hurt him. He, unfortunately, didn't give a fuck."

Winter crawled across the bed on her hands and knees. "That adrenaline you were telling me about kick in yet?" Viper watched intently as she unknotted her towel, baring her body. "Of course, if you're too sore, I can understand. Want me to see if I have a pain pill left?"

"No. I took some Ibuprofen. How many beers did you drink?" Viper questioned her.

"A couple. Why? You think I'm drunk?"

"No, I think you're horny. I've noticed beer does that to you." He watched as her finger traced her nipple, her fingernail leaving a faint white line.

"It's not the beer, it's your cock," Winter smiled, in the mood to be naughty while also loving the reaction it was bringing out in Viper.

"I can solve that problem real quick," he said, getting to his feet. Pulling off his vest, pants and boots, he stood naked in front of her. He turned off the lights by the door, leaving on only the small lamp by the desk.

"Shade told me I must not be doing something right if you thought sex lasted only ten minutes."

Winter tensed on the bed. Damn, Shade. She had known that he had accepted giving her his vote too easily. The big tattle tale must have figured out she had set him up.

Viper opened the bedroom door before joining Winter on the bed.

Thinking at first that he was joking, Winter didn't realize that he was serious. Hastily crawling toward the end of the bed to run and close the door, Viper leaned down, grabbed an ankle and then pulled her down the length of the bed until she lay by his side.

Before she could protest, his mouth covered hers in a deep kiss that sent passion racing through her bloodstream. Taking his mouth away, he went to his knees, spreading her thighs before going down on her.

Winter tried to jerk her pussy away from him, but he latched onto her clit with his teeth and she went still immediately. Viper scooted her hips closer to him as he gently sucked on her sensitive bud while his tongue slid inside her slick sheathe. Winter couldn't help the moan slipping from her throat. His hands moved, placing a leg over each shoulder.

"Pretty girl, you're going to come in my mouth." Winter's head shook back and forth across the blanket.

She looked down to see him between her spread thighs. The erotic picture almost drove her into an orgasm, but seeing Knox and Jewell entering the bedroom door, had her lying still as Viper worked her clit into a frenzy of need.

"Bed or couch, Viper?" Knox asked.

"Couch," Viper muttered, taking his mouth away from her damp flesh.

"Viper..." Winter started to protest, watching Knox pulling Jewell down on his lap. Taking her top off, Knox stared at Viper between Winter's thighs as Jewell rubbed her pussy against the thigh she was sitting on.

Viper's mouth returned to play with her clit as one of his hands pulled the flesh back, exposing it to his torture. When his teeth grazed the sensitive bundle, Winter screamed her release into his mouth.

Not waiting for her to come down from the ecstasy he had expertly drove her to, he flipped her to her stomach then slid her down the length of the bed until he was able to stand. Viper maneuvered Winter to her knees. Her body was still giving her tiny shudders from her orgasm when he drove his large cock into her with a series of hard pumps.

"Bed or couch." Winter heard Cash's voice from behind Viper. Winter started to scramble forward, but a hard hand in her hair stopped her, holding her head down on the mattress, her face turned toward the sitting area.

Knox's eyes were trained on them as Jewell jacked him off. Winter's eyes moved toward Cash who had taken a seat on the chair with Natasha between his sprawled thighs, whose experienced fingers released his cock before eagerly taking him into her mouth. Cash's eyes were now also on Viper pounding his cock into her pussy. Winter closed her eyes.

"Open your eyes, pretty girl."

Winter opened her eyes to see Knox was getting close, she could tell from his expression. He jerked a condom from his pocket and handed it to Jewell, who carefully rolled it onto Knox's pierced cock. Jewell moaned as she lifted her skirt and Knox circled her waist with his strong hands, held her in the air and then turned her until she faced Winter. Knox impaled her on his cock, Jewell cried out as he lifted her up and down, his strong arms holding her entire weight. Winter shoved her ass back harder onto Viper's cock.

"Want me to stop?" Viper's hand caressed the tattoo on her back, on the exact spot that had almost made her a cripple, before sliding forward to tightly pinch her nipple.

"No..." moaned Winter.

"You going to give me any shit for fucking you in front of them?"

Winter didn't answer, so Viper pinched her nipple harder. Her pussy was boiling, she wanted to come so badly. She had never felt so needy of his cock, as if she would die if he didn't keep going at her.

"You going to give me shit?" Viper repeated his question.

"No..." Winter screamed as he released her nipple. Winter lost track of time as his thrusts intensified while he continued holding her still, pumping inside of her. Her orgasm had her screaming until she shoved her hand over her mouth.

"Move your fucking hand," Viper snarled, trying to keep himself from coming.

The feel of her tight pussy on his naked cock was a feeling he had never experienced. They had only received their medical forms this morning, giving them the all clear and Winter had already seen to birth control.

"I want to hear you scream. It lets me know you want my cock in your needy pussy."

Winter just held onto the side of the bed as he continued to fuck her. She was expecting him to come. Surely he couldn't last much longer, but he did, merely keeping at her with a steady pace.

"Viper, you need to come," Winter pleaded.

Viper looked down at his cock sliding in and out of her pussy. "Pretty girl, I'm not going to come for a while," he warned.

Winter's screams could be heard down the hall, begging him to come as sweat glistened on her skin. Knox and Jewell left to find a bed of their own at the same time that Evie came in alone to sit on the couch, watching Viper fuck Winter. Natasha had finished off Cash and was lying on his lap with his hand buried in her panties. Evie rose from the couch, going to Natasha, pulling off her panties, and providing everyone in the room with a view of Cash with his fingers fucking the woman into an orgasm. When Natasha lay still, Cash got up from the chair carrying Natasha to the couch, sitting her on the end. Turning, he quickly shoved Evie over the couch arm, keeping her legs together with his on the outside, he swiftly thrust his cock into her pussy.

Viper was still playing with Winter.

"I know what I want for my birthday. You're going to get this little tidbit pierced for me."

"No," Winter wailed, not wanting to let a needle anywhere near the sensitive flesh he was stroking.

"But it's what I want for my birthday and, Winter, just think how I can play with it when I go down on you," he cajoled.

"When's your birthday?"

"A couple months away," Viper answered.

"I'll think about it," Winter stalled.

"Then I'll only think about going down on you until you have it done. I plan on playing with it a lot, if that makes you feel better," he promised, increasing the strength of his thrusts.

Viper hit her high in her sheathe, drawing her away from the conversation and back to his plunging cock, forcing another orgasm from her quivering pussy.

"Do you think I've been fucking you longer than ten minutes, Winter?"

"Yes…" Winter's orgasm overtook her mind, body and soul, leaving her exhausted. Viper, taking in her shattered expression, finally allowed himself and his aching cock their release.

Leaning over and kissing her neck, he trailed his finger down her spine before circling her waist and lifting her into his arms. Carrying her to the couch, he sat down, placing her on his lap. Softly teasing her breast with his fingertips, they watched Cash fuck Evie into an orgasm.

"I'm hungry. Let's go raid the kitchen," Cash said.

Cash zipped up his jeans, pulling Natasha to her feet. "I'll fix you a sandwich, Natasha," he offered.

Winter saw something flash in Natasha's eyes, as Evie finally had enough strength to walk to the door.

"Raci," Winter told them as the nickname popped into her mind. It had just occurred to her that Natasha was a little wicked and had the energy of a speed demon, so that name would be perfect.

"What?" Cash asked, Evie hesitated at the door with a smile.

"Raci, her nickname is Raci." Winter looked at Natasha who was beaming with happiness that they all were able to see.

"Let's go, Raci," Cash said, taking her hand.

"Close the door," Viper ordered.

Cash closed the door as they filed out.

"I'm proud of you. I thought you would have been screaming hysterically by now." Viper was waiting for her reaction.

Surprised at herself, Winter agreed. The dignified woman who was always so cautious of every move she made was gone. The night she had been attacked, she had lain on that ground, wanting to give up. The only thing that had given her strength was the courage her mother had used to fight her breast cancer, Winter had known she couldn't do any less.

The other reason was Viper. Every time she had closed

her eyes that night, she thought she had seen his face for the last time. Afterward, the time in the hospital and rehab center had been humiliating, her body no longer her own as different aides saw to her physical needs, which had caused her natural shyness to be ripped away. Her attempts at escape from the clubhouse had been half-hearted at best. She admitted to herself she needed Viper and The Last Riders to make her whole again.

"I guess, watching them the last few months, I realized that they all are very respectful of each other. It isn't a dirty thing with them, Viper."

"No, it isn't," he agreed. "So has your curiosity been satisfied?"

"Yes, it has." Winter buried her red face in the curve of his warm shoulder.

"Ready for bed?" Viper brushed his cheek against the top of her head.

"More than ready," Winter groaned.

Viper carried her to the shower, gently moving the showerhead of hot water over her body in a steady stream. Her eyes were closing as he dried her off, helping her to slide under the covers.

"Good night, Winter," he said tenderly, pulling her close.

"Goodnight, Loker."

CHAPTER TWENTY-FIVE

The Last Riders were gathered into the hallway, ready to leave for Beth and Razer's wedding. They were waiting for Razer while Winter and Evie admired each other in their peach dresses.

"Ready?" Viper asked Winter as Razer came downstairs, dressed in his tuxedo.

Winter turned at Viper's question, admiring him in his suit, nervously plucking at a crease in her dress.

"We're ready," she answered. Viper lifted her up into his arms.

"Viper, I don't need you to carry me anymore," she protested.

He stopped. "There's no reason to tire yourself going down those steps." The only obvious result left of her attack was the steps. She would often have to stop and get her balance.

The Last Riders went out the door with Viper bringing up the rear of the line with Winter.

Viper noticed the members stood blocking his bike at his approach. Stopping as they neared, Viper was aware that they were hiding his bike from view. He looked down at Winter who, with an apprehensive look on her face, was trying to wiggle from his arms. He put her down, sensing something was about to happen from the tight faces of his brothers.

"Viper," Winter drew his attention back to her. "I hope you won't be angry with something I've done, but I couldn't stand you riding on that motorcycle any longer. Please don't be mad. If you don't like it, we can get another. Please don't be mad," she ended on a whisper.

The Last Riders moved until he could see what they were blocking from his sight.

"Rider tried to fix your bike, but you had damaged it too badly. He suggested we send it off to a restorer, but by the time they would have finished, not much would be left of the original bike."

Viper stared at Gavin's motorcycle. Someone had recently had it polished and shined, obviously preparing it to be ridden. Viper felt his heart catch as he stared at it sitting in the lot, as if waiting for Gavin to laughingly climb on for a ride. In his mind's eye, he remembered the many times he had seen Gavin riding the Harley. They had gotten out of the service a month apart, but Gavin had waited until Viper had come out to purchase his bike. They had purchased their bikes the same day from the same dealer.

Gavin's bike had sat in Ton's garage since Viper had asked Cash to have it transported from Ohio at Ton's request. No one had ridden the motorcycle since Gavin's death. Viper reached out touching the handlebar, swallowing hard.

"Are you mad?" Winter whispered with tears in her voice at seeing the grief on his face.

"No, I'm not mad," Viper said hoarsely.

Winter wrapped her arms around his waist from behind, her head falling forward to lie against his back. "Rider told me when he couldn't fix your motorcycle that a true biker becomes part of his machine. I thought you could bring a part of Gavin back to The Last Riders."

Viper's head lowered for a second, his hand on the handle bar tightening.

"Let's ride," he ordered and then all the guys mounted their motorcycles.

The women were riding in cars so their hair and clothes wouldn't become disheveled. Winter moved to go to Evie's car with her head down, brushing a tear off her check.

Viper's hand caught hers in his tight grasp. "Ride with me?" Viper asked.

Winter nodded, waiting for Viper to get on before climbing on behind him. After putting on her helmet, she grasped his waist tightly. Then the brothers all turned their bikes to face the road, throttling their motors.

Viper's shoulders pulled taut as his head went back in pride while throttling the bike. He pulled out of the parking lot with Cash by his side and two-by-two they drove down the mountainside with Shade and Razer at their back.

* * *

Beth looked beautiful standing with Razer. Winter could only cry as the couple exchanged their vows, not able to hold the tears back when she heard Razer's voice break as he slid his ring onto Beth's finger. Pastor Dean performed the traditional ceremony that was over too soon. The wedding ceremony was held in the huge backyard of the church, allowing those who attended to eat afterward at the tables, which had been set up with flower centerpieces.

Winter sat down next to Lily as pictures of the bridal party were taken after the ceremony. There were several photos taken in various positions. First the whole bridal party, then the bridesmaids, then groomsmen, then the groomsmen and the bridesmaids.

Winter hid her smile as the groomsmen became increasingly aggravated, wanting the food at the table they could see clearly from their position. It didn't help that the guests had begun eating without them.

"Let's finish this up," Razer warned Beth, seeing their threatening glares.

"All right, all right, just a few more," Beth soothed.

Winter had taken a picture with Rider. It was Lily's turn next. The photographer decided to take pictures of her with Shade as they were standing next to each other exactly like the others had during their pictures.

"Last one," the photographer said, moving to a different position.

Charles, hearing the photographer, moved closer, waiting for Lily who gave him a sweet smile. Shade's eyes narrowed as his arm slid around Lily's waist, bringing her flush against his side. Lily stiffened within his grasp, her hand going to his chest, though she didn't pull away, thinking that Shade had simply made the change for the photographer.

Her smile became more nervous. Shade's face became a different matter, giving a clear warning to the young man standing beside Winter. To give Charles credit, he didn't run when the photographer finished, taking Lily's hand.

"Let's get something to eat." Charles led her away to the buffet tables, giving Shade a gloating smile over his shoulder.

Not liking the look in Shade's eyes and not wanting Beth's wedding ruined, Winter moved to block his path.

"Hey, Shade. It was a nice ceremony, wasn't it?" Winter winced at her too cheerful voice.

Winter saw the look of sanity come back into his eyes.

"Beth and Lily looked beautiful, didn't they?"

Shade's eyes went to Razer and Beth standing together as their friends congratulated them.

"Yes," he growled out.

"They all are so happy, Beth with Razer and Lily finally settling into college. Their lives are merging, yet still fragile. It could be hurt irreparably if she feels he's putting a friend's wants over her sister's needs."

Shade's body stiffened, standing still.

Winter shrugged, deciding to be blunt. "It's not like you're deprived of female companionship. Lily will be out of school in two years with a degree she's wanted since I've known her. By then, you might not want her anymore." Which was what she was hoping would happen.

Shade gave her a look that had her taking a step back, the blaze of possession in his startling blue eyes was evident as he looked at Lily and Charles sitting at one of the tables. Winter was aware in the instant that the chances of Shade changing his mind were nil. Shades eyes turned back to her to make sure she understood his silent message. Winter was no rocket scientist, but she was smart enough to back off. Satisfied, Shade left, going in the opposite direction of Lily and Charles, and leaving Winter shaking in her shoes.

Winter let out a sigh of relief at his departure, deciding to find Viper. Seeing him sitting at a table with Ton, big plates of food in front of them, she decided to fix herself a plate of food before sitting down.

"Did you two get enough food?" Winter teased as she pulled out the chair next to Ton.

"Ton, Viper, I would like you to meet my Aunt Shay." Mrs. Langley sat down next to Ton, placing her plate on the table while Winter took the other chair sitting down next to Viper.

Eating her food, she watched as Ton and her Aunt began to talk. Her shy aunt was slowly drawn out of her shell by the gregarious man. Winter smiled, pleased, catching herself when Viper gave her a speculative look. Winter tried to appear innocent, yet she didn't think she had succeeded.

The music started as Razer and Beth moved out onto the dance floor that had been placed down in the grass. Winter watched as they glided across the small floor.

"Want to dance?" Viper asked.

"Yes, I do," Winter said, getting to her feet

immediately.

Viper held her close as they danced. The reception lasted several hours, in which they were dodging Beth's biker women friends who, after loud protestations from Beth, promised to leave Bliss alone. They then turned their attention to Shade and Pastor Dean. Winter noticed Beth didn't rescue them.

The sheriff stopped by their table once to tell them that Jake's charges had been reduced after Winter visited his office to explain how her memory had returned and that it wasn't Jake who had assaulted her. He didn't ask many questions, drawing only enough answers in order to get the charges dropped. Jake still had to face arson charges, but at least it wasn't on Winter's conscience that he was serving time for a crime he hadn't committed. As Winter had left the sheriff's office, she had passed the empty deputy's desk. The sheriff didn't blink an eye when he told her Deputy Moore had disappeared after an argument with his father.

Winter and Viper decided to leave not long after Razer and Beth left for the airport, going to Vegas for their honeymoon. They said their goodbyes to everyone before giving her Aunt Shay, who was still sitting with Ton, a quick hug.

The parking lot was filled with flower petals and ribbons that she was sure Pastor Dean wouldn't be happy cleaning. Driving out of the church parking lot, Winter could barely hear his voice with her helmet on and the rushing wind.

"Feel up to a moonlight run before going back to the clubhouse?"

Her head fell to his back, her arms tightened, holding him closer.

"Always, Viper."

CHAPTER TWENTY-SIX

Winter strode angrily towards the kitchen. It wasn't fair. She wasn't going to take a punishment that wasn't her fault. She fumed angrily to herself. It was Rider's freaking fault she was in trouble anyway, throwing away another one of her baskets from the dollar bin that she had purchased for the hundredth time. It wasn't her fault she had lost her temper and, after taking the basket out of the trash, had banged it against the offending member.

Everyone kept stealing the damn things, using them to organize their crap and leaving her damn seeds unorganized. She always somehow managed to draw them as punishment. Well, not today. Last time she had noticed that everyone else's papers had been folded multiple times while hers was smooth. They had conspired against her so that she was always the one drawing the hated punishment. Not freaking today.

Winter stood against the wall. She didn't have time for this, she needed to balance Riverview's budget. The school board had given her the job without telling her the school had been given the shaft where funding was concerned. *That crap is going to change, too*, she thought. *Viper doesn't know it yet, but he is going to be making a large donation*, she thought in revenge.

"Evie." Evie moved to take her slip of paper before sitting back down.

"Bliss." Winter rolled her eyes at that one.

"Rider." Winter could barely restrain herself from flipping him off.

"Pretty girl." She didn't try to hide her resentment as she went to the hated red punishment bag, dipping her hand inside. Her finger couldn't find any slips of papers in the bag, instead brushing a small box. Pulling it out, she held the small box in her hand before opening it. Inside lay an emerald engagement ring.

"Will you marry me, pretty girl?" Viper asked as The Last Riders waited for her answer.

Winter flung herself into his arms to the loud cheers inside the room.

"Yes, I'll marry you," Winter answered, staring up into his eyes.

Viper gave her a teasing grin. "I'm you're punishment," he said with the red cloth bag still in his hand.

"No, Viper," Winter said. "You're my reward."

ALSO BY JAMIE BEGLEY

THE LAST RIDERS SERIES:
RAZER'S RIDE

VIPER'S RUN

THE VIP ROOM SERIES:
TEASED

THE DARK SOULS SERIES:
SOUL OF A MAN

ABOUT THE AUTHOR

"I was born in a small town in Kentucky. My family began poor, but worked their way to owning a restaurant. My mother was one of the best cooks I have ever known, and she instilled in all her children the value of hard work, and education.

Taking after my mother, I've always love to cook, and became pretty good if I do say so myself. I love to experiment and my unfortunate family has suffered through many. They now have learned to steer clear of those dishes. I absolutely love the holidays and my family put up with my zany decorations.

For now, my days are spent at work and I write during the nights and weekends. I have two children who both graduate next year from college. My daughter does my book covers, and my son just tries not to blush when someone asks him about my books.

Currently I am writing three series of books- The Last Riders that is fairly popular, The Dark Souls series, which is not, and The VIP Room, which we will soon see. My favorite book I have written is Soul Of A Woman, which I am hoping to release during the summer of 2014. It took me two years to write, during which I lost my mother, and brother. It's a book that I truly feel captures the true depths of love a woman can hold for a man. In case you haven't figured it out yet, I am an emotional writer who wants the readers to feel the emotion of the characters they are reading. Because of this, Teased is probably the hardest thing I have written.

All my books are written for one purpose- the enjoyment others find in them, and the expectations of my fans that inspire me to give it my best. In the near future I hope to take a weekend break and visit Vegas that will hopefully be next summer. Right now I am typing away on Knox's story and looking forward to the coming holidays. Did I mention I love the holidays?"

Jamie loves receiving emails from her fans,
JamieBegley@ymail.com

Find Jamie here,
https://www.facebook.com/AuthorJamieBegley

Get the latest scoop at Jamie's official website,
JamieBegley.net

Made in the USA
Middletown, DE
17 November 2017